Jane
AND THE
Final
Mystery

BOOKS BY THE AUTHOR

The Merry Folger Nantucket Mystery Series
Death in the Off-Season
Death in Rough Water
Death in a Mood Indigo
Death in a Cold Hard Light
Death on Nantucket
Death on Tuckernuck
Death on a Winter Stroll

WRITTEN UNDER THE NAME
STEPHANIE BARRON

Being the Jane Austen Mysteries
Jane and the Unpleasantness at Scargrave Manor
Jane and the Man of the Cloth
Jane and the Wandering Eye
Jane and the Genius of the Place
Jane and the Stillroom Maid
Jane and the Prisoner of Wool House
Jane and the Ghosts of Netley
Jane and His Lordship's Legacy
Jane and the Barque of Frailty
Jane and the Madness of Lord Byron
Jane and the Canterbury Tale
Jane and the Twelve Days of Christmas
Jane and the Waterloo Map
Jane and the Year Without a Summer
Jane and the Final Mystery

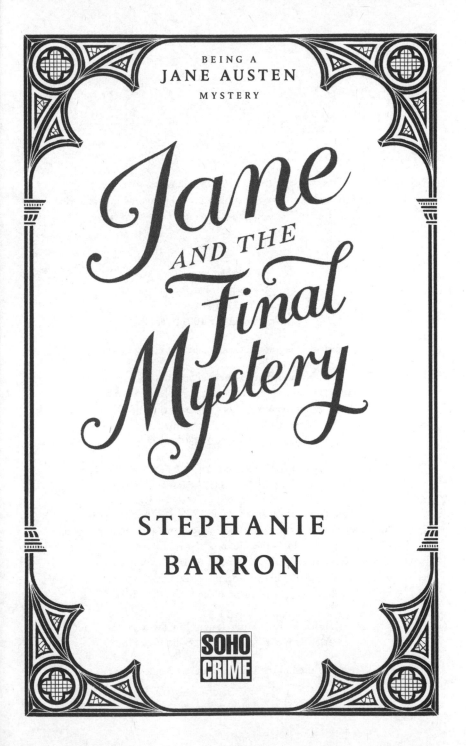

BEING A
JANE AUSTEN
MYSTERY

Jane
AND THE
Final
Mystery

STEPHANIE
BARRON

SOHO
CRIME

Published by
Soho Press, Inc.
227 W 17th Street
New York, NY 10011

Library of Congress Cataloging-in-Publication Data

Names: Barron, Stephanie, author.
Title: Jane and the final mystery / Stephanie Barron.
Description: New York, NY : Soho Crime, [2023]
Series: Being a Jane Austen mystery
Identifiers: LCCN 2023014657

ISBN 978-1-64129-617-5
eISBN 978-1-64129-506-2

Subjects: LCSH: Austen, Jane, 1775–1817—Fiction.
Women novelists—Fiction. | LCGFT: Detective and mystery fiction.
Historical fiction. | Novels.
Classification: LCC PS3563.A8357 J3299 2023
DDC 813/.54—dc23/eng/20230331
LC record available at https://lccn.loc.gov/2023014657

Interior art and title design: Jim Tierney
Interior design by Janine Agro, Soho Press, Inc.

Printed in the United States of America

10 9 8 7 6 5 4 3 2 1

For Stephen

Like Jane, you left this world too soon.
Love you. Miss you.

PROLOGUE
THE SOLICITUDE OF OLD FRIENDS

Monday, 27 January 1817
Chawton Cottage

Having endured over one-and-forty years on this earth, and observed much of human existence, I may state with confidence a peculiarity of our condition: one has only to be thinking of a person or event to conjure it immediately to life. A sporting relative mentions the winner of the St. Leger at Doncaster this past September (The Duchess, by Cardinal, out of Miss Nancy), and but a day and a half later one glimpses Mr. Sutherland's aquatint engraving of the very same animal, displayed at the stationer's in Alton. The *Morning Gazette* publishes an intriguing article on Sir Joseph Banks's eucalypt, a plant of which one has never heard; the following week one's niece announces she intends to plant a eucalypt at her father's Kentish estate, if only he may obtain a specimen from the Botanic Gardens at Kew.

By such mysterious workings of the Universe, I had despatched a letter to my dear friend Alethea Bigg this Friday last, only to observe her to pull up in a hired chaise before my very door on the Monday. I need hardly add she had neither received nor read my charming missive. This was tiresome, as I had written purposely to request her receipt for Seville Orange wine, my brother Charles having presented his sisters with a quantity of the fruit at Christmas, and we having quite outrun our powers of invention in consuming them.

Alethea's sudden appearance, however unlooked-for and delightful, is what we in the Austen household must regard as a sad waste of energy and hot-pressed paper. Naturally, she had come away without her receipt.

"Mrs. Heathcote accompanies her," Cassandra observed from her position by the dining parlour window, as Alethea and her sister were handed down from the carriage, "and Master William. He does not look very much grown since last we saw him. Indeed, he is positively slight in comparison of our nephews. How old must he be now, Jane?"

"Fifteen at least," I replied after an instant's calculation. I was unmoved to learn that William had not grown; Elizabeth Heathcote's son is forever being apostrophised as *delicate*. "They will have set out from Streatham on Saturday and stopped in Basingstoke. By this time"—for it was nearly one o'clock—"they will be famished for a nuncheon."

"Sally," Cassandra said to our maidservant, who was tidying the remains of a late breakfast from our table, "we have guests. Pray set the kettle to boil, and look out the last of the mince-pies."

I hastened to the front vestibule and drew back the front

door. Alethea Bigg stopped short on the gravel that separated the cottage from the Winchester Road, and extended both arms in greeting. "Jane!"

She was looking handsome, in a warm winter pelisse of cherry wool lined with swan's-down, and a square-crowned bonnet of *gros de Naples* in a slightly deeper shade. She had contrived to visit a London milliner while celebrating Christmas with her Streatham relations, I guessed. Alethea is both the youngest and the slightest of the Bigg sisters, and at nine-and-thirty has acquired a becoming dignity to her countenance. I have been acquainted with her from the age of seventeen, when she made her debut at the Basingstoke assemblies, and must prefer her present gravity to her girlish simper.

We might once have called each other *sisters*.

This chimerical thought, rising unbidden to the mind, I swiftly suppressed. Yes, nearly fifteen years ago I had entertained the absurd marriage proposal of Alethea's little brother, Harris Bigg-Wither—a youth just down from Oxford, unschooled in address, but indubitably the heir to Manydown Park, an ancient and respectable manor in my home neighbourhood. He was far too young to marry, and I was probably too old; in any event, tho' I accepted his offer at first, I rejected it at last, and have never regretted my single estate—when the price for exchanging it must be Harris.

I will admit to a few pangs of regret for Manydown and its comforts, which marriage should have secured me; but am privileged to retain the best of them, in the friendship of the Bigg ladies—which endures despite my snub of their brother. Harris, for his part, proved successful in winning the heart of another—and has succeeded some years since to his father's estate.

I grasped Alethea's gloved hands in my bare ones, heedless of my want of a wrap against the January wind. "How good of you to break your journey to call upon us! We did not look for the honour!"

Her warm brown gaze swept my face, and some emotion suffused her own; but she mastered it swiftly. What might a younger and less controlled Alethea have betrayed? Anxiety? Horror? *Pity?*

I looked past her, my smile fixed upon my lips, and saw the naked shock in Elizabeth's countenance. It has been many months since the three of us have met—and I read the alteration of my person in their surprize. I have always been slender, but am now thin to the point of gauntness; my gowns hang upon my frame, and my visage is grown sharp and peaked. My colour is indifferent, tending towards the sallow, and my eyes, although they retain their brilliancy, appear sunk in their sockets.

The Biggs' apprehension of my illness must be the crueler for being sudden, whereas my sister Cassandra's daily exposure to it, has inured her to its effect. So, too, with my mother and our companion Martha Lloyd; when from weakness I take to my bed, and refuse all nourishment, they cluck their concern, but dismiss it from their minds once I am well again. Alethea and Elizabeth have no shield against the blow, and I may measure my diminishment in their unease.

"Mrs. Heathcote!" I cried roundly, with a show of pleasure as Elizabeth embraced me. "And Master Heathcote! Fresh from your Christmas holidays, and full of plum pudding. Come within-doors, before this wind freezes you to the marrow!"

Elizabeth stared directly into my eyes; then, regardless of what she read there, stepped past me to greet Cassandra. Little would be mentioned, I was certain, of my health or prospects; we would share a brief interval of cheer and laughter; then the ladies and their charge would be once more upon the Winchester Road, headed south to their comfortable home in the Cathedral Close. They should reach it well before nightfall.

All the confusion of shedding outer garments in the vestibule; my mother's delighted halloos from above-stairs, and her abjurations to Sally to fetch her dressing gown; Martha bustling about with a beaming countenance, and a lavish hand with the confections; Master William's schoolboy sufferance of a party of ageing ladies assuring each other of their continued vigour; and at last, a settling in our various chairs before the drawing-room fire, with the pleasantish view of the winter garden through the peaked Gothick window.

"And how does Kitty go on?" Cassandra enquired once our guests had accepted a cup of tea and sampled some of Martha's little almond cheesecakes.

Elizabeth glanced at her son; the boy was endeavouring to make a friend of Cass's dog, Link, with the inducement of a scrap of cold ham. "William," she said, "do you take the animal out into the back garden for a romp."

"There is also a pair of donkeys in the stable," I offered. "Cook will give you an apple for them."

He rose at once, inclined his head with a blush, and was gone in a trice; at which, Elizabeth sighed. "I did not like to discuss my sister's condition before the boy. She is in *that way* again, and at her advanced time of life"—Kitty is the same age as I—"it seems a pity that Mr. Hill proves incapable of controlling his urges. She has presented him *already* with five sons and a daughter, and the latter is as yet a babe in arms!"

"The elder boys are delightful," Alethea supplied doubtfully, "but I will admit that six children under the age of seven make for a boisterous household."

"Kitty is fortunate that the fact of Mr. Hill's holding *three* livings, affords him ample income to provide for servants," Martha observed.

"However little he may spiritually offer his parishioners," I murmured into my tea. I knew the reverend Mr. Hill to preside over churches as distant from one another as Hampshire, Hereford, and Surrey—and doubted whether he earned his keep. Curates held his place in the pulpit, and the little Hills were their beneficiaries.

"Any lying-in may be perilous," my mother mused (she had survived eight), "but at Catherine's age, must be doubly so. I shall pray for her."

Alethea affected a shudder. "I confess, I am never more thankful for having failed to marry, than when I observe poor Kitty's haggard appearance over her needlework of an evening, when domestic cares and the demands of her husband have wrung the last particle of spirit from her frame. Elizabeth and I go on *quite* comfortably in our little establishment in Winchester—as I am sure you ladies do, here in Chawton—without the claims of a lord and master!"

Judging by the admirable state of her dress, Alethea is privileged, I must suppose, to a private settlement of funds from her late father. Even if modest in the eyes of the Great World, her circumstances supply the elegancies of a genteel household. But the household itself is a credit entirely to her sister.

Nearly twenty years ago, fresh from the same Basingstoke assemblies, Elizabeth Bigg chose to ally herself with a "lord and master"—William Heathcote, the second son of a baronet and rector of a fine parish, as well as a prebendary of Winchester. He was a strikingly handsome fellow, much addicted to the hunt; that he departed this life in the full flush of youth, when his son was but ten months old, was regarded as a tragedy. Elizabeth bore her loss with fortitude, however, and preserved her energies for the rearing of young Master William—betraying not the slightest inclination to assay the married estate again.

Her jointure allowed for the leasing of a respectable home within the Cathedral Close, and the provision of her son's fees as a Commoner of Winchester College. It is a peculiarity of the school's founding in the fourteenth century that a clutch of prelates were named to oversee the instruction of a fixed number of charity boys, and each priest was awarded a house within the Cathedral's walls.

But as the centuries wore away and the school's administration diverged from that of the Church (the schism from Rome, the Dissolution of the Monasteries, and the college's acceptance of expensive gentlemen's sons, bearing no small part in this), the Close's homes were increasingly viewed as spoils, for their owners' mercenary use. Elizabeth leases No. 12 from its prebendary, Dr. Williams, who cannot be troubled to occupy it; he finds his living at nearby Compton more to his taste.

An excited bray from the rear of the house informed us that the donkeys had scented Cook's apples. I hoped that Master William, however delicate, was stout enough to brave their gaping yellow jaws.

"Your son is admirably behaved," I told Elizabeth, who rose from her seat on the sopha by my mother and moved to one of the straight-backed chairs drawn up beside my own. "A paragon of virtue, in fact, compared to my brother Edward's hellions!"

"I wish he were in as boisterous health as they," Elizabeth confided in a lowered tone. "Indeed, it was anxiety for his welfare that dictated my choice of a home within the Cathedral Close when he took up his place as a Commoner at Winchester. I could not be easy about William adventuring into the world otherwise."

I have not a mother's tender feelings, it is true. But Elizabeth's words must occasion surprize. I have been accustomed to various male Austens embarking on their careers at Winchester, and eventually achieving their places at Oxford, with no greater misadventure than a few colds, beatings, and fisticuffs. Certainly, their mothers felt more relief than apprehension when the time came to pack their trunks and launch them upon the world. Elizabeth has never been one of your die-away misses, either, who must suspect a fearful danger in the sunniest of days. She possesses a tranquil if keen understanding, a resolute temper, and some familiarity with the Great. Why, then, this over-active sensibility with regard to her son?

"Is William ailing?" I enquired. He was thin and pallid of complexion enough to suggest ill-health, but few youths of his age are Adonis-like; it is an awkward period.

Elizabeth hesitated, her eyes drifting to her sister's face. Alethea was engrossed in Cassandra's admiration of her bonnet. "Not in body, no. But I sometimes fear for his spirits, Jane. He has suffered a good deal of anxiety in recent months."

"Has he, indeed?"

"William shares his Uncle Harris's propensity to stutter."

I felt my heart sink. Impossible not to recall the agonised dismay of Elizabeth's younger brother, under the eyes of a room full of family and acquaintances, each judging and pitying him his choked and halting speech. For years, his childhood intellect was dismissed as wanting. The underside of his tongue was cut by an over-zealous surgeon, who insisted the fault was mechanical; and he was frequently whipped to discourage a laziness of articulation. Harris's intervals of formal tuition were eventually abandoned in favour of private instruction at home with a tutor from Cambridge, who professed to be adept at curing defects of speech. Whether the man succeeded in ameliorating the youth's condition I cannot say; I know with certainty that even as a gentleman of twenty, Harris exhibited a painful shyness among strangers—who frequently judged his brain to be as impaired as his conversation. The terrors of public speech led him to embrace solitude: riding, hunting, fishing, and reading in blessed silence, free of the interrogation of a single soul.

When he offered for my hand, I was moved to accept in part from pity. Harris was truly a creature of peculiar loneliness, dating from childhood, and it was an anguish I might have assuaged. Reflection, however, led to regret; I pitied, but did not love him. I must hope his chosen helpmeet felt entirely otherwise.

"I am sorry for it," I said now. "Schoolboys may be thoughtlessly cruel. I hope that William is not miserable?"

Elizabeth's gaze settled once more on my own. "Oh, he is quite tormented! Called every sort of derisive name, from half-wit to gabble-tongue, that the human mind may summon! He was only admitted to the college, I believe, due to Dr. Gabell's affection for my late husband. But I do not think William would be such an object of general ridicule, were the Headmaster more adept, and the college in better order! Did your nephew Edward say nothing during the Christmas holiday, of the school's ungovernable state?"

James-Edward, my brother James's only son, left Winchester at the close of the last Michaelmas Term, and is now gone up to Exeter College, Oxford. I recollected that young William Heathcote, tho' two years his junior, had been an especial friend from Edward's school days; naturally Elizabeth would ask after him.

"I do not recollect him speaking of Winchester at Christmas," I said, "and tho' he has been staying with us so recently as last week, his conversation *now* is all of Bag-Wigs and Proctors and the junior common room. He is full of Oxford, and nothing but Oxford, as must be natural."

"And as one would wish him to be." She made a slight movement with her hand, as tho' dismissing whatever worry had been in her mind, and said resolutely, "But that is not why I exchanged my place for one beside you. How is your health, Jane? You have been, I think, a little indisposed?"

When in truth did my ill health begin? —Last winter, when the cold was so acute that the Thames froze, and London celebrated a Frost Fair with booths and skating on the ice? —Or was it last spring, when all hope seemed stillborn in the face of a brutal and persistent rain? I, who had enjoyed a riotous constitution throughout my four decades, had felt so little like myself in the previous twelvemonth that I found it hard to remember being free of pain. Never one to fancy myself ill or spend my existence in languishing upon a sopha, I had taken the unusual step last May of decamping to Cheltenham Spa to drink the waters—which were nauseating, and of dubious benefit. My sister Cassandra had returned to Cheltenham in September, but I did not accompany her. Throughout the autumn I suffered from pains in my back and an unsettled digestion. I was frequently tired and wanting in energy, and found it difficult to walk the three miles into Alton and back, to see my niece Anna and her children, or my brother Frank and his family. We had adopted the practice instead of driving the donkey-cart to the neighbouring village, but in the winter season when the roads between Alton and Chawton are mired in mud, such an expedient must be impossible. My nephew Edward had promised to return at the Easter holidays, and teach me to ride the donkey—I, who have never been fond of horses—

The thought of Edward's laughing countenance, his good-humoured gaze, and his ready tongue returned me to sensibility of my companion. I clasped Elizabeth's hand gently, then released it.

"You are very good to concern yourself. But I assure you, I am perfectly well. I was a little troubled with bilious attacks before the Christmas holidays, but am much recovered in recent weeks."

She narrowed her eyes shrewdly. "Are you writing?"

I hesitated. Of *The Elliots*, completed last summer and set aside to mature in peace, I said nothing.[1] But I *have* other schemes at hand. "I am. Is it so obvious, in my air of broody distraction?"

"Capital!" she cried. "It has been too long since we have had anything from your pen. I liked your *Emma* very well, but I am impatient for the next of your progeny. What is this one's name to be, and when may we celebrate her birth?"

I laughed. It is a measure of the depth of my friendship

---

1 *The Elliots* was Austen's working title for *Persuasion*, published along with *Northanger Abbey* in 1817.—*Editor's note.*

for all the Biggs that they are admitted to the secret of my authorship; and Elizabeth has honoured me by expending actual *coin* for her volumes. "I have devised no real heroine, as yet, worth the name. This tale is rather a set-piece, about a peculiar group of adventurers intent upon bringing a seaside village of no particular merit, into prosperity and Fashion. It shall be my commentary on the delusions of watering-places, where all the world flocks in pursuit of dissipation, and calls it health! My interval in Cheltenham supplied the idea, but the creatures who populate the story are entirely my own."

Elizabeth sipped her tea. "Drawn from the eccentrics of your acquaintance, I daresay. But I shall not look for myself among them; the portrait might be so like, as to make me uneasy. Ah, here is William, looking half-frozen!"

The boy, his cheeks flushed and his hands reddened from exposure, brought the scent of snow and hay and warm animal hide into the sitting room, to the delight of all the ladies present. When he had warmed his chilled fingers at the blaze and reluctantly answered my mother's questions about his House and studies, succumbing to the torture of his wretched tongue only half-a-dozen times, our guests rose to take their leave. Already the shadows of early afternoon were beginning to lengthen, and the family party had a full sixteen miles yet to travel before they should reach their own hearth.

"If there were the slightest possibility that you and Cassandra would desert your mother for an interval, I should urge you both to stay with us at the Close," Elizabeth said as she donned her cloak. "At Easter, perhaps, or later. Alethea is to travel upon the Continent this spring—and I shall be quite alone."

"The Continent!" Cassandra cried, all astonishment. "How very daring, Alethea!"

"It is at the invitation of friends," she admitted, "and not so *very* daring now that the Monster is safely exiled to St. Helena. I must wish, however, that Elizabeth accompanied me."

"But not enough to forego the treat!" her sister teazed. "Say that you will condescend to visit, Jane, so that Alethea may be envious!"

"With pleasure," I assured her, "—if my health permits." We had enjoyed the hospitality of the Close before, and I should be happy to see Winchester again.

"As to that—" Alethea waved her hand airily, "we know an excellent surgeon, Mr. Lyford, should you wish to consult him. He has proved a saviour in even the most hopeless of cases!"

Cassandra drew a sharp breath; there followed an awkward silence, heavy with unspoken thoughts. Martha broke it by appearing from the kitchen passage, her arms filled with wrapped bundles. "I took the liberty of putting aside some treats for you to share with the other boys at school," she told Will. "There are apple pasties and jam-tarts."

"Miss Lloyd is the only baker worth the name in this household," I advised him, "so make off with your prize before I snatch it from you."

"Th-th-thank you, Miss Lloyd." He bowed, his cheeks flaming with embarrassment. He quitted the house before the rest of the party, trudging to the carriage under a peculiar cloud. With a bright, oblivious smile, Alethea followed.

"Poor fellow!" Cassandra observed. "He looks as tho' he goes into exile, rather than to his studies!"

"Thank God, he has only one year remaining," Elizabeth murmured. "Then he shall be safe."

"Safe?" I repeated. "It cannot be so bad as that, surely?"

She glanced at me, her eyes sombre. "I hardly know. There have been strange rivalries among the schoolboys, and troubling mishaps, poorly explained. To hear William tell it, a state of open warfare exists among the various camps, and persecution is the favourite pastime! Do say you will come to us at Easter, Jane—I believe I should benefit from your advice."

"What can I possibly know of schoolboys?" I scoffed, as I kissed her cheek. "They are all Latin and Greek, of which I remain ignorant."

"Until they become men," Elizabeth sighed, "and their vices both common and apparent. With these, Jane, I suspect you are well acquainted. You have brothers, have you not?"

AND SO I RETURN to the observation with which I opened this passage: one has only to be thinking of a person or event to conjure it into life.

Elizabeth and her deep anxiety for her son were much in my thoughts in the days that followed her visit; but it was not until two months later, and from a very different source, that I was to hear of actual violence at Winchester College—and the death of an unfortunate schoolboy.

1

MR. CURTIS IS BAFFLED

Chawton Cottage
Tuesday, 25 March 1817

"That is a handsome saddle, Aunt." Edward led the younger of our two donkeys, the dun-coloured one called Bottom, up the muddied lane towards Alton.

"I had it made especially," I managed, from my cramped and terrified position above, "by Mr. Jenkins the saddler. He fitted me for it"—I emitted a gasp as the donkey's head jerked unexpectedly up and down, and it brayed with ear-splitting effect—"but a fortnight since."

My right knee was hooked around the side-saddle's horn, while I clung desperately to the same feature with both gloved hands. This is *not* the accepted approach to equestrienne stile; it was expressly *not* as Edward—who, like his father, is accustomed to break-neck hunting with The Vyne—had urged me to proceed.

"Hold the reins in both hands," he instructed. "*Loosely*, Aunt. Not as tho' you wish to tie off a bleeding man's stump."

Like all the Austens, Edward has a way with words.

I forced a game smile, and struggled to relax my fingers.

Almost immediately, a sensation of dizziness assailed me. I dropped the reins and clutched instead at the donkey's thick mane.

"You're perfectly safe." Edward's tone might have been employed with an infant. "The poor beast is barely twelve hands. You could step straight out of the saddle to the earth and come to no harm!"

It is true that I swayed a mere four feet above the ground; but there was something about Bottom's lurching, ungainly motion that heightened my sense of precarity. Although rigid with fear, I forced myself to glance stiffly at Cassandra, who was sauntering alongside. She frowned. "Do sit up, Jane! We shall reach the outskirts of Alton soon! Do you wish the entire world to die of laughter?"

I have ventured on horseback on only rare occasions in my life—at my brother's estate of Godmersham, in Kent, for instance, where the mounts are well-bred and smooth goers—but it is many years since I trusted my life to a beast of unpredictable whims and tempers. One of my dearest friends, Anne Lefroy, died after being thrown from her horse. And *she* was regarded as an accomplished rider! Did I mention that my back ached with every jolt from the devilish beast? It has ached abominably these past several months, from trouble no doubt in the kidneys.

But Edward was whistling now as he strode along, and the donkey attempted a skittish little jog, and Cassandra exclaimed, "Is it not *lovely* to be out of doors in the sun at last, after such an interminable winter?"

She had set aside her mending and stillroom duties to

trudge through the mud of late March. Edward, down from Oxford at the close of Hilary Term, had taken several days away from his family to visit Chawton. They had both put themselves out to entertain and accompany me—to supply me with needed air and exercise—and I was behaving badly. Even Bottom showed more spirit.

I set my jaw, forced myself upright from my hunkering posture over the mane, and took up the reins.

"I expect," Edward said in a conversational tone, "that if you look straight ahead rather than at the ground, it will go rather better with you, Aunt."

How did he *know* where I looked? His back was firmly set to my pathetic form, his attention fixed on the road ahead. Perhaps he merely *assumed* I was like every other poor gudgeon who suffered a dread of being run away-with. I studied the posterior of my nephew's head, or what could be glimpsed of it below his stylish new hat. He is a typical Austen—in appearance very much like his father James, with auburn hair and hazel eyes—but his grin is wider and his temper infinitely sweeter. I noticed that the collar of his coat was bottle-green velvet. He had acquired a decided air of Fashion in a few short months at Exeter; another year, and I should hardly recognise my nephew in the Corinthian.

"All serene?" he threw over his shoulder.

"Decidedly," I asserted, unwilling to appear a Poor Honey.

"I doubt that very much. But I intend to keep walking. In revenge, Aunt, you may abuse my prose this evening. I expect your opinions to be quite *bracing*."

Being James's son, Edward is naturally addicted to his pen. My brother published a satirical sheet he called *The Loiterer* while at Oxford, a literary triumph he never allows me to forget. Rather than ape his father, Edward is attempting a novel—which he freely shares with us of an evening. I hope he meets with greater encouragement at my hands than James's; too often, my brother damns with faint praise.

I am frequently astounded, in fact, that with two such parents as James and Mary, the one exceedingly pompous and the other decidedly lachrymose, Edward and his little sister Caroline should prove so charming! Perhaps their unfeeling household has worked as a sort of tonic. Met with indifference and self-absorption at home, they have studied wit and smiles as passports to the broader world.

A less optimistic character than Edward might have found much to resent in the happier fortunes of his Kentish Knight cousins, his schoolfellows at Winchester, who were born to wealth and unquestioned social position. But Edward regards himself as *dashed fortunate*. "No brothers to wrestle for the Pater's favour. And all the liberality of a gentleman's education at the finest schools in England. I may yet escape hanging, Aunt."

Bottom stumbled, and I drew a sharp breath. Instantly, my hands tightened on the reins, and the blasted donkey tossed its head. "I have forgot to tell you," I blurted out hurriedly, in order to distract myself, "that we saw your old school-friend William Heathcote a few months since."

"Will! How does he go on?"

"Well enough, despite his unfortunate tongue. Tho'

his mother would have it he is beset with worry, uneasy in his mind, and . . ." what had been Elizabeth's word? —"*Unsafe.*"

If I expected Edward to laugh aloud, I was disappointed. He was oddly silent for several paces, his stride slowing, and I had the impression his well-tailored back had stiffened. "Did she say—did Mrs. Heathcote give some hint as to her meaning?"

It was Cassandra who answered him. "The other boys teaze him, as I'm sure you know, on account of his stuttering."

"He's not the only fellow who stammers," Edward retorted. "I should have thought the juniors would be accustomed to the extraordinary phenomenon by now. Was that all that disturbed Mrs. Heathcote? —Will's tortured consonants?"

"Elizabeth *did* mention strange rivalries and mishaps," I admitted. "Boys' mischief, I must suppose, but clearly troubling to her mind. She seemed rather to wonder at your having heard nothing of what she called the college's *ungovernable state.*"

"She would do well to remove herself from the vicinity of the school altogether, and leave poor William to his pursuits!" Cassandra exclaimed. "There is such a thing as *too much* maternal care."

"I daresay she is a source of endless mortification to the boy," I agreed. "No youth of nearly sixteen wishes to be tied to his mamma's apron."

"Will is excessively fortunate to have her near," Edward returned brusquely. "I cannot tell you how many school holidays I met with relief, in knowing I should be invited to Heathcote's for a feast, and an entire day of indolence. To have somewhere to go, outside of college—a refuge . . ."

I glanced sidelong at Cass. *These* were confidences we had never been treated to before; our various Knight nephews being less intimate with their aunts than Edward, rarely divulged the stuff of their school-days. We were fortunate merely to catch a glimpse of their handsome faces en route to school, as they sped by on the Mail as it bowled down the Winchester Road.

"You never professed a dissatisfaction with Winchester while a Commoner there," I observed.

Edward shook his head. "I should be the most ungrateful scrub alive if I did! Consider the push my Pater was put to, to scrape together the fees, Aunt. He is not one of your fashionable vicars with livings strewn all over the Kingdom. I daresay he and Mamma made do with less coal and leaner joints than they ought, to give me a gentleman's education. They still must do so, if it comes to that, to bear my Oxford expence."

He exaggerated, I suspect—James was ever of a saving nature, and Mary is equally guarded in her purse; they should make a point of impressing upon poor Edward the sacrifices necessary to his career. But Lord in Heaven! They possess but *the single son*. Upon whom else should their guineas be spent? Certainly not poor Caroline, whose only doll is a gift from Cassandra and me.

"Were you unhappy at Winchester?" Cass demanded bluntly.

Edward shrugged. "Is happiness to be expected? Such places are not formed for the joy of their charges. They exist, rather, to toughen and harden them to the Great World. Fail to endure the daily drudgery, and you shall most certainly expire under the weight of mature existence. I knew from the first day—nay, the first hour!—that happiness was irrelevant to my success as a Commoner."

I was intrigued. "What qualities served you better?"

"Ruthlessness," he returned immediately, "and the ability to witness fellow-suffering without being fool enough to intervene."

Cassandra gave a little moan of dismay. Edward turned upon her a satiric look. "Aunt! Do not say that you have been mistaking me for a Hero! My study of Latin and Greek do not extend so far."

"What sort of suffering?" I persisted.

"The usual kind common to Englishmen: the imposition of slave labour upon those too weak to rebel, at the hands of those too powerful to notice."

The donkey stopped abruptly and dropped its head to a tuft of spring grass, tearing at it with stumped brown teeth. I released the reins and let it feed. "What does that truly mean?"

At last, Edward turned around in his path and faced us. But he kept his gaze, usually so lively, fixed upon Bottom's head. "Do you know how a junior Commoner spends his entire first year?"

"I have heard some reference to *fagging*," I said, "which I apprehend refers to the fetching of firewood and the running of errands."[2]

---

2 This term, which has developed a pejorative connotation in American English, is commonly used in Britain to describe wearisome or boring tasks. It derives from the centuries-old practice of younger public schoolboys performing manual labor for older ones.—*Editor's note.*

"It does," he agreed. "Also, the preparation of a senior Commoner's breakfast—to include the toasting of and buttering of bread, the fetching of coffee from a provisioner in town, the filling of the senior's tankard with his daily ration of beer, and the serving of each cooked meal—before ever tasting a morsel of bread oneself. Then there is the mending of the senior's wardrobe, the tending of his fire, the polishing of his boots, and the fetching of his letters, whose postage must first be paid by said junior. I have known juniors to pen all of their seniors' essays, regardless of how little Latin they may yet command, when they are not consumed with the duties of their seniors' laundry, or repairing their torn shirts. No junior's hours—or so few as may be counted on one hand—are actually spent in lessons for himself; and if he fails to give satisfaction, he may be whipped by his prefect before the entire school. Indeed, prefects expend a sum of cash each term in the purchase of ash rods intended for such beatings, as they are a privilege reserved to prefects alone; the masters believe that by learning to administer justice, we become better Englishmen."

"This is what your father's fees secured?" I was aghast.

"As a junior, certainly. I returned to Steventon that first year much thinner than I had left, on account of the scarcity of food, and the unremitting fatigues of my station. I may also say I possessed more stripes on my backside than any of Uncle Frank's Ordinary Seamen. It is possible to be beaten five times each day. I have seen waistcoats sliced to ribbons from fifty lashes."

"How dreadful," Cassandra murmured faintly.

Edward resumed walking, and the donkey, its appetites momentarily sated, consented to be led. I considered the intelligence my nephew had imparted, my gaze fixed thoughtfully once more upon his back.

"But if this is the usual run of a schoolboy's lot," I ventured, "—one Elizabeth Heathcote's husband himself must have known and condoned—why should she be especially anxious for young William's safety? Generations of Wykehamists have lived and died, apparently none the worse for the regimen."[3]

We had reached the edge of Alton, and I had been so much absorbed in our conversation that I had ceased to think of Bottom's lurching, or my own fear of a bruising fall.

Edward took his time, and some care, before answering.

"Not every Commoner is as impervious to abuse as I may have been. I was older when I arrived in college—full sixteen to many Commoners' thirteen years—and prepared for what I must expect, by the instruction of my Kentish cousins."

Of course. Four Austen-Knight boys had preceded Edward at Winchester, and then again at Oxford. A fifth son, Charles-Bridges, was in his first year at the school even now—and I shuddered suddenly in apprehension of his lot, with no elder relative to shield him.

"I must write to Will," my nephew said now, "and learn more fully how he does."

---

3 Winchester College was founded by William of Wykeham, Bishop of Winchester, in 1382. Former students are referred to as Old Wykehamists.—*Editor's note.*

"You only quitted Winchester in mid-December," I pointed out. "How did the boy go on during the autumn? Surely the change cannot be so very great!"

Edward's left hand clenched briefly, straining the leather of his glove. "Will was ever the target of a particularly brutal fellow named Prendergast—a prefect in a house different to ours. I had thought him warned off his persecution at the end of my final term; but I collect I was mistaken."

"Could you not protect the boy? Surely you were Prendergast's peer?"

"I was not a Prefect," Edward said briefly. "There are only a small number of those, you know, set up to rule their fellows—and they are chiefly appointed from among the sons of titled gentlemen. The preferment of noble scions is customary, as the masters receive an emolument for it—including, alas, even Dr. Gabell."

Gabell is the present Headmaster.

"But why?" Cassandra demanded. "Surely the posing and airs of a few well-born youths can be of no interest to true scholars!"

Edward laughed out loud, a sound of genuine mirth untinged by bitterness. "My sainted and adorable Aunt! You must know that at not too distant a date, these well-born youths will turn to men—and command England's every corridor of power! Naturally, their instructors should wish to be remembered with gratitude!"

We were nearly to the High Street, and my own unfortunate errand. "Tell me of this Prendergast," I said.

Charles frowned. "I confess no deep acquaintance with

his character, Aunt; we are very different men, and I admit to a distaste of his company. But I should say that Prendergast is all for ambition, and ruling the lives of others; I once witnessed him engaged in a high-spirited race, with a junior for his horse, goading the little fellow with spurred boots in his sides. The lad cried out piteously each time the spurs lashed his thighs. He was sent to Sick House afterward, torn and bleeding."

"And nothing was done to Prendergast?"

"Nothing at all. He had every right to use his junior as he chose; no Master, and certainly no other Commoner, should have dreamt of interfering. Prenders's horse won the race, after all, and a few days later, discharged from Sick House with gashes healing, was pathetically proud of its feat."

Edward halted before a shopkeeper's door. We had achieved No. 4, the High Street—the premises of Mr. William Curtis, the fourth generation of that family to serve as Alton's apothecary. I have been his patient now for over a year.

My nephew tied the donkey's lead to a post, then helped me down from my handsome side-saddle. I confess I was aching and stiff from the brief period on Bottom's back. And there was yet the return to Chawton to endure before I should be done! Perhaps a draught from Mr. Curtis would fortify me.

"Aunt Cassandra intends to fetch the post while I stop here," I told Edward. "I do not expect to be long. You might look into the public house in the interval."

"YOU HAVE BEEN INDISPOSED, Miss Austen?"

Mr. Curtis received me in his back room, a consulting office safe from the prying eyes and ears of the entire town, which circulated through his shop in search of everything from *Dulcamara* to *Extractum Stramonium* to *Folia Sennae* in his carefully labelled rows of jars. His apprentice, a lad of twelve, measured out the powders on brass scales and put them up in twists of paper. There were other preparations as well—Olympian Dew, Milk of Roses, and Gowland's Lotion for the removal of freckles; pomatum and hair powder; vials of lip salve and rouge.

Indisposed.

For nearly a fortnight I had been in and out of bed, suffering fever and bilious attacks that prevented me from taking sustenance. Inactivity bred weakness, which indisposed me further. Having felt well enough in January to undertake the project of my new novel—which I am calling *The Brothers*—I had got barely as far as the description of Mr. Parker and his Trafalgar House schemes before abandoning my work to illness. I have not the energy for composition beyond the necessary letters to friends and family.

I lifted my shoulders in an expression of indifference. "A week ago I was very poorly. I have had a good deal of fever, and indifferent nights."

He peered at me narrowly through gold-rimmed spectacles. "Your skin has certainly darkened, Miss Austen, tho' as it is hardly the season for tanning, you cannot be excessively exposed to the sun. We have experienced so much rain of late!"

We were blessed with yet another damp spring. And I had spent most of it within doors—in the confines of my bed, to be exact. But I knew that Curtis was correct: indeed, my face appears black and white and every wrong colour, mottled as a brindled dog's. "I must not depend upon ever being very blooming again."

"Such a complexion suggests a surfeit of black bile," Curtis said, "one of the sad effects of advancing age. It contributes lamentably to melancholy. Have you found that your spirits are as oppressed as your bowels and frame?"

Naturally my spirits are oppressed! To think on Death will dash the heart of the most insensible and hardened among us. But I said only, "What ought one to do for an excess of bile?"

Curtis sighed, and threw up his hands. "One cannot turn back the clock. It is, as I have said, a condition of advancing age. But you might avoid red meat. And submit to a regular practice of blood-letting. That is the only true method of ridding the body of pernicious humours."

I compressed my lips. There is nothing so lowering as the arm stretched out over the basin, the sting of the lancet, and the dark, animal blood spooling across white porcelain.

"I could bleed you immediately," he offered, "but you will experience a faintness in the head afterwards, and I do not like to think of you adventuring back to Chawton in such a state. Better, perhaps, that I should call upon you tomorrow at home, so that you may rest once the blood-letting is done."

"You cannot prescribe a paregoric draught?" I suggested feebly. There were, after all, scores of labelled jars in the adjoining room; surely some concoction of miscellaneous Latin might relieve my symptoms?

The apothecary shook his head. "I am afraid, Miss Austen, that there is nothing more my draughts may offer you. Unless you are experiencing excessive pain . . . you have referred to your back, in the area of your kidneys . . . in such a case a dose of laudanum, to be taken in water, will alleviate the acutest symptoms."

I like laudanum even less than bleeding. I have known of women addicted to the subtle poison, and to the indolence it produces; I refuse to spend my final months in a fog of benign stupidity.

"In that case, I shall waste no more of your time." I rose from my chair and curtseyed politely.

Mr. Curtis bowed. "Shall I attend you at home on the morrow?"

He has bled me repeatedly over the past six months, and I perceive no lasting benefit.

"I must decline," I said, "as we have company in the house. Illness is a dangerous indulgence at my time of life—I prefer to be merry with my guests. Surely laughter may do as much to dispel black melancholy as the sharpest steel!"

"We must hope that is the case." But the apothecary's voice was solemn, and he did not appear to share my views; indeed, I believe he has washed his hands of me.

2

THE PASSING OF MR.
JAMES LEIGH-PERROT

Chawton Cottage
Thursday, 27 March 1817

Edward returned to Steventon yesterday, the morning after our donkey-jaunt into Alton. I had barely an interval to consider of rest, and the gloomy prospect of Mr. Curtis and his lancet, before the mail was brought in. We received ill-tidings from my aunt Leigh-Perrot at Scarlets: my uncle James is failing and in danger of his life.

James Leigh-Perrot is my mother's elder brother. He and Aunt Jane were never blessed with children, and my widowed mother has long regarded their property as her rightful inheritance—or as that of her eldest son, James. As Uncle Leigh-Perrot's namesake, my brother must be gripped in considerable suspense as to the outcome of events; and as my uncle is fully two-and-eighty years of age, that outcome cannot be long delayed.

Edward writes this morning to inform me that his father has actually gone into Berkshire, presumably to hold vigil—or my unfortunate aunt's plump hands—until such time as my uncle expires. That James should undertake such a journey, in poor weather, when he has been suffering from indisposition himself this winter, is a testament to fine family-feeling and the duty one owes one's elders—or one's pocket. The rest of us are resigned to await the sad intelligence from Scarlets through the more usual medium of the post.

My mother suffers a good deal of apprehension, not solely from solicitude for her purse. From my bedroom window, I may observe her to take repeated turns around the garden, wrapped closely against the wind in an old velvet cloak of a now-indeterminate colour. She and her brother are fond of one another, as the sole remaining siblings of a family ought to be.[4] For many years, particularly during our residence in Bath, we were intimate with the Leigh-Perrots. We attended their card-parties and suppers when they quitted Scarlets during the winter to take Bath's waters (the source, perhaps, of my uncle's remarkable longevity), and danced constant attendance upon them at concerts and plays. My Aunt Jane, who was born in the Barbados and sent back to school in England at the tender age of six, knew hardly any other family than ours. She married my uncle when she was but twenty, and was the concentrated object of his affection and indulgence for more than fifty years. It has perhaps made her think too highly of herself and her position, a complaisance that has in later years blinded her to advancing age, diminished looks, and even a questionable

---

4 Jane's mother Cassandra Leigh Austen had an elder sister, Jane, who predeceased her, and a younger brother, Thomas, who is described as "imbecilic," and was placed in care along with her son George, who was similarly disabled. Although Thomas Leigh was still alive at this time, he was not part of Cassandra Leigh Austen's life.—*Editor's note.*

sanity. Tho' a wealthy woman, she is never generous, and her whims are peculiar. I cannot forget that my aunt was tried for theft at the Winter Assizes of 1800—a milliner on Pulteney Bridge insisting she had palmed a card of lace—for which she might have been transported to the Antipodes. My uncle was steady in his support of her innocence, going so far as to lodge with her gaoler a full seven months. Her trial ended in acquittal; but she remains a subject of familial uneasiness. There was the additional episode of a purloined plant, spirited from a hothouse under my aunt's cloak, that has never been adequately explained, tho' probably silenced by my uncle's liberal application of coin in necessary quarters. At the prospect of losing him, Aunt Leigh-Perrot will be prostrate, and overcome with predictable terrors. I do not envy James his dutiful errand.

My mother has come to a halt now in her perambulations through the withered grass, and appears to be contemplating the bed in which she cultivates her potatoes. I have not burdened her with speculation—but I cannot be sanguine that my uncle's death will benefit even one of us. He suffered a reversal when my brother Henry's banks failed last year, having pledged ten thousand pounds in surety of Henry's loans—a ghastly sum that was lost when Henry was declared a bankrupt.[5] It is possible that my uncle regards his duty to his sister's children as entirely at an end.

There is a sudden volley of fists upon the front door, below-stairs, and I rise from my chair to answer it—but

---

5 Ten thousand pounds in 1817 is a sum roughly equivalent to £950,000 today. —*Editor's note.*

perceive that Cassandra is before me. The caller is a messenger, come on horseback with an express from James for my mother.

Cassandra carries the missive immediately out to the back garden, without staying to shrug on a pelisse. Her countenance, glimpsed even from the remove of this upstairs window, is mournful. My sister stands in the chill, hugging her elbows, as my mother adjusts her spectacles with gloved hands. Her face is pinched and aged, her eyes heavy-lidded. The paper trembles in her fingers. Then she drops it to the ground unheeded and reaches for Cassandra.

I know without having to enquire that my uncle is dead.

Here I sit, in contemplation of future events—and they have already occurred. Regardless of how we may hope to dispose of our remaining days, their end is preordained.

I shiver suddenly, and draw away from the glass.

MY BROTHER JAMES NATURALLY communicated the melancholy intelligence to Steventon rectory, and to my brother Frank's establishment in Alton, at almost the same moment he sent it to ourselves. A flurry of family missives, by courier and manservant, is the result.

Frank is determined to journey into Berkshire to assist James and my aunt Leigh-Perrot with the preparations for my uncle's funeral at Scarlets. He has invited Cassandra to accompany him—and James's wife, Mary, insists on going along, too. She should never miss an opportunity to condole with the Bereaved, and appear important in black bombazine, for the gratification of mourners.

The entire party intends to be present for the reading of my uncle's will.

"I wish I might accompany them," my mother said falteringly, "that I might condole with sister Jane and support her in affliction; but I fear I am unequal to so fatiguing a journey, and ladies do not attend the obsequies, after all. You will write to me, Cassandra, and tell me how the corpse appears?"

Cassandra said all that was proper, in assuring my mother that she need not exert herself beyond what is seemly in a lady of eight-and-seventy. I am sure Cass will report that my uncle's countenance is all that is serene in death.

I am not to accompany my family, being as little inclined as my mother to the Berkshire Road. It is some forty miles to Scarlets, and tho' Frank means to hire a post-chaise and complete the journey in three stages, changing horses in Basingstoke and Reading, it will prove a punishing day of driving. My back should suffer too much; but I may make an excuse of attending upon my mother, whose advanced years demand every consideration.

My nephew Edward has written to say that, as his mother is being taken up in Frank's carriage at Basingstoke, he means to drive over with his sister Caroline in the pony-trap tomorrow, and keep us company during his parents' absence. I confess that I shall be happy to see him back, tho' indeed he left us only yesterday, and for the pleasure of twelve-year-old Caroline. If we *must* put on our dreary old black gowns for Uncle James, at least the girlish laughter of my niece will lighten our hearts.

3

A SUMMONS TO WINCHESTER

Chawton Cottage
Friday, 28 March, 1817

"Are you at liberty to read a bit of prose, Aunt Jane?" Edward stood in the drawing-room doorway, a page of foolscap in his right hand. His chestnut curls were more disordered than was usual, even for his fashionable stile of hair-dressing, and his fingertips were stained with ink. He had not been arrived at the house above an hour, and already he was bent upon writing.

"I am always at leisure to be entertained," I replied, struggling to sit upright. I had been lying across three straight-backed chairs set out in a row, to ease the ache in my back.

"Why are you not lying upon the sopha, Aunt?" Caroline enquired curiously. She had trailed along behind her brother, to his obvious annoyance; after her initial delight in arrival, the child was more than usually dismayed by a want of occupation, without her mother to scold her and set her tasks. "I am sure it must be more comfortable."

"The sopha is your grandmamma's place," I explained in a lowered tone, "and if I once usurped it, she should never rest there again. We cannot have that, Caroline; Age must always take precedence over Beauty."

Caroline wrinkled her nose at my feeble joke—she must regard me as equally old and ugly as her grandmother. She slid past Edward to fling herself on the aforementioned sopha. "That is as nonsensical as Edward giving precedence to Miss Smith, when he goes in to supper at The Vyne on Hunt days, because her aunt is Mrs. Chute."

"Mrs. Chute is the mistress of The Vyne, and her husband the Master of the Vyne Hunt," I said reprovingly. "Edward merely secures the privilege of chasing foxes, and drinking excellent claret after, by allowing Miss Smith to go before him to the dining parlour."

Caroline sniffed her contempt. "There are far too many Smiths. I will not allow them to be any better than Austens. And certainly none of them is a *Beauty*, no matter what her age."

"Miss Emma Smith is a charming girl," Edward retorted hotly, "and the respect I accord her is none of your business, minx!"

He had entirely forgot his prose. Indeed, his fingers crushed the paper deplorably.

"Pray take Link for a walk, Caroline," I suggested, "as he will be missing Aunt Cassandra exceedingly, and we do not want him moped to death. Do not neglect to wrap up warmly, and enquire of Cook whether she has any errands for you."

The girl flung a sigh, but took herself off in search of the dog, without protest. I trusted Cook would give her a penny, to be spent at the Chawton bread-baker's.

"Now we may be private." I was sitting fully upright; my backache I chose to disregard. I searched my mind for the names of Edward's characters. "Have you more to relate of the delightful Mr. Reeves, and his adventures in Sport? —Or am I to abuse the preoccupations of the intimates of Culver Court?"[6]

"Neither." Edward unclenched his fingers and smoothed the paper, no doubt relieved that I did not teaze him for particulars of Miss Emma Smith's charms. "I have here a letter from William Heathcote, that I believe demands your peculiar attention. I received it at Steventon yesterday by the morning post, and its contents have never been far from my mind in the hours since. Indeed, it was partly from a desire for your opinion that I descended on Chawton."

"And here I flattered myself it was for my company." I frowned as I took the foolscap from him, and glanced at the closely-written lines. Master William's fist was legible, tho' from its raggedness, I discerned anxiety or haste in the composition.

---

6 Austen mentions both Mr. Reeves and Culver Court in reference to James-Edward Austen's fiction, in a letter dated 27 January 1817.—*Editor's note.*

Gabell's House
Winchester College
Wednesday, 26 March 1817
My dear Austen—

I learned of my Mother that you were down from Oxford for the Easter holiday, and so direct this missive to the rectory at Steventon in the hope I shall catch you idling there. It feels an age since we have met, tho' you have been gone only since the close of Short Half. I shan't deny I envy you your freedom, and the rigs and grigs you must get up to now that you may spend your allowance as you chuse, and are at liberty to lark about the country without regard for Masters or Prefects and their beastly rods. I am sure you never wish to darken the doors of Winton again.

It is only that if you should be bored in your Easter rustication, and casting about for something to do, I should dearly love your advice.

You will remember Prenders, the ugly villain? Dashed if he hasn't made away with himself—and contrived to make it appear as tho' I am to blame! The whole school is in an uproar already, without my Mother fretting I shall be hauled before the Magistrate and transported or hanged. I cannot think to whom I should appeal for help, as Dr. Gabell only looks grave and preserves a dignified silence when I broach the subject, or says we must Await the Event of the Inquest. That is to be Monday, at the White Hart.

Gabell has been ever a lick-spittle and a coward, and I would consult old Clarke instead, but he is in as bad a case as myself, being blamed for Prenders sneaking out of college and drowning himself. As if Prenders cared for Clarke's good opinion! He was a Prefect, after all, and bowed to no Master but Urquhart, as all the world knows.

Pray write to say that you shall Succour me in my Hour of Need. Mamma shall see you right and tight at No. 12; Aunt Ally has fled to the Continent, and Mamma must have someone to Coddle.

Yours ever,
Heathcote

I read the letter a second time, concentrating on the passages that seemed most wildly phrased, then glanced up at Edward. "Master Will expresses himself more comprehensibly in print than he does in conversation. Who is Prenders?"

"The senior I mentioned, Arthur Prendergast, who fagged his juniors unmercifully."

"The one with a taste in spurs." I folded the foolscap gently and held it out to my nephew. "I apprehend that he has died?"

"And apparently by his own hand—tho' how Heathcote can fear that he is to be held responsible for self-murder, much less transported or hanged, is beyond my comprehension."

Thus speaks eighteen, of the terrors of mere adolescents.

"Dr. Gabell is the Headmaster?"

Edward nodded. "Young William was taken into his House as a special favour to his Mamma, owing to Gabell's feeling for Will's father. They were at Oxford together, I believe—you know the sort of thing."

"I do. Was Prendergast also under Dr. Gabell's jurisdiction?"

"He was not. Prenders lodged in Clarke's House—the fellow Heathcote says is under a cloud."

"Is Urquhart also a Master?"

Edward looked shocked. "Not at all, Aunt! Urquhart is a Scholar in College—and one of the most dazzling. A charming fellow, blessed with easy humour and an excellent understanding. I called him a friend, indeed, tho' we were never housed together. He has often stood buff when Will Heathcote was subjected to teazing, and defended him even from the intimates of Clarke's House. I do not know a better fellow—on good terms with the whole world, including even Prendergast."

"A paragon, I collect! Do the college masters hold him in equal esteem?"

"It is believed Dr. Gabell will propose Urquhart for a place at New College next autumn, and speaks of him as certain to win it. Urquhart also has been a great favourite of Mr. Clarke's from the moment of his entry upon Winchester; indeed, I believe it was Clarke who proposed him for Scholar. You will know, of course, that Scholars pay no fees."

"I had thought them usually Founders' Kin," I mused.

Such boys are descended from the original prelates who established Winchester, and preferred above all other scrubby youths, regardless of origin.

Edward wrinkled his nose. "I have never heard anyone speak particularly as to Urquhart's *family*. He is one of those whose natural achievements are recommendation enough."

"His amity for the villain Prendergast does not argue a *discerning* character."

"On the contrary, I suspect it was Urquhart's influence that exercised what little restraint Prenders managed. They were both Prefects, tho' one is a Scholar and the other a Commoner. If Prendergast was distinguished by tyranny, Urquhart was known for his mercy. Will Heathcote would tell you the same."

"And yet, you describe the prefects as friends."

Edward's brow furrowed. "I believe Urquhart was often staying with Prendergast's people during term-leave. Perhaps his sense of obligation dictated his tolerance."

"Perhaps." I considered this an instant. "Is it possible Prendergast was not *entirely* a villain?"

Edward looked dubious. "He was certainly no angel, Aunt."

"But self-murder, Edward! What urged him to so desperate an act? Should you have said Prenders was of a melancholy disposition? —Prone to poetical despair?"

"An apprentice of Byron's, do you mean? Lord, no!"

"You are surprized, then, to learn he made away with himself?"

Edward tucked Heathcote's letter into his waistcoat.

"Had the intelligence come from anyone other than Will, I should not have credited it. Prenders was more likely to do murder than . . ." He faltered.

". . . submit to injury himself?"

"Exactly. I should describe him as tenacious of life, as in life he was tenacious of power."

I glanced at my nephew admiringly. "Oh, well-phrased! We shall make a novelist of you yet. If suicide is unlikely, perhaps Master Prendergast met with an accident. Or was set upon by a junior who resented his bullying—and died defending himself from mortal peril!"

"That junior is hardly William Heathcote," Edward objected. "Prenders outweighed him by several stone, and should have swatted Will aside as he might a fly."

I reflected on my last glimpse of Will: flushed with embarrassment as he stammered, then bowed in gloom as he trudged to the carriage. The poor fellow was hardly carefree in the easiest of times; but his apprehension now must be extreme.

"Heathcote must be dashed anxious, to have written such a letter," Edward mused, echoing my thoughts.

"He cannot truly be in fear of being taken up, however," I reasoned. "What can have occurred between him and Master Prendergast, that he should refer to transportation and hanging?"

My nephew turned restlessly before the hearth. "That is what disturbs me, Aunt. No fellow of Will's age and cares will be bothered with scrawling a note to an old schoolfellow, without there is great need. He endeavours to appear stout-hearted—but I'll wager he's living in dread of the Law. You will note how he refers to Monday's inquest. Absurd as it appears, he must believe himself caught in this snare."

"But what can he expect you to do, Edward? You have not yet achieved your majority, and can have no influence with the coroner. Young Will requires the counsel of a male relative—and that relative's solicitor." I rose from my makeshift couch. "I shall write immediately to his mother."

"Stay, Aunt." Edward extended his hand and halted me. "If *you* have discerned the need for a male relative, no doubt Mrs. Heathcote will have already done so. If you must write to her, let it be to inform her of our imminent arrival at No. 12, The Close."

"I?" The word came out on a squeak. "Travel to Winchester? I have only just refused to go to Scarlets!"

"The two cases are not the same. Winchester is but sixteen miles from this door, a few hours' journey over excellent road. We may set out after breakfast, and be arrived in time for a nuncheon."

"You intend to accompany me?"

"Better than that. I shall drive you in my trap."

"But what about Caroline?"

"She may serve to amuse my grandmamma."

I sighed. "Your grandmamma will be most put out, to discover herself the sole guardian of a teazing child!" Martha Lloyd, who might otherwise have amused my niece, was absent on a visit to her relations.

"Caroline shall have Link. They shall succour each other in the absence of dearer friends."

I stared at him.

"Will's mother was already gravely concerned for his welfare when last you met," Edward said gently. "She shall welcome you now with relief."

Elizabeth certainly had urged me to stay with her at Easter. Alethea was gone to the Continent, as Master Will's letter declared. My friend was marooned in a silent house, fear rising like fog in the deserted rooms.

"We must allow a day for her receipt of the post," I mused. "And that means losing tomorrow. We shall be forced to Sunday travel. And it is *Palm* Sunday! Your father will scold, Edward."

"—If ever he knows of it. And I am sure I cannot see why he should. Consider the drive to Winchester an act of charity on our parts rather than a blasphemous indulgence—for the inquest is to be held Monday, recollect." He patted his waistcoat pocket. "We cannot in conscience delay."

I considered for an instant, while my nephew waited amiably for me to fall in with his plans. The reprobate grinned at me.

"We are safe through Easter at least, Aunt, for having only just arrived at Scarlets, our family party is unlikely to quit it before the funeral-baked meats are entirely cold. They will not return to Hampshire until Easter Tuesday at the earliest. And as that is the day I must return to Oxford . . ."

We might just manage an adventure if we acted with decision. I should have to prevaricate a little to my mother—Elizabeth Heathcote indisposed, her sister absent, her son requiring Edward's companionship, being sadly moped while home at the Easter holiday . . . but would it serve?

And would I suffer unduly from the jolting pony trap, over the course of a few hours of *good road*?

"It cannot be more injurious than a quarter-hour of riding Bottom," I muttered under my breath.

Edward laughed. "Brava, Aunt Jane! I shall undertake to charm Caroline and Grandmamma into believing this is entirely their own scheme, while you write to Winchester. If I carry the letter directly to Alton, we shall make today's post!"

4

A SUMMONS TO DEATH

No. 12, The Close
Winchester
Sunday, 30 March 1817

There is nothing so wearying as carriage-travel, particularly when one is subjected to my brother James's trap, which is the sort of ancient equipage only a clergyman could regard as anything but a penance. I have seen smart traps in my time, with gleaming leather cushions and stylishly-dressed ladies holding the ribbons, but that is not the vehicle poor Edward is obliged to drive when he is at home. James owns a vastly nicer closed carriage, and a pair of horses he may put to it, but rarely suffers either to churn the mud of country roads. I have no idea what he is saving them for.

But the journey south in the open cart, behind Edward's trusty pony Shadow, on a (thankfully!) cloudless spring day, proved bracing rather than injurious. Being a well-travelled route for the Mail, the Winchester Road is in excellent repair, and the pony's pace was hardly break-neck. One is able to see so much more of the country, too, from an open vehicle. On every side, the soul was refreshed by signs of spring, in the delicate green tracery of leaves among the copses, and the blowsy beauty of daffodils tossing among hedgerows. I was devoutly glad it did not come on to rain.

Edward handed me down from the trap before the door of No. 12, and stayed only to make his salutations before driving round to the Close's stables. Elizabeth ran down the few steps and embraced me fervently.

"You have come!" she said breathlessly. "If you knew how I have *longed* for this visit! But I was certain you should never fail me, Jane!"

Any doubt I felt at having solicited my invitation to Winchester, I immediately put aside.

"I am sorry to see you dressed all in black," Elizabeth said as she led me into her home. "My condolences on the loss of your uncle. I am sure you are all anxiety for the grieving family party assembled at Scarlets—which makes your willingness to travel to Winchester at such a time, all the more precious."

"I might as easily await news of my uncle's funeral rites in Winchester as Chawton," I assured her. "I wrote to my sister Cassandra, and begged her to direct her correspondence here for a time."

"How does your Aunt Perrot go on?"

"Cassandra would have it that she is deeply affected by my uncle's loss—which makes us love her better. In the usual way, Jane Perrot is entirely self-absorbed; a sincere grief may be the making of what years she has left."

"Jane!" Elizabeth looked torn between amusement and reproof. "I hope you mother is grown accustomed to her brother's loss? She will not be unhappy this week, being quite alone?"

"She will be occupied by her granddaughter Caroline, who is perfectly formed to both teaze and cajole her out of all misery. And do not forget that she is in momentary expectation of an important communication, by Express from Berkshire: she looks for a considerable legacy from my uncle's estate."

"The Perrots were childless, I recall," Elizabeth said. "What a security it should be for Mrs. Austen, to have a fund put by against advancing age!"

"My brother James expects any legacy to come to *him*," I added, "as my uncle's namesake, and rejoicing as he supposes in many more years of life than poor Mamma may reasonably expect. Observe the speed with which he departed for Scarlets at receiving the intelligence of a mere illness! My uncle had not even breathed his last."

"One cannot blame James, I suppose."

"One can," I corrected, "and one does. It is not as tho' my uncle may appreciate James's zeal in observing the obsequies, after all. Nor may he amend his will in James's favour, on account of it. My brother ought to have stayed quietly at home, and expressed his sympathies on a black-edged mourning card. My sister Cassandra I cannot censure; her motives in journeying into Berkshire were anything but mercenary, and indeed, verge on the selfless. She went only to support my aunt—who, being insensible to the misery she habitually occasions others, cannot appreciate the depth of Cass's sacrifice."

When I had removed my wraps and the two young men had joined us, our party shared a nuncheon of bread, cheese, and sherry. But the atmosphere was uncongenial. Young Heathcote was looking hagged—I imputed the cause to poor sleep—and Eliza was worse. Her pallor was dreadful, and her right eyelid twitched in an alarming manner I am sure she was ignorant of. Her inattention to the general conversation was remarkable.

When the serving girl had retreated to the kitchens, Will set down his tankard. "Ed-d-ward will have t-t-told you what h-h-happened to P-p-prendergast, M-m-miss Austen?"

"In a manner of speaking, William. He allowed me to read your letter. It was lacking in detail, but suggested that Master Prendergast is dead."

The boy swallowed a bit of bread with difficulty. "As a d-d-doornail."

"William," Eliza murmured in faint distress.

The boy screwed up his mouth, his face working vigourously as he attempted again to speak. A series of inarticulate grunts emanated from his throat, and then with explosive effect: "Y-y-yes, Mamma, I am a-w-wware that I offer the f-f-fel . . ."

Confounded, and with evident exasperation, Will reached for a tablet of paper and a pencil and dashed off the remainder of his thoughts, which he then held up for all our party to peruse. . . . *the fellow faint respect. But I never liked Prenders, as you very well know; he was a complete villain, and I will confess my first emotion upon learning he was dead was one of relief.*

"Do not be saying so beyond these four walls," I cautioned. "However your intimates may excuse the justice of your feelings, the broader world will condemn them."

"What we do not fully apprehend," Edward added, "is *how* Prendergast died."

Will began to scribble furiously again.

"Are the facts generally known?" I asked Elizabeth.

"Dr. Gabell has done what he can to quell rumour before the inquest tomorrow. But as is so often the case, his efforts have merely encouraged all manner of wild speculation," she replied. "I am told the boy was absent from his bed Tuesday night, but from one cause or another was not looked for until the following morning, when he failed to present himself in Hall."

Will held up his tablet, with its pencil scrawls. Edward took it from him and read aloud: "Insley Minor bade the juniors to keep mum that night and stick a bolster in Prenders's bed. Wherever Prenders had got to, Insley said, was his business entirely. Old Clarke quizzed his boys after breakfast, but none could say where Prenders was. General search of buildings. He did not turn up."

"Who is Insley Minor?" I asked.

"Peter, the younger of the two Insley boys in school. Insley Major was my year," Edward supplied, "and is gone up to Magdalen."

"Has anyone interrogated Minor as to his special knowledge of Prendergast's movements?"

Will lifted his shoulders to convey ignorance. *He is*

Prenders's chief booby and loyal shadow, he wrote. *He'd enjoy lording it over the others, in Prenders's absence.*

"Around four o'clock," Elizabeth continued, "the parish constable arrived with a report for Dr. Gabell, who had apparently ordered a broader search of the town. Master Prendergast's body was discovered drowned in a culvert at some remove from the school."

Will's pencil was flying again.

"In Pot," Edward read, from over his shoulder. "Or rather, the culvert below."

I glanced from one boy to the other. With a nod, William gave the office of explanation to my nephew.

"You will know, Aunt, that when we have a holiday or a Remedy—that is, a special day free of lessons—we are released to Hills," Edward said.

"What is Hills?"

"The college's preferred exercise-ground. Properly speaking, it is St. Catherine's Hill—about a mile's walk to the south. When given leave, we all march over in a column, Prefects on the road and the rest of us on the footpaths, and lark about in the meadows. The ruins of an ancient fort are at the hill's summit, and the Itchen at its foot."

"And 'Pot?'"

"A particular lock, in the system of cuts that are known as the Itchen Navigation—some ten miles of canals running alongside the river itself, Aunt, that permit barges full of commerce to move from Winchester to Southampton, and the sea."

"Allow me to conjecture," I said. "The boys make a dare of jumping from the bank to the barges, and back again."

Edward grinned. "Certain among us have been known to do so, from time to time. But Pot is in general a perfect bathing-pool during the summer months. The only defect is the presence of a sluicegate that controls the lock's water level; when opened, the rush of the current may be quite strong. An inexpert swimmer may be swept through the lock and into a culvert, some ten feet in length."

"Is it also a dare to open the sluice upon the head of some unwitting junior?"

"I *have known* stronger swimmers to deliberately ride the current through the tunnel, for the sheer adventure; but I suspect not every boy is so brave."

I looked at William. "Was Master Prendergast a strong swimmer?"

He lifted his shoulders helplessly, by way of reply.

"In your letter to Edward," I said, "you suggested self-murder was suspected."

William bent to his tablet. His mother issued a small sigh of exasperation.

"Speak, William! You know that your defect will only mend if you *practise*."

"H-h-haste," he retorted, and displayed his tablet.

"Suicide, on account of it being the wrong month for bathing, and the water so dashed cold," Edward read aloud. "And he was fully dressed. Sodden wool, in the torrent of the sluice, should have dragged him down; but his boots—!"

"He went into the water thus by choice, accident, or at the malicious hands of another," I concluded. "Let us take the first proposition. Cast your mind back a week, Will, and tell me if Master Prendergast was in a morbid state of mind?"

William's brows drew together in perplexity.

"Blue-devilled," Edward suggested.

His friend's face cleared. "He was n-n-not. —Boasting of the m-m-mill his cousin m-m-meant to take him to, on the Easter h-h-holiday, which none of us cr-cr-credited for a m-m-moment."

"Mill?"

"Prize-fight," Edward offered. "If he was not claiming to be a rum go at cock-fighting, or tipping a Charley when he was up in Town, or betting at vingt-et-un, Prenders was always sure to have witnessed Abey Belasco level the Nonpareil. We none of us believed such tosh."[7]

So much schoolboy cant made me smile. "Master Prendergast aspired to the Corinthian Set, I collect. His spirits, then, were very much as usual? There was nothing to suggest a crushing blow, black despair, or a mind at its tether's-end?"

Will shook his head.

"Very well. We must agree, then, that suicide is unlikely. Could it have been an accident? A careless slip, for instance, on soft ground near the sluicegate?"

---

7 Abey Belasco (1797–1830) was a bare-knuckle fighter, among the top five rated pugilists in London in 1817. Jack Randall, known as the Nonpareil, fought from 1815–1822 and retired undefeated.—*Editor's note.*

"I daresay that whoever pushed him, hoped it would be deemed so," my nephew interjected.

I lifted my brows. "You are all for the strong hand in the small of the back, then, Edward?"

"Well, that is how one usually goes into Pot, without one is tossed in by the collar! Recollect, Will, when Fflagg-Winters navigated the tunnel? He spit out the other end like a ball from a duelling pistol, his hair all over green from river-weed!"

Both young men laughed heartily, while Elizabeth and I exchanged stares of consternation. But it emerged that being nearly drowned in Pot, if not a dare, was nonetheless a rite of passage at Winchester College. Most of the junior boys were subjected to dunkings at the careless hands of elders; those who could not swim, quickly learnt, by trial and error; those who could, were suffered to prove their mastery with a quarter-mile exhibition from Tun Bridge above the lock, to Pot itself—and then were declared free of the general humiliation.

"Fflagg-Winters was such a one," Edward concluded. "He was set upon by a pair of seniors and summarily sent down the sluicegate torrent. That was in summer, naturally. No one would think of plunging into Pot in March, as Prenders did—he'd end in Sick House, with an inflammation of the lung."

Or drowned.

"We cannot rule out accident," I said thoughtfully, "but cannot exclude the possibility of a *push* either. The mere fact of its being a prevalent practice among the schoolboys, should make it the whim of a moment—easily acted upon. But should it not have been *witnessed*? Are there not generally a number of boys taking exercise in the neighbourhood?"

"Not on a lesson-day in this season," Edward replied. "Hills is a treat reserved for free days, or the long evenings of June and July."

"At present, the light begins to fade at half-past five," I mused, "and by seven o'clock it is generally dark. That may account for the body lying undiscovered until the following day. Who found the corpse?"

Will cast his mother an enquiring look. This was a detail he could not supply.

"The lock-keeper," Elizabeth said. "Apparently the boy's coat snagged on something within the culvert, that kept the body from floating free. It was only when the sluice was opened again on the Wednesday, for the accommodation of a barge, and the culvert failed to drain, that the keeper investigated the blockage, and discovered the young man's body."

She paused, and fumbled for a handkerchief. "When I consider of his family—how the dreadful intelligence must have fallen upon them, in an Express despatched by the Headmaster—"

Her speech was momentarily suspended.

"How did you learn so much, Elizabeth?" I enquired.

"Dr. Gabell," she replied. "He shared the particulars when he waited upon me here Wednesday evening."

"The Headmaster took you into his confidence, regarding Arthur Prendergast?" I frowned. "Why should he do so?"

She hesitated an instant, the fine skin drawn tightly over cheekbone and jaw. "Because he suspects my son of contriving the boy's end."

I looked from her stricken countenance to Will's flushed one. "How?"

"P-p-prenders had m-m-my note in his p-p-pocket," he said grudgingly, "s-s-summoning him to his d-d-death."

NOW, THE TABLE WAS cleared of its repast, and the serving-girl unlikely to disturb us further. It was time, I judged, to grapple with ugly truths.

Will's note—for he admitted stoutly that the handwriting was indeed his—was found in Prendergast's waistcoat when the unfortunate lad was fished from the culvert. Will insisted, however, that it had not been directed to the dead boy at all.

"It was a s-s-sentence or two only," he explained, "m-m-meant for B-b-badger—"

"That will be Charles Baigent," Elizabeth supplied, "another junior in Will's house."

"Capital fellow!" Edward exclaimed. "How does old Badge go on?"

"S-s-splendidly." Will bent once more to his tablet.

We had waited all winter to launch a model frigate I had of Uncle Gilbert when he was last turned on shore. It has been raining for ages—and the fine weather this week could not be trusted to last. As the Easter holiday meant Badger should be sent home to his people, I proposed we meet at Pot once our lessons were done, to sail the ship.

"What day was this?"

"M-m-monday l-l-last."

And to arrange the meeting, Will had resorted to pen and paper, as he frequently must. It was obvious he preferred the fluency of the written word to the trials of his tongue.

"'I was hit with the notion in the midst of Vulgus,'" Edward read aloud. "—That's our set Latin composition, Aunt. 'Jotted the words on parchment and pitched the roll over Badger's scob.' —That is a work desk, in normal parlance. 'He met me after Toytime—' that is, our studies—'and we stole off with no one the wiser.' How did she sail?" Edward demanded.

"S-s-sweet as you like! My uncle is a p-p-post-captain on the East India S-s-station, you know, and h-h-had the m-m-model from a M-m-malay c-c-carver—"

"I collect this missive you tossed to your friend somehow went astray," I interjected, "if it was later discovered in the dead boy's waistcoat."

More writing, offered this time to the table generally.

Badger thought he put it on the fire, but could not perfectly swear to it. Either Prenders picked it up and pocketed it for reasons I cannot explain, or Another gave it to him. Doctor Gabell says, however, that as I am responsible for Prenders being on Hills without leave, I shall have to account for myself to the coroner."

"I see no help for it." I was purposefully brisk. "But as one who has given sworn testimony in the past, in places akin to the White Hart, I may assure you that the coroner will be all that is correct. Such men are not bogeys, William, intent upon seizing your soul. Are you able to recall the language of your stray missive?"

Will nodded and resumed his pencil. *Meet me at Pot after Toytime. We'll launch her in the drink.*

"And this was enough to draw the unfortunate Prendergast away from school?" I exclaimed. "He wanted little inducement!"

"Many of the fellows slip out of college betimes," Edward explained. "Prenders must have thought he'd been invited to a lark."

"Is such leave generally granted?"

Elizabeth snorted. "Not at all, if one refers to Dr. Gabell. But the little choristers are constantly jobbing up and down the town's streets—fetching coffee and Sally Lunns from one shop, or their seniors' coats from a tailor. And the older boys are willing to take their punishment at the rod, in exchange for a stolen interval of leisure. College is as porous as a sieve."

"The existence of the note should be as nothing, did Dr. Gabell credit William's word of honour—and his claim of innocence," I persisted. "Is there some reason for the Headmaster to doubt either? —Some history of enmity between Prendergast and yourself, Will?"

His eyes dropped to his tankard, and he fingered the rim.

"There is not a fellow in college that did not detest Prenders like the plague," Edward said into the silence.

"Insley M-m-minor," Will objected.

"True." Edward frowned. "I wonder what he makes of all this. No one else is so well acquainted with Prendergast's character or interests. I rather wonder, indeed, at his failure to accompany his friend that afternoon to Pot."

"We cannot know whether Prendergast informed him of the appointment," I observed. "Perhaps we shall learn more at the inquest. But to return to the point: William, was there particular enmity between you and Arthur Prendergast, that might justify Dr. Gabell's suspicions?"

The boy drew a sharp breath, and resorted to a flurry of written words.

That is a question better asked of the Dead. Had it been my body found submerged in Pot, I daresay none of my fellows should have expressed surprize—and all should have known who was culpable.

5

THE MEMORY OF FIRE

No. 12, The Close
Winchester
Sunday, 30 March 1817, cont'd.

My back ached deplorably, but I knew that it should improve if I took some judicious exercise. When Elizabeth suggested an airing, therefore—or perhaps a nap before dinner in the privacy of my bedchamber—I pushed my chair back from the table and waved a dismissive hand. "Rest? Fiddle! I have been at my leisure all morning, I assure you. And the grounds of the Close are so lovely at this time of year."

The young men had left us, to tramp towards St. Catherine's Hill through the waning light of the spring day. Edward wished to look over the ground where Arthur Prendergast met his end, and as so strenuous a walk was beyond my powers, I was content for him to be my proxy.

I tied my bonnet strings beneath my chin and drew on my gloves. I was garbed in black, of course, in respect of my uncle Leigh-Perrot, but my pelisse was the usual checkered silk I had worn for the last three Easter seasons. Unlike her sister Alethea, Elizabeth favoured a sober stile of dress, which lent her station of widowhood dignity. Her day gown was of dull blue wool, trimmed in black braid, and her velvet cloak was the colour of ashes.

"Shall you be warm enough?" she asked.

"If we walk briskly."

She slipped her hand through my arm and we set off.

THE INNER CLOSE OF Winchester Cathedral is a walled sanctuary for those privileged to live there. Laid out to the south of the great church, it falls roughly into four parts: the Deanery and its out-gardens across from the south transept, where the stables and Nos. 1 through 3 may also be found; west of these, Nos. 4 through 6, running up to the wall at St. Swithun Street; just to the north, across Dome Alley, Nos. 7, 8, 9, and 10—and more northwards still, hard by the west door of the cathedral itself, Nos. 11 and 12, set in the angle of the Close's protective wall. Elizabeth Heathcote's house—or perhaps I should properly refer to it at Dr. Williams's house, as it is he who lets it to her—is by far the most private of the prebendaries' residences, tho' it is one of the more modest. It has a large back garden running west to Symonds Street.[8]

We might have taken a turn there, and admired the crocuses and daffodils lifting their heads to the sun, but Elizabeth led me purposefully towards the central green

---

8 No. 12 was renumbered as No. 11 in the last century and is still in private hands, as are Nos. 1 and 10. Most of the houses Jane references, however, no longer exist as she knew them. The Deanery, administrative home to the cathedral's dean, remains as No. 2, along with a few structures repurposed for cathedral use.—*Editor's note.*

behind No. 11. This was a withered square of lawn, edged by trees, and bisected by a pair of paths—one leading diagonally to the Deanery, the other to Curle's Passage, the slype a long-dead prince of the church blasted through the cathedral's flying buttresses.[9] The south transept rose in Gothick magnificence at the far end of the green, and I saw that Elizabeth was intent upon the slype rather than the imposing edifice of the deanery. I was happy enough to saunter through its enfilade of stone; ghosts drift and whirl in the slype's shadows.

"I am relieved that Will and Edward took themselves off," she began, "for if I do not unburden myself, Jane, I fear I shall go mad. Thank God you are come! It is impossible to relate my anxiety fully in a letter; mere words render the truth absurd. At every attempt to set pen to paper, I tossed the result onto the fire."

"We have been intimate our entire lives, my dear. I should be a poor friend, did I fail to support you *now*."

She sighed. "I could never have conceived of the present storm over our heads, had I drifted in phantasy a twelvemonth. I am aware that you have endured such crises in the past—that you are acquainted, however improbably, with violence and murder—and I know you have met adversity with a sanguine temper, and malevolence with a shrewd mind. That is why I wish to consult you."

---

9 A slype is an arched gothic colonnade or passage between a cathedral transept and an adjoining charterhouse. At Winchester, it was deliberately cut through the cathedral's south buttresses around 1650 to provide townspeople with direct (exterior) access to the Close. Prior to this, most foot traffic used the (interior) south aisle of the cathedral as a shortcut.—*Editor's note.*

"My powers, such as they are, are at your disposal."

She drew breath. "Then I shall begin as seems most logical—with the fact that someone hates my son. I do not know my enemy's name, nor his motives, but I am certain of his purpose. Young Prendergast's death is merely the culmination of a campaign that commenced the moment William passed through the college gates."

Had I read such a declaration in a letter, I might have exclaimed aloud, or dismissed Elizabeth's fears. I might have demanded *Who could wish to harm a schoolboy?* But mindful of the past hour's revelations, I did not teaze her patience with such nonsense. I merely said, "Tell me the whole."

She glanced at me sidelong. "Thank Heaven, you do not abuse me as an hysterick. For nearly three years, Will has been subject to relentless attacks on his spirit, his mind, and his standing in the world."

"You suggest something more profound and malevolent than the abuse he endures, on account of his regrettable speech defect?"

"I do. That abuse is both casual and general, widespread among his schoolfellows, despite the fact that a number of them suffer from similar impediments. They are not at all uncommon, Jane, and having been reared with a brother who is similarly afflicted, I have more patience and sympathy for the condition than is usual. I have encouraged William to draw strength from his uncle's example—to know that one may lead a happy, regular, and admirable life regardless of the defect. I congratulate myself that I have in large measure succeeded; William has gained in confidence, and counts several excellent young men as friends, not least of them your nephew Edward. But there are other influences at work. I fear, Jane, that *one* intends to ruin my son's position and reputation in the world."

"To what end?"

Her brows came together at my words. "That is just it—I cannot apprehend *why* someone should wish to harm a boy of fifteen, the fatherless son of a clergyman. Will cannot be a threat to anybody."

"Perhaps if you describe the nature of these attacks, the purpose will become clear."

By this time, we had traversed the oblique gravel path to Curle's Passage, and the first of the stone arches soared above our heads. As we stepped into the slype, light and shade flickered through the gaps in the colonnade; the chill was palpable. Winter held on here still, tho' spring gained ground outside.

"Last night, having received your letter and aware that I should be able to consult you soon, I cast my mind back over the course of Will's years in college," Elizabeth began. "He was not long in residence before the episodes began, but they were such minor incidents as might readily be dismissed as the usual lot of a first-year schoolboy. His Greek lexicon went missing, and was discovered sunk in a privy, irretrievable. His clothes were stolen, so that he was forced to seek his Master's help while yet in his nightshirt, to the ridicule of all in Hall. He was made to look responsible for minor infractions or neglect that won him beatings almost daily, but all of that I should have dismissed."

"I am astonished you even heard of such things," I observed, "given the usual code of schoolboy silence."

"Indeed, I learnt of them solely when Will shared them with your nephew, while the two dined here on Remission days. He related them with pride, if you will believe. Only once did Edward come to me in private and confide that he believed William to be the object of particular malice, worthy of my vigilance or even investigation. That was in the autumn of my son's second year."

"Eighteen hundred and fifteen?" I asked.

"You will have heard of the fire in school that November, two years since?"

"Of course. My nephews wrote of it. The same week as Bonfire Night, was it not?" Fire had broken out in one of the school dormitories, and the boys had been sent barefoot into the streets a few hours before dawn. "We most of us dismissed it as a late Guy Fawkes prank, gone sadly awry."

"—and the culprit was never named. Dr. Gabell chose to blame one of the masters—Mr. Clarke, in whose set of rooms a fire was left burning."

Old Clarke. In his letter to Edward, Will Heathcote had referred to the Master as being *in as bad a case* as himself with regard to Arthur Prendergast's death, without further elucidation. I must hope that my nephew was able to draw out his friend during their walk beyond the Itchen; he was likely to learn far more of a private nature than Will's overanxious mamma.

"The fire was accidental?"

"At the time, I was certain of it—for who, man or boy,

was likely to deliberately destroy an entire building of the college, much less threaten the lives of its inhabitants? Only a criminal or a madman should contemplate such wickedness, Jane, and I had not been used to regarding my neighbours as either. We in the Close are in general respectable, well-meaning, and quiet in our living; we lack the wealth and ambition for vice."

"But your confidence wavered?"

"Yes," she agreed in a troubled tone. The end of the slype lay just ahead, and a lozenge of greensward was visible beyond. "It was your nephew Edward's belief, he informed me, that William was meant to be suspected of setting the fire."

I stopped short on the gravel. "You cannot be serious!"

"Edward discovered my son's pocket-watch where it should never have been—in the passage leading to First Chamber, in the midst of the blaze. Edward was one of those who formed a bucket brigade in the first attempts to subdue the fire, as you may know."

"I was unaware of that." I resumed walking. "Is William's watch so immediately identifiable?"

"It was his father's," Elizabeth said, "a gift from me at our wedding. It bears my late husband's initials engraved on the case—initials which are identical to William's. I purchased it from Rundell and Bridge, while in London for my wedding-clothes."

"Of course," I murmured. "It could not have slipped from William's pocket in the normal course of a day in college?"

"William did not lodge in Chamber Court, where the

fire broke out. He should have no business to be there at any time, much less three o'clock of the morning, when the first cries of *Fire!* went up."

"Pray recount all you know of the event," I said. "My nephews wrote of it to their people, but my intelligence is second hand, and as such imperfect."

"Mine as well," she admitted. "I was from home at the time—on a visit to my brother at Manydown. William sent an account of all he observed, in a letter delivered to me the following day, but mentioned nothing about his watch being missing."[10]

"That is hardly surprising." My voice was dry. "He should not wish to inform you his father's heirloom was lost—and by the time he sat down to write to you, Edward may already have restored the pocket-watch to him."

"Very true. There is nothing like a boy for sins of omission."

"Or a man, for that matter."

"They are forever claiming to *spare us* the exposure to some indelicacy or another!"

"—When in fact, they are responsible for most of them. But the fire, Elizabeth?"

"—erupted in Chamber Court, near Mr. Clarke's set of rooms. Both First and Second Chamber, which lie in that part of college, had recently been subject to redecoration, and the paint being not yet dry, fires were lit in every hearth during the night to temper the walls."

---

10 A copy of this letter may be found in William Heathcote's biography, *A Country Gentleman of the Nineteenth Century* (F. Awdry, Warren & Son, Winchester, 1906), p. 14.—*Editor's note.*

Paint, I thought, meant other things as well: oiled rags and turpentine, left behind by the labourers. Highly flammable, if put to malicious use.

"How did they determine Clarke's rooms were the source of the conflagration? Did he own the truth himself?"

"Having taken lodgings in town during the renovations, he was not even resident in college at the time. Indeed, he hosted a final dinner for friends that evening in his lodging-house. His absence was a mitigating point in his favour when some among the Trustees called for his dismissal as recompense for the damage sustained to Chamber Court. The poor man lost all his possessions—worth some *six hundred pounds.*"

It was a considerable sum. "I do not apprehend how he could be blamed."

"No—but he took it very much to heart, I believe. When the blaze went up, the entire town was alerted, and Mr. Clarke made his way immediately to college from his lodgings, despite the fact that it was the middle of the night. He was nearly prostrate to discover that the roof had already fallen into his own set of rooms—and that all was lost. He is elderly, Jane, and of a delicate and nervous sensibility. It required two fellow masters to support him from the scene."

"No one can say how the fire jumped from Clarke's hearth, to engulf Chamber Court? It appears to have spread swiftly."

"A spark or ember, perhaps, flying from a log to a hearthrug . . . and there was a delay, you see, among the pumping engines. The college owns one, but its pipes were unequal to the task. Those belonging to the private insurance company could not be got through the college gates. It required, eventually, the bringing of an engine from the local garrison—with a complement of soldiers to work it—before water could subdue the flames."[11]

"Hence the bucket brigade."

"The older boys, and the masters, assembled it. A number of townspeople, too, assisted the efforts."

"Was your son involved? That might explain the presence of his watch."

Elizabeth shook her head. "William's dormitory is on the opposite side of the school. He lodges in what is called Gabell's House, because the Headmaster and his wife have a commodious set of rooms there, comprising the entire ground floor."

So Dr. Gabell, who was uneasy enough in his mind to inform Elizabeth that her son must account for himself before the coroner's panel, had served *in loco parentis* over the boy for nearly three years. What, I wondered, was his intimate view of William Heathcote? Was the Headmaster in possession of facts he had *not* shared with Elizabeth?

"Did Will write to you of his own actions during the night of the fire?"

"He and his fellows were held in readiness of evacuation, lest the fire spread. He was in some anxiety throughout the early hours of morning, being able to see the flames over

---

11 Public fire brigades did not exist in Great Britain at this time, but private ones supplied by insurance companies would battle blazes that occurred in clients' properties.—*Editor's note.*

Chamber Court, but being physically absent from the scene, and thus in considerable ignorance of what went forward."

"The boys were not turned out of Gabell's, however?"

"There was no need. By mid-morning the fire was subdued, and most of the school was saved. Chamber Court was a shambles, naturally, and Middle Gate was entirely under water. But the chapel and library were completely untouched—save for a persistent odour of scorched wood, that lingers to this day."

"Was anyone injured in the fire?"

She shook her head. "The violence was directed only at the school."

We stepped out of the slype into weak sunlight, partially blocked by the high wall that bordered the Deanery's grounds. I had thought Elizabeth might be guiding me towards the cathedral's eastern front, but she turned south instead along a carriageway that took us past the handsome front of No. 1—a substantial home in the Queen Anne stile—and the smaller, tho' no less attractive, pair of buildings that comprised No. 2. Ahead of us lay the bulk of No. 3, and beyond it—

"They have been rebuilding what was lost," Elizabeth said, and came to a halt in full view of the college's spires.

I had seen Winchester school before. It has been a number of years since my brother Edward Austen-Knight sent his eldest son here; and indeed, the fact that he had so many boys to educate privately, at a short remove from his Hampshire estates in Chawton, may have persuaded him to offer his widowed mother and unmarried sisters a comfortable freehold in Chawton village. Self-interest has always a part to play in generosity; my brother knew that he should often be upon the Winchester Road throughout the year, and with Chawton Great House frequently let to tenants, having a bedchamber and a place at our table always to hand, must be a comfort.

I had not glimpsed the college in several years, however, and must confess that I was surprised to see the skeletons of raw timbers rising above the ancient grey stone of Chamber Court. The damage had indeed been extensive.

"I suppose they have also profited from necessity, to improve the interior of the buildings?"

"I have heard that nearly four thousand pounds has been expended in making Chamber Court habitable again," Elizabeth said, in an awed tone.

That was a princely sum; I hoped the boys privileged to lodge there were grateful for the luxury.

"The majority of the buildings are stone," I mused. As should be natural, in a school built nearly five centuries ago.

"Externally, yes," Elizabeth agreed. "But within they are all old oak panelling and fusty scobs."

"Scobs?"

She smiled faintly. "That is what the boys call their desks. It is *boxes*, spelled phonetically and backwards. A term of art for Old Wykehamists."

"Would the wood have gone up like paper, do you think? —From misadventure with a popping ember, as was thought? —Or did such a conflagration require a deadlier agent?"

"Dr. Gabell supported the notion of an accident. But your nephew and I, aware that Will's watch was deliberately pilfered and left as evidence in First Chamber, believe the fire was set on purpose. Had the watch been discovered by a Master, Will should certainly have been interrogated—possibly even charged with arson," Elizabeth asserted. "I have an idea he would have been dismissed from the school, and his mother served with a civil suit for recovery of damages. Such a monetary judgement against me should have ruined me, Jane—I have not the resources to meet such an expence, as the rebuilding of Chamber Court demanded."

"Your late husband was the son of a baronet," I said thoughtfully. "Could the object have been the extortion of funds from Sir William at Hursley House—or even, perhaps, from your brother Harris, at Manydown?"

"I do not think so," Elizabeth said in a troubled tone. "Any such funds must go to Winchester College, after all. I cannot believe the Headmaster, or the Trustees, should deliberately besmirch my son's reputation in order to fund a new building. Such a plot appears to me incredible."

"To me as well," I admitted. "Far more likely that Will should be targeted by an enemy his age—a schoolboy whose mischief proved diabolically destructive."

"That has been my conclusion."

"Did you inform the Headmaster of the watch's discovery in First Chamber, and a possible intrigue against your son?"

"Are you mad?" Elizabeth stared at me, aghast. "I should never so incriminate William! I was only too thankful that it was Edward found the pocket-watch, and not another who should have falsely exposed my son to blame!"

Her sentiments were natural in a mother, I supposed. But had the pilfered watch been revealed to authority, its movements might have been traced. After the lapse of so many months, however, discovery of the thief must be impossible.

And by a logical progression of thought, the thief must also have set the fire.

"Mr. Clarke—the Master charged with governing First Chamber—numbered Arthur Prendergast among his boys?" I queried. "Prendergast was therefore present in the dormitory when the fire broke out?"

"He was. I cannot say whether he was responsible for kindling it, however."

"And it is impossible now to enquire of Prendergast himself. What of the boy named Insley Minor?"

"I am uncertain whether he was yet a student at the school two years since. But William will know."

I turned away from the prospect of the college. I was suddenly overwhelmed with fatigue, a flagging of both body and spirit that weakened me at the knees. "Elizabeth, if you have no objection, I should like to return to the Close."

6

A SCHOLAR AND A GENTLEMAN

No. 12, The Close
Winchester
Sunday, 30 March 1817, cont'd.

"I have wearied you unforgivably!" Elizabeth exclaimed. "Of course we shall turn back to the house—and you shall have a tot of brandy, as a restorative."

She gave me her arm as we toiled back up the slight rise in the direction of the cathedral. I confess I leaned upon her more than I should have liked. To divert my mind from my swimming head and tumultuous pulse, I said, "Were there other incidents of malice you regard as directed at William, between the fire eighteen months since, and the drowning of Arthur Prendergast?"

"One during the spring of last year, and another around the anniversary of the fire this past autumn. It was the latter that inspired so much unease in my bosom over the Christmas holidays—which I could not suppress when we visited you in Chawton, on our road home."

"The particulars, as precisely as possible."

"William befriended a stray dog," she said, "and took to feeding it scraps when it appeared in the Close. I did not like to take it into the house, of course, with William living generally at school—and the animal was indifferent to my existence in any case, being devoted to Will alone."

"Link is much the same. He adores Cassandra and barely glances at me."

Elizabeth nodded. "The night after William returned to College from the Easter holiday last year, he found the dog lying on his bolster when he turned back the bedclothes. It had been strangled with fishing line."

"Good God!" Revulsion strengthened my accent. For some reason, the wanton cruelty required to dispatch a dumb animal, and deposit it in a boy's bed, impressed me more forcibly than the tipping of Arthur Prendergast into a sluicegate's rapids. More than malicious or murderous, it was . . . *evil*.

I drew a steadying breath. We were passing once more beneath the arches of the slype, the Close's central green before us. I knew that once the house was achieved, I should have only as much strength as was necessary for the stairs to my bedchamber, before closing my eyes in exhaustion. "And the second incident, this past November?"

"Was of an entirely different, but no less repugnant a nature," Elizabeth said. "A straw figure—such as one might burn in effigy as a Guy on Bonfire Night—was discovered hanging from a rope from the rafters in Will's dormitory. It had been strung up as tho' hanged from a gallows, Jane. A length of parchment was pinned to it. Someone had scrawled *Heathcote* on it."

I stopped short, momentarily too dizzy to walk further.

The curve of grey stone above our heads seemed to bend and sway in my vision.

"Someone is dangerously fond of throttling things," I observed.

"Yes." She shivered. "You apprehend, now, my anxiety when we met in January. Will told me nothing of the hanged dummy when the incident occurred. It was only in my sister's house at Streatham, over Christmastide, that I understood that something was wrong. He suffered nightmares, Jane—crying out in his sleep. A persistent midnight terror of a rope around his neck."

"He has been afraid," I murmured.

"As I have never known him afraid before. He is nearly sixteen, after all—no longer a child. But—"

"He has been threatened, Elizabeth. I wonder that he was able, in his heart and mind, to contemplate a return to college after the holiday."

"It is a point of pride with him to betray nothing of his enemy's success. When I tasked him with the idea of leaving school for a time, he retorted hotly that if he did so, *they would win.*"

"But he put no name to his tormentors?"

She shook her head.

"Do you think he is truly at a loss? Might it have been Prendergast? Or Prendergast and his friend Insley?"

"It might. But in the case of Arthur Prendergast, I must hope otherwise," she admitted. "For he is dead, Jane, and by violence. I do not want my William implicated."

WE WALKED ON SLOWLY to the slype's end. A little effort more, and we achieved the entry of No. 12—with thankfulness on my part. I thought Elizabeth, too, looked the better for having unburdened herself. Her colour had improved, and the lines of care eased about her nostrils.

Upon entering the hall, we discovered the young men returned from their survey of the Itchen Navigation. Edward and William were seated by the drawing room fire, their boots upon the fender. And a third young man was with them: a clear-eyed, smiling youth blessed with handsome looks and a buoyant manner. All three rose immediately at perceiving us, and the newcomer bowed.

"Master Urquhart!" Elizabeth exclaimed. "How delightful to see you!"

"Mrs. Heathcote, your servant."

"I must make you known to my aunt." Edward gestured at me. "Thomas Urquhart, Miss Austen. Aunt Jane, my very good friend, Urquhart."

"A pleasure." Urquhart was taller than either Edward or Will, and had the figure of a nascent Corinthian: broad of shoulder, strong of limb, with a mobile, handsome visage. His tailor had done justice to his form, with a neatly-fitted blue coat and buff breeches that would not disgrace a countess's receiving-room. His eyes were blue, his hair guinea-gold, and his expression open as a sunny day. I judged him older than William Heathcote—of an age with my nephew, in fact, and appearing as one already at Oxford.

"I did not know you were yet in Winchester," Elizabeth said. "How do you spend your Easter leave-out?"

"In miserable solitude," Urquhart admitted, "and a sad lack of victuals. I have been haunting the coffee-houses with hang-dog looks."

"Then you must certainly remain to dinner!"

Urquhart's countenance flushed with pleasure. "I will accept your kind invitation with alacrity, for conversation as much as sustenance! I confess I am moped to death, Mrs. Heathcote, and could not credit my good fortune when I encountered these two excellent fellows."

"We found Urks taking the air on Hills," Edward explained, "and carried him with us to examine the ground near Pot. Any marks of a skirmish Tuesday, however, have since disappeared in the rain."

"I wonder you could bear to venture there," Elizabeth said. "The associations—too painful . . ."

A cloud moved swiftly across Urquhart's countenance. "It afforded me no happiness, indeed. I saw it rather as a duty. I was to have spent the holiday in Wiltshire, at Avebury Court. I have written my condolences instead."

"Lord Beaumont's seat," Elizabeth nodded. "But surely the unhappy parents will be arrived in Winchester already, for tomorrow's inquest?"

I must have looked bemused, for Edward supplied, "Prendergast was Viscount Beaumont's heir, Aunt."

"And his only son," Urquhart said soberly. "Unfortunately, his lordship is detained in Wiltshire due to ill-health. The viscount suffered an apoplectic attack at learning of Arthur's death—and is not expected to long survive him."

"How dreadful!" I exclaimed.

"Jane, you must sit down." Elizabeth supported me towards the chair lately occupied by her son. "Will, allow Miss Austen a place by the fire."

"With p-p-pleasure," he said. "And I shall throw on a log."

As he stirred up the flames, the others seated themselves, and Elizabeth ordered tea and brandy of her maidservant, Mariah.

"My sympathy, Master Urquhart," I said as the warmth of the hearth made itself felt in my chilled frame. "This must indeed have been a difficult period. You were intimate with Arthur Prendergast, I collect."

"As much as anyone could be, perhaps," he returned. "Prenders revealed himself to few beyond his family circle."

"He valued your company enough, however, to admit you to his home?"

"As to that—" Urquhart paused a moment in reflection. "There were few young men of his age and standing Prendergast deigned to call *friends*. For reasons I cannot explain, he accorded me influence over his whims, and appeared to weigh my counsel."

"T-t-t-too m-m-modest," Will interjected brusquely. "Urks k-k-kept us all s-s-safe."

His friend smiled crookedly. "I do not deserve such praise, nor Prenders such censure. I tried, perhaps, to urge on his better angels—and shield those whose happiness he governed. But did I truly *know* the fellow? I cannot have done, Will, for never, in an hundred years, should I have suspected Prenders capable of self-murder!"

"Nor I," Will agreed. "Ned?"

My nephew sighed. "One never looks for that degree of misery or self-loathing, to be sure. But I could make a case for it. Consider, Urks, how unhappy Prenders must have been, to tyrannize over the boys in his house as he did! And not only Clarke's. He made a point of persecuting every junior who fell in his way. And they hated him for it! Possessed of a similar nature and hideous popularity, I should have done away with myself long since, I daresay!"

"Perhaps you are correct." Urquhart's expression was sombre. "The bitter truth cannot lessen the tragic consequence for his father, however."

His compassion momentarily silenced speculation. Mariah then appearing with a tray of tea and cakes, all conversation was suspended. I drank my cup in peace, delighted to find that Elizabeth had dosed it liberally with brandy, and at our guest's then questioning Edward about Exeter and Oxford life, was content to listen. I excused myself not long thereafter, and made my way upstairs for an interval of rest.

But as I lay down on my bed, I reflected that contrary to Edward's opinion, young tyrants thrive on their grasp of power. Far from taking their own lives in remorse, they move purposefully from strength to strength. Such careers, in my experience, end only in a battle to the death—at the hands of a victim, or a rival.

7

GABELL'S FORCES

No. 12, The Close
Winchester
Monday, 31 March 1817

There is a refreshing novelty to a coroner's inquest when one is not obliged to give testimony. However much anxiety I might feel regarding young Will Heathcote's circumstances, I felt none for myself; and thus was able to support Elizabeth as she sat, with compressed lips and fixed gaze, on a rough pine bench in the middle of the White Hart's public room. Elizabeth had eaten very little of her buttered toast this morning and was no doubt suffering from a nervous stomach; she certainly was incapable of conversation. Sitting next to her was William, and next to him, at the end of the bench, my nephew Edward. Thomas Urquhart was also present, but having arrived a trifle later than ourselves, was towards the rear of the room. Glancing over my shoulder at the growing crowd, I glimpsed the flash of his golden hair.

Being too distant from my nephew to converse sensibly, I contented myself with surveying the townsfolk and black-gowned Winchester College masters. I could assign professions to most of them, except for one: a ginger-haired gentleman in a dark beaver, who had seated himself next to my nephew Edward, at the far end of our bench. He looked entirely the gentleman, but I noted a black armband on his right coat sleeve. *Mourning.* Perhaps he was an emissary of the dead schoolboy's family, detained as they were by the viscount's illness.

The appearance of the coroner put an end to my musings.

Mr. Pelham, who serves as a coroner for Hampshire, must move about the county a good deal, assembling panels for the inexplicably deceased in various towns from Basingstoke to Portsmouth. In the course of his office, he will have encountered any number of dead youths— those knocked down by drover's carts, those fallen into wells, those burned from their clothes catching light on the kitchen hearth. Such episodes are but too usual in the country. As Winchester is the centre of our law courts, however, his proceeding on the present occasion might fall under the scrutiny of local judges—and Arthur Prendergast being a nobleman's son, attached to the college, lent the inquest particular gravity. The coroner therefore was immaculately dressed in white linen and a black coat, with a starched cravat, his hair obscured by a silver periwig. He was, I judged, barely in his fourth decade—trim, energetic, and purposeful. He heard his panel's sworn oaths, then conducted them out of the public room to view the drowned boy's body.

They were soon returned. Pelham seated himself at a deal table, steepling his hands. The men of the coroner's jury—all freeholders of Winchester—arrayed themselves on a bench to his left.

The first person Pelham called was one Matthew Harper, lock-keeper of the Itchen Navigation.

"You tend to the lock below Tun Bridge?" the coroner enquired.

"I do."

"Did you observe anyone loitering near the sluicegate before dusk, Tuesday last?"

"I was downriver all that day, tending to a broken gate at Twyford. I did not reach home until nearly seven o'clock."

"But you were present at Pot the following morning?"

"Aye."

"Tell us what you discovered there, Wednesday last."

Harper duly recounted the arrival of a barge, at roughly half after two o'clock; the opening of the sluicegate to fill the lock; the passage of the barge to the next cut in the Navigation; and the subsequent failure of the lock's waters to drain through the culvert tunnel, as Harper expected.

"I spied into the tunnel with a lanthorn," he said, "and saw a bundle of rubbish at the far end, shunted up against the ironwork. So I sent my boy down to fetch it."

The boy, it appeared, was a lad of seven, small enough to move at ease within the culvert, but powerless to drag a dead youth of seventeen back out into the lock. Harper had been forced to employ a rope and grappling hook, a procedure he described with relish.

"I turned t'corpus over and saw he was blue and staring," he said, "so I sent my boy at a run to the constable."

The constable, when called, swore he had detected in the corpse the lineaments of a Winchester college youth, and had informed the Headmaster. Doctor Gabell had accompanied him immediately to the ground.

The Headmaster of Winchester was then called, spoke his oath, and awaited questioning.

"Doctor Gabell," Pelham said, "can you put a name to Deceased?"

"He was the Honourable Arthur Prendergast, aged seventeen years, son and heir to Frederick, Fifth Viscount Beaumont, and a Commoner and Prefect of Winchester College." This grand declamation inspired a ripple of comment throughout the assembly.

"What was your feeling, upon perceiving Deceased?"

"I may say, horror. I have experienced nothing similar in my years of governance over the school."

Pelham smiled thinly. "And what did you then?"

"Ordered the corpse removed to Sick House, and saw the surgeon summoned."

"The name of this surgeon?"

"Giles-King Lyford, of the Winchester hospital. He pronounced life to be extinct."

The coroner removed his spectacles and deliberately folded them, as tho' they were of no further use. "And how do you account, Dr. Gabell, for the presence of a young nobleman in your charge, so perilously near the Itchen Navigation?"

"I cannot account for it. No boy is given leave to quit the school premises alone, without express direction from a parent or guardian, or at the discretion of his particular Master."

"You were, I collect, in authority over Deceased?"

"Inasmuch as I am Headmaster of Winchester, and he a Commoner, that is true; but Master Prendergast was not housed directly under my care. He was lodged with Master Clarke, in Chamber Court."

"Have you any knowledge of the day or hour when Deceased quitted Winchester College?"

"I have not. His absence was discovered in School—that is the building where Commoners habitually study—at approximately nine o'clock in the morning, Wednesday last."

"But presumably his presence was recorded before the school's candles were doused?"

"As to that . . ." Gabell hesitated. "I cannot perfectly say."

Pelham looked all his amazement. "Is there no curfew at Winchester College?"

"Naturally, there is."

"—But you *cannot perfectly say* whether Master Prendergast was recorded present?"

"It is not my province to determine whether or not he was so. That is the province of his Master, Ruthven Clarke."

"Then the unfortunate boy might have been lost any number of hours?" Pelham demanded incredulously. "Are standards so lax in *your province*, doctor?"

Gabell stiffened. "I myself knew him to be present during lessons on the Tuesday."

"And when do those end?"

"At approximately four of the clock."

"Can you say, at least, whether Master Prendergast took his *dinner* in hall?"

Gabell hesitated. "I cannot say. I myself dined out of college that evening, being entertained in the company of my wife at the home of friends."

Pelham's expression was one of irritation. "Is there no one who may say when Deceased was last seen?"

"For that, you must consult Deceased's Master, Mr. Clarke, who is responsible." Gabell fixed the coroner with a defiant stare.

"Very well. You may stand down."

At this, Mr. Pelham called Mr. Ruthven Clarke, Master of Winchester College.

To my surprise, the elderly man was wheeled into the room in a basket chair, his bandaged right leg elevated before him. A choleric expression suffused his countenance. The serving-lad who propelled him must have jostled his leg, because the Master suddenly exclaimed, "Insufferable jackanapes!"

"Gout?" I whispered into Elizabeth's ear.

She inclined her head. "Clarke is a martyr to it, as he is to his stomach. I believe he is known for his fine taste in wines, and his infinite care for his victuals."

"Hence the dinner party in his hired rooms, the night of the school fire."

There was no time to say anything further. Clarke swore his oath in a high, irascible voice, and Mr. Pelham immediately enquired when he had last seen the Honourable Arthur Prendergast.

"Tuesday last, as he quitted Chamber Court a quarter-hour after lessons were concluded."

"That would be at what time?"

"I should say a quarter after four, or thereabouts. The bells had just rung the quarter-stroke."

"And you saw Deceased leaving Chamber Court. Did you speak to him at that time?"

"I did not. He appeared to be in considerable haste, and had a junior in tow."

Pelham's brows rose. "Indeed? Did you recognise Deceased's companion?"

"His usual acolyte. Insley Minor."

The coroner glanced at his clerk, who was diligently transcribing testimony. "You are the Master of said court?"

"My good man, there is no such thing." Clarke smiled thinly, as tho' he smelled something foul. "I am the *Second Master* of Winchester College, deferring only to the Head-master, Dr. Gabell, whose deputy I am."

The coroner's brows drew down. "I distinctly understood that you were responsible for Deceased's welfare while resident in the school."

"Oh, indeed I *was*," Clarke agreed. He probed his waist-coat with swollen fingers, and withdrew a tin of snuff. He opened it, and held a pinch to each nostril, inhaling noisily and pressing a handkerchief to his nose. I judged that we were about to receive tuition, from a man accustomed to dispensing it.

"It is a delicate distinction, however. As Second Master, I sit in jurisdiction over the boys known as *Scholars*, who are appointed members of the College for their deserving merits—that is, boys who pay no fees. They lodge to a man in Chamber Court." Clarke's thin, reedy voice penetrated to the very back of the room; a lifetime of speaking over the din of boys had schooled him in being heard. "I also lodge there, in a set of rooms above First Chamber. You will know, Mr. Pelham, that Chamber Court is a quadrangle, formed by the Chapel and Hall to the south and the kitchens to the west. The remaining two sides are composed of six chambers running east and north, where the boys both lodge and take their lessons."

"Master Prendergast was therefore a Scholar?" Pelham enquired.

"He was not." Another thin smile. "He was a Commoner—a boy who pays for his education. There are any number of *those* at Winchester, scions of the Great, and some of them are what is known as members of Mr. Clarke's House."

Pelham consulted his notes. "Master Prendergast therefore lodged in First Chamber, where your rooms are located?"

"No, no, no." Clarke looked pained, as tho' the coroner were particularly wretched in his Latin declensions. "Commoners lodge in *Sixth* Chamber. My set is as far from them as it is possible to be, and yet remain within the Court. I could not possibly *live* with the boys. I merely . . . accept them into my orbit. It is a matter of survival, you see."

"Mr. Clarke, I understand nothing of what you are telling me," the coroner returned sharply.

The Master blinked, his small mouth pursed, and lifted his hands as tho' confounded. "I perceive, sir, that you have not the benefit of a public school education."

Pelham controlled himself admirably, but I saw his nostrils flare.

"You are woefully unfamiliar with our traditions. In places set aside for the education of England's Future Leaders, the Scholars benefit from Appointment to the school. They are in general what is known as Founders' Kin—descendants of the original signers of the school's charter, dating from 1382, and thus guaranteed a place free of charge. Scholars are destined to move on to New College, Oxford, with whom we have been affiliated since its foundation—where they will study similarly free of expence."

"And Commoners?"

"—Are those boys who must offer coin for their place. In the main, they live in Commoners—a separate quadrangle entirely from College—except for those Dr. Gabell and I deign to accept as personal charges."

"What is your basis for so doing?" Pelham demanded.

Clarke's visage assumed a woeful expression, and his fingers fluttered like a maiden aunt's in search of smelling salts. "It pains me to disclose, sir, but the Headmaster and I are but poorly remunerated under the foundational charter. I am given a mere 35£ per annum for my numerous labours, and the Headmaster little more. We rely for our sustenance, therefore, upon the fees we receive for the boys we consent to educate."

Pelham sighed. "All of which is to say: Arthur Prender-gast lodged in your court, but not in your chamber, and was therefore not under your eye Tuesday night last, when he went missing, despite your *paid responsibility* for his welfare."

"Exactly so," Clarke replied, and took a second pinch of snuff.

The coroner's equanimity at this point deserted him. "The young man is dead, sir! You appear singularly unmoved by the result of your carelessness!"

Mr. Clarke's thick white brows rose in surprise. "Never call it so! Master Prendergast was a prefect, and as a leader of his fellows, ought certainly to have been present at the curfew hour, as you should perfectly apprehend, had you been raised a gentleman! To castigate *me*"—here, the Master's voice rose querulously—"for gross neglect of Prendergast, when in fact he had stolen without leave from school, in defiance of every stricture known to Commoner or Scholar, is beyond the pale! The boy knew, I assure you, that he was entirely in the wrong. He knew that he should be beaten if he were discovered, and yet persisted in his defiance! I may say that he reaped his just reward. It is Master Prendergast, not I, who lamentably forgot his duty to Winchester!"

"As you say," the coroner replied evenly. "Tell me, Mr. Clarke—how long were you acquainted with Deceased?"

"Some three years."

"How should you describe him?"

The Master considered the question while mopping his brow with his snuff-stained linen. "He was not unintelligent, but lacked application. A penchant for mischief, of a particularly ingenious kind. A natural leader—due, no doubt, to the superiority of his birth—and any number of boys were eager to follow him. All too often, however, Prendergast led in the wrong direction."

"I am sorry to hear it," Pelham answered. "Perhaps if he had received sterner guidance—"

Clarke slapped his palm on the arm of his basket chair with remarkable force. "The world is determined to make me its scape-goat, for every manner of crime; but I am innocent of wrongdoing, and indeed am the object of the grossest ill-usage, indecent at my time of life, and impossible to be borne!"

"Do you never ascertain whether the boys in your charge are safely secured within Chamber Court by nightfall?"

"That is the duty of the prefects."

"Of which Deceased was one?"

"Unhappily. A gesture to the beneficence of his father, Lord Beaumont."

"And his companion, Insley . . . *Minor*." Pelham looked from his scribe to Mr. Clarke. "He was presumably returned to Chamber Court Tuesday, tho' Prendergast was not?"

"As to that—I cannot attest myself." Clarke's spectacles glinted as he cast about the room. "But you may enquire of him yourself. He is sitting over there."

A slight stir as half the occupants of the room followed the direction of the Master's upraised arm, and discovered the pale visage of a boy crushed between two black-clad academics. It appeared from their stony looks as tho' Insley Minor had been conveyed to the inquest unwillingly.

"One final question, sir," Pelham said. "Did you notice any alteration in Master Prendergast's spirits prior to his disappearance? Did he seem troubled, despondent, or agitated beyond what you should judge usual?"

"I should say that he was as arrogant and boisterous as

ever. I had the beating of him Monday in Hall, and he was indifferent to pain as ever."

"Up to the hour he disappeared?"

Clarke looked peevish. "I cannot tell. I do not perfectly know what hour that was! Do *you*, Coroner?"

Pelham audibly sighed. "In your opinion, Master Clarke, was the Honourable Prendergast of a temperament to do away with himself?"

"Not at all. Indeed, on the very Tuesday morning, when he ought to have been working on his recitation, I discovered him plotting a fresh campaign in his perpetual battle against his rivals in Dr. Gabell's House."

"His rivals?" Mr. Pelham's attitude was all attention. "Pray explain, sir."

Clarke took his third pinch of snuff. "The usual business. Prendergast's forces—which included every boy in Clarke's House—were sworn to bedevil the boys in Gabell's. The two sides were ever working pranks and mischief against each other, and of late Gabell's House had shown the upper hand. When I learned Prendergast was missing on Wednesday, indeed, I was certain he was being detained somewhere at the hands of his chief enemy."

"His chief enemy?" Pelham repeated. "And who should that be, Mr. Clarke?"

The Master's eyes drifted over the townsfolk assembled to hear his testimony, lingered briefly on my visage, and then slid away. "The leader of Gabell's band, naturally. Master William Heathcote."

8

TORTURED TESTIMONY

No. 12 The Close
Winchester
Monday, 31 March 1817, cont'd.

"I am W-w-william H-h-heathcote, f-f-fifteen years of age, and a C-c-commoner of W-w-winchester C-c-college."

As he choked out that first sentence, an uneasy murmur rose up from the townsfolk seated around us, and I saw more than one glance significantly or whisper to a neighbour. A stammer will never command respect. William stood at the coroner's right hand, facing the assembly, his thin face drawn and pallid. A slight figure of adolescence, with the spotty complexion common to youth, and a hunted expression in his eyes, he did not inspire confidence. I saw that Will kept his gaze fixed upon my nephew Edward rather than his mother's agonized countenance, and hoped that my nephew's assurance might support his friend.

Elizabeth's gloved hand gripped my own like a vise. She had clutched it in the first instants of surprize at Mr. Clarke's revelation that her son was a leader of a desperate band of committed warriors. That she was ignorant of the charge I was certain; that both William and Edward accepted it, I knew at a glance. Edward, too, had been a member of Dr. Gabell's House in his day; if there was such a thing as "Gabell's Band," I surmised that Will was his chief lieutenant, and had assumed Edward's duties when my nephew quitted the school. Hence their intimacy, the letter sent to Steventon imploring support, and Edward's insistence that we impose ourselves upon the household at No. 12. It was a matter of martial brotherhood.

Will had sworn to Almighty God to tell the truth, however, and he was the sort who would never perjure himself. Mr. Pelham should elicit more truths from the boy in the next half-hour than I would in a week.

"You were acquainted with Deceased?"

"Th-the-these th-th-three years, sir."

"And what was your opinion of him?"

"Th-th-that he should be a b-b-better man, were he h-h-humbled, sir."

Pelham's gaze sharpened, and his frame straightened a trifle in his chair. "Humbled? Why should he be humbled?"

Will's lips furled in exasperation, and he glanced about with increasing anxiety.

His tablet, I thought. *His pencil.*

As tho' the thought had communicated itself to Edward, he rose from his place and lifted his hand to draw the coroner's attention. "I beg your pardon, Mr. Pelham, but if I may approach the bench?"

"To what purpose?" the coroner demanded testily.

"The assistance of the witness. May I suggest that if he

were to write out his answers to your questions, your interrogation might proceed more smoothly?"

"We deal in oral testimony, sir," Pelham said dismissively,
and looked again at Will.

"His written answers might be read aloud immediately
for the benefit of the panel," Edward persisted.

The coroner stared at him, brows drawn down in a
frown. Then he gestured to his clerk. "Let paper and pencil
be provided the witness."

The man drew a tablet from a leather satchel at his feet,
and offered it to William, who bowed his thanks.

As the boy's pencil flew furiously across the page, the
uneasy thread of muttered comments swept once more
through the surrounding townsfolk.

"Imbecile, he is," I caught one whisper.

"Fancy, the son of a gentleman unable to speak!" said
another.

"Sounds like a gobblecock," a third said far more loudly,
and several people tittered.

Elizabeth's hand spasmed in mine, and she returned it
stiffly to her lap.

William handed his answer to Mr. Pelham, who narrowed his eyes to make out the schoolboy scrawl.

"He set himself up in defiance of the masters, sir, and
believed them inferior to himself and his authority. Such a
boy is exceedingly troublesome when ruling over others,"
the coroner recited. He stared at William. "How did Master
Prendergast manifest this rebellious spirit—if, indeed, he
did so?"

The colour had flooded back into William's cheeks; he had chosen his line of testimony, I saw, and thus felt more confident. Again, he handed Pelham his answer.

"Rebellious is the very word, sir," the coroner read aloud. "Some five-and-twenty years since, Winchester suffered a Great Rebellion, when a group of seniors, angry that masters they regarded as social inferiors, should be permitted to discipline them, armed themselves with clubs and pistols and barricaded the gates of Winchester College. For several days they held all within hostage. They rampaged, smashed windows, and threw desks into the quadrangles to burn. The High Sheriff and a detachment of militia were necessary to subdue them." Pelham sighed gustily and tossed the paper on the desk before him. "What can this history have to do with the death of Master Prendergast?"

His haughtiness, I observed, was ill-placed. Any number of older townsfolk in the room recalled the Great Rebellion, I surmised—including, no doubt, several members of the coroner's panel sitting in judgement this morning. William was scribbling once more, his head bent.

"Prendergast spoke continually of leading another such rising," Pelham recited. "He resented the masters' authority; he called it an insult to his honour and his birth that *mere jumped-up tradesmen*, as he called them, should set limits on his behaviour. I thought him an influence for disorder, and a danger to the school."

Pelham smiled grimly. "Now we come to it. You bore Master Prendergast personal animus, and determined to bring him to heel. You have heard Mr. Clarke describe a campaign of mischief, between those who lodged in his house and Dr. Gabell's. What do you know of *Gabell's Band*?"

"It is t-t-true, that certain of our f-f-fellows met the p-p-pranks of tth-theirs with equal v-v-vigour," William said aloud. Two bright spots of colour burned in his whitened cheeks, but he held his head high.

Beside me, Elizabeth repressed a moan.

"How long has this enmity between the houses existed?"

"As l-l-long as I have been a C-c-commoner in the sch-sch-school. That is to s-s-say, nearly th-th-three years."

"Did the rivalry originate with yourself?"

William shook his head emphatically. "With P-p-prendergast!"

"Mr. Clarke names you as the leader of Dr. Gabell's band."

William smiled faintly. "He d-d-does me too m-m-much honour, sir."

It was the sort of answer a courtier might make—suddenly charming, consciously deflective, and far beyond Will's years. For an instant, I recognised the dead father in the boy. Elizabeth's lost husband had been all that was easy and handsome, as I recalled with a pang.

Pelham led the boy through a description of the tricks and stratagems deployed from one House to another: compositions rendered illegible by spilled bottles of ink; bedcovers soaked with ice-water; the ruin of a hapless individual's dinner or the destruction visited upon his clothes. Will resorted once more to a written account, but owned to every prank.

The crimes he credited to the Clarke's House boys were of a different order, however. They aimed to wound.

There had been the time a letter was received, purportedly from a family seat in Herefordshire, falsely informing a junior in Will's house of his mother's death in childbed. Another boy awoke to rampant rumours of his noble father's bankruptcy at cards. A third learned from signs posted in Hall that his sister, in her first London Season and lately presented at Court, was got with child by a stable-lad.

In every instance, the matter was a lie; but the damage before the lie was discovered was considerable. The nastiness of such pranks was shocking; and in the looks of those who listened to the testimony, I detected a dismay as deep as my own.

"Whom do you regard as responsible for these vile outrages?" Pelham asked.

"I c-c-cannot say, sir. Th-th-they were all of th-th-them anon-non-ymous."

"Were you ever the object of such an attack, Master Heathcote?" Pelham enquired.

Will hesitated. "I w-w-was."

"What was the nature of it?"

The boy grimaced. "I d-d-do not w-w-wish t-t-to say."

"I must remind you, young man, that you are under oath."

"I d-d-do not w-w-wish to give p-p-pain to—to anyone p-p-present in the room." In frustration, Will snatched up his pencil.

"I may assure you that the charge was again a vile

falsehood," Pelham read out, "regarding a member of my family, and intended purely to bring shame upon the Heathcote name. To repeat such untruths is to give them renewed life. There can be no value, and much harm, in so doing."

Pelham considered this, his pen tapping ruminatively against his inkstand. "Very well," he said at length. "The particulars cannot bear directly on the present matter. Suffice it to say that you have reason to hold the members of Clarke's House in disregard. Mr. Clarke suggests that Arthur Prendergast was their leader. Do you dispute this?"

"I d-d-do not."

"Have the disagreements between you ever resulted in physical violence?"

There was a pause; Will's eyes darted once more to my nephew Edward's countenance. I observed Edward to nod slightly; some nerve in the other boy's frame relaxed.

"N-n-naturally, sir. I am a g-g-gentleman. I h-h-have on o-c-c-ccasion resorted to f-f-fisticuffs, when an insult p-p-proved too great for honour to b-b-bear. There is not a b-b-boy in G-g-gabell's House who would not sw-sw-swear the same—we are all of us h-h-handy with our f-f-fives."

"Your fives?"

"Our f-f-fists, sir."

"*Manners maketh man*—that is the motto of your school, is it not?" Pelham's tone was contemptuous. "Master Heathcote, are you aware that a written message was discovered in Deceased's waistcoat pocket?"

Will nodded.

"Speak," Pelham said sharply.

"I am, sir."

"I ask you to look at it now."

Pelham placed a small roll of parchment on the desk before him and smoothed it flat. Will stepped closer and glanced down at it. "Th-th-that is m-m-mine."

"You admit to writing it? You agree that it is in your hand?"

"I d-d-do. But n-n-not f-f-for P-p-prendergast."

Pelham turned to his panel. "The ink on this parchment is naturally blurred from damp, but the fact of its having been folded inside a coin-purse, secured in Deceased's waistcoat pocket, has preserved it from complete disintegration. Pray note that it contains the lines: *Meet me on Hills after Toytime. We'll launch her in the drink,* and that Master William Heathcote admits that he wrote it." Then with a look for Will: "Explain yourself, sir."

"I g-g-gave that note to a f-f-friend, Charles B-b-baigent. We m-m-meant to sail a m-m-model f-f-frigate in P-p-pot after lessons."

"When was this written?"

"A w-w-week since. M-m-monday last."

"And did you and Master Baigent meet on St. Catherine's Hill, near the Navigation lock known as Pot, that day?"

"W-w-we d-d-did."

"And yet, this note was found on Deceased's drowned body, after it was taken from the culvert below the same lock, Wednesday morning."

Will bent once more to scrawl his reply.

"I cannot explain it, sir," Pelham recited. "I may only assume that Prendergast found the discarded paper and pocketed it for some purpose." The coroner lifted his eyes from the testimony. "You deny that you gave Master Prendergast this message, Master Heathcote, with the express intention of drawing him to the lock, where he was drowned?"

"I d-d-do d-d-deny it."

"Did you see or speak to Arthur Prendergast on Tuesday last?"

"I saw him in H-h-hall, as we w-w-went about our l-l-lessons."

"Did you speak to him?"

"I n-n-never d-d-did so, sir, if I c-c-could h-h-help it."

"What was your opinion of his spirits?"

William shrugged.

"Speak," Pelham ordered again, and wearily.

"M-m-much the same as always. He was b-b-boasting of t-t-treats in st-st-store over the Easter l-l-leave-out."

"You saw no indication of distress or melancholy?"

"N-n-none, sir."

"Master Heathcote, were you within college the entirety of the period between your studies and retiring for bed, Tuesday since?"

A hesitation. "I w-w-was not, sir."

"You left the school?"

"I d-d-did."

Elizabeth drew an audible breath.

"At what hour?"

"I qu-qu-quitted Gabell's House a qu-qu-quarter before the hour of f-f-four o'clock."

"And where did you go?"

"I c-c-cannot say, sir."

"William," Elizabeth murmured in agony beside me.

"Come, come, Master Heathcote. You are required to answer my questions truthfully and fully."

Will compressed his lips, his countenance appallingly white.

"You refuse to answer?"

Again, not a word passed William's lips.

"I am forced to instruct the panel that Master Heathcote refuses to disclose his whereabouts at four o'clock on Tuesday last. Will you tell me, Heathcote, when you returned to college?"

William expelled a gusty breath, as tho' he had been holding the air in his lungs for the past several seconds. "Just before six, sir, by the bells."

"You were absent, then, nearly two hours!" Pelham's looks were grim. "I must put to you the question, Master Heathcote: Did any matter lie between you and Deceased, that should be cause for violence? —Remember, you are *under oath to your Lord God Almighty.*"

Will was silent an instant. "My oath is s-s-sacred, sir. No such m-m-matter lay b-b-between us."

Pelham sighed. "Very well," he said. "You may take your seat. I call Master Peter Insley to approach the panel."

9

THE TYRANT'S DISCIPLE

I turned my head to watch Insley make his way to the coroner's position, and felt Elizabeth do the same. He was both younger and shorter than her son William, perhaps fourteen years of age, well-fleshed and rubicund of countenance, with slightly protuberant eyes and an unfortunate tendency to breathe heavily through his mouth.

"Are you at all acquainted with him?" I whispered to Eliza.

She shook her head. "He is no friend of William's."

"Master Insley," Mr. Pelham said, "you are what is known as a Commoner of Winchester, and are housed in Chamber Court?"

"Yes, sir. In Sixth Chamber."

Pelham consulted a sheet of paper on the desk before him. "That was also where Arthur Prendergast lodged?"

"Yes, sir."

"Master Insley, you were observed departing the court with Deceased a little after four o'clock Tuesday last. Where were you bound?"

"For a . . . a walk."

Pelham frowned. "A walk?"

"To take . . . exercise." Insley darted a glance about the public room as tho' in search of an ally. It did not appear that he found any. He clutched his hands together; they were red and plump, and I suspected rather damp.

"In company with Master Prendergast?"

Insley nodded.

"Speak up, boy."

"Yes. With Prenders."

"Were you often in the habit of doing so?"

"Never, sir. I abhor exercise."

A ripple of laughter moved through the room; Insley looked at first startled, and then gratified. It was not often, I gathered, that he was regarded as a Wit.

"As Nature abhors a v-v-vacuum," murmured William, from Elizabeth's other side.

"What spurred your perambulations on this occasion?" Pelham asked.

Insley stared. "Beg pardon?"

"Why did you quit the school for a walk?"

"Prenders wished it."

"And you did so, without begging leave of any kind?"

The boy nodded again unhappily. "Knew I'd fetch a beating, of course, but it was a mark of distinction—to be asked to go. I was *lieutenant*. Naturally, I kept mum."

"Distinction," Pelham repeated. "—to accompany a fellow boy on a walk. Why should this be?"

"Prenders meant to meet the enemy. Said he required support. I carried his rod."

"His rod?"

"Beating stick. Mark of a prefect. Never without it."

"I see. And why did he require support?"

Insley shrugged. "He was to *meet the enemy*. Absurd to venture alone, in such a case."

"The enemy. Could you put a name to this person?"

"Heathcote." The response was immediate, and offered with confidence.

"You refer to Master William Heathcote, of Gabell's House?"

"Yes, sir. He and Prenders—Master Prendergast—are always at daggers drawn, so when I learned he'd writ to Prenders to set the time and place, I knew it was my duty to stand buff."

"We have heard some mention of a note, discovered on Deceased's person. Is this what you refer to?"

"Aye. *Meet me at Pot after Toytime,* it said, *and we'll launch her in the drink.*" He recited the words from memory.

Pelham held out Will's scrap of paper for inspection. "Is this the note in question?"

"It is. I recognise Heathcote's fist." Insley smirked, playing to his crowd. "Better with his fist than his tongue, I reckon."

"I take it your walk was in the direction of the specific lock on the Itchen Navigation, known to you as Pot?"

"It was."

"Please relate to the panel what occurred there."

"Well, we found the place deserted—Heathcote must've known the lockkeeper was called away—and took up a position behind the keeper's hut, to keep a level eye on the ground, so as not to be taken unawares."

"What time was this?"

Insley's forehead wrinkled. Sparse strands of brown hair clung to it; he was sweating freely under the coroner's interrogation. "A bit after four. I cannot precisely say."

"And did Master Heathcote indeed appear at the lock?"

"Not while I remained. Prenders and I waited some time before I was obliged to beg off, owing to an appointment with my Greek tutor. We threw stones, and talked Strategy a bit; he meant to get the girl away, you see, but it was vital Heathcote be made to pay."

"The girl," Pelham repeated. "To what girl do you refer?"

"Why, the one Heathcote meant to drown."

A positive whirl of comment met this startling statement, and William started from his chair. Edward grasped his wrist, and pulled him back down.

"Explain yourself, Master Insley," Pelham charged severely.

The boy looked directly at William. "He wrote it himself. *Launch her in the drink.* Heathcote has a taste for meddling with tradesmen's daughters. Prenders said he'd got a woman of the town with child, and rather than do the honourable thing, he meant to cast her into Pot and release the sluicegate. Prenders was to save the girl from drowning, and bring Heathcote to justice. It should be a fine coup for Clarke's House. —Only after I left, Heathcote must have killed them both."

"G-g-good G-g-god!" Will cried, surging to his feet once more. "He l—l-lies!"

Elizabeth's hand was on his coat sleeve; with a look at his mother's troubled visage, Will sat. But I noticed the faces of the onlookers had hardened. No townspeople like to think their daughters the prey of indolent schoolboys. Will was the object of more than one censuring look.

"Were you also aware of this . . . dalliance?" Pelham demanded.

Insley's gaze drifted over our bench. "I saw Heathcote in close conversation with a girl several times in recent months, when we were sent out to Hills for a Remedy."

"What is the name of this young woman, pray?" the coroner demanded.

"I should be the veriest scrub, sir, if I owned it," Insley replied sanctimoniously. "A gentleman never speaks ill of a lady."

"Very well. You shall tell me privately, Master Insley. At what time, do you judge, did you quit St. Catherine's Hill?"

"It wanted a quarter to five o'clock, sir. The Bishop expected me at five. I heard the bells, and made off, tho' I was loath to miss the fun."

"The Bishop?"

"Mr. Huntingford, sir. He tutors Greek."

"And how long should you say you were with him?"

"Not above an hour. I dined in hall, at six."

"Master Prendergast had not then returned?"

Insley shook his head. "He was not at dinner, sir. Nor at lights-out. I stuffed a bolster in his bed and told the other fellows to keep mum, if they wished to avoid Prenders's wrath. Nobody chose to invite it."

"It did not occur to you to inform the Master, Mr. Clarke?"

Insley looked horrified. "As much as my life is worth, to peach on Prenders! I should never betray him to a soul."

The coroner paused, and studied Peter Insley. "You held him in such respect?"

The boy hesitated. "In a manner of speaking. No one crossed Prenders. He was the mightiest Prefect in School."

"Should you have said he was in good spirits, of late?"

"He was looking forward to thrashing Heathcote."

"You do not believe him likely, then, to make away with himself?"

"Never!" Insley was all astonishment. "Why should he? Heir to a viscount, plump in the pocket, and the ruler of all! Prenders led a charmed life."

"Until Tuesday last, when he drowned," Pelham observed. "Master Insley, you may stand down."

THERE REMAINED BUT ONE more person to be sworn before Pelham's panel: Giles-King Lyford, Surgeon-in-Ordinary of the Winchester County Hospital. The name was not unfamiliar to me. There have been Lyfords in Hampshire forever—and their chief passion is the curing of their neighbours' ills by any means possible. I have known Lyfords who were apothecaries, Lyfords who were clergymen—but the present Mr. Lyford is quite a formidable man of science indeed. He is nephew to Mr. John Lyford of Basingstoke, who was kind enough to listen to my mother's innumerable complaints while we were yet living at Steventon rectory.

Giles-King was a stout, grey-haired man in his fifties, I should judge, whose face was lined with weariness, and hardened from exposure to the world's troubles.

"You examined Deceased's corpse once it was drawn from the Navigation lock?" Mr. Pelham asked.

"I did."

"And what did you determine was the cause of death?"

I am sure that everyone in the White Hart's public room expected Lyford's answer to be "drowning." But he surprized the world by saying, "A blow to the head."

Pelham's gaze lifted from his pen and paper. "Indeed? What part of the head?"

"The posterior base of the skull."

"And you believe this blow was severe enough to cause death?"

"The bone was crushed. Deceased would certainly have lost consciousness the moment the blow was inflicted."

"—and falling into the lock, was then drowned?"

"Perhaps. He might also have died of the blow, with his corpse then placed in the lock, to encourage the idea he met with accident."

"You are suggesting the boy was *murdered*?" Pelham demanded.

"It is certainly possible. Without anatomising the body, I cannot reach an accurate conclusion."

A murmur went round the assembled townsfolk at Lyford's words; anatomisation, the cutting up of corpses to examine their organs, is a feared and loathsome practice. Surgeons are known to be addicted to it, and to abet the equally heinous expedient of grave-robbing, to supply them with specimens. No parent would be likely to subject a dead child to the outrage, particularly a viscount. But I detected in Mr. Lyford the frustrated ambition of a natural philosopher.

"Could Deceased have struck his head as he fell into the lock?"

The surgeon's brow furled. "It is just possible. Although in that case, I suspect the injury would differ. Deceased's bruise is both broad and long, and struck with considerable force—as tho' inflicted by a cricket bat. Had Deceased struck the edge of the sluicegate, I should predict a sharper, shallower wound—to the forehead or temple, rather than the posterior of the cranium."

"The constable discovered nothing like a cricket bat lying abandoned near the lock," Pelham persisted.

"Perhaps the assailant took it away with him."

"Could the blow have been delivered by a Prefect's rod?"

"I am not familiar with such a thing," Lyford said stiffly. "But if it resembles a bat . . ."

The coroner steepled his fingers, dabbing with them at his nose. "You are persuaded, then, that self-murder is out of the question?"

"I am," Lyford said.

He was dismissed.

Pelham turned to instruct his panel. The faces of the men were grave, and I noticed more than one studying Will Heathcote with wary looks.

"Arthur Prendergast, a blameless youth and heir to a noble title and fortune, is dead," Pelham said. "The immediate cause of his taking-off, and all guilt for it, are uncertain. If you believe that death was accidental, you must return a judgement to that effect. If you find the idea of suicide more persuasive, despite Mr. Lyford's testimony, you return a judgement of suicide. If, on the other hand, you believe death was at the hands of a person or persons unknown, render that judgement, and we shall be satisfied."

Here he paused, for greater effect.

"But if you determine that the cause was murder, with malice aforethought, then you must say so. And if you find evidence enough to put a name to the murderer—then before God, I abjure you, gentlemen, speak that name, that Justice may be done in the eyes of this assembly, and the Almighty."

10

THE SURGEON PROPOUNDS HIS VIEWS

No. 12 The Close
Winchester
Monday, 31 March 1817, cont'd.

Elizabeth pressed her gloved hand to her lips as the panel filed out of the public room. "What a terrible duty is theirs," she murmured. "For who can possibly know what happened that fateful evening? You do not think, Jane, that they will believe *William* responsible for that unfortunate boy's death?"

"I am sure they will not." I rose from the bench, doubtful of my own bracing sentiment, and intent upon obtaining exercise, for my back was aching again. Edward and Will were also on their feet. I detected in my nephew an attitude of care for his younger friend, a shepherding through the crowd.

"But the testimony!" Elizabeth exclaimed. "Surely they will apprehend that Insley is speaking lies, from beginning to end!"

"Come and take the air, Mamma," Will urged.

Edward offered me his arm. We followed the Heath-cotes out of the public room, avoiding the scrutiny of the curious at every step. When we had gained the fresh air and paving, a flash of gold alerted me to the presence of Thomas Urquhart—who clapped Edward on the shoulder.

"What a farce!" he exclaimed. "As tho' Heathcote should have anything to do with the muslin company, to be sure! I nearly rose in my place and disputed the testimony—but doubted the coroner would listen."

"I cannot tell whether Insley believes his own story, or has simply got it off by rote, at Prendergast's direction," Edward agreed, frowning.

"You must tell me everything you know of Insley, by and by," I interjected. "But first—Did you expect the Master, Mr. Clarke, to disclose the war between his and Gabell's houses?"

"I thought him too dim to perceive it," Edward admitted. "But as Prenders was in some wise his responsibility, Clarke must be eager to shift blame for the fellow's death. He's not the sort to preserve a dignified silence in respect of Winchester's reputation. Clarke would peach on his own mother, I daresay."

"You apprehend, Miss Austen," Urquhart said with a smile, "that your nephew is one of the most celebrated of Gabell's generals? A formidable opponent, indeed, whose departure for Oxford was met with relief!"

Edward laughed. "The rivalry is ancient and honourable, Aunt, as Urquhart knows—or was, before Prendergast came to power."

Spying Lyford the surgeon before us, I dropped Edward's arm and hastened forward. "Mr. Lyford!"

He turned, hesitated at perceiving a stranger, then bowed. "At your service, ma'am."

"I must beg your pardon, sir—but I hoped you might clarify a point of testimony."

He frowned, debating whether I was an impertinent woman or merely a curious one—and whether he should encourage either.

"You said that only anatomisation should determine the cause of Master Prendergast's death. I am wondering what the practice, in this case, might reveal?"

"Why do you wish to know?" he demanded bluntly.

I glanced at Edward, who raised his hat to Mr. Lyford. Urquhart had hurried to the support of Elizabeth and William.

"James-Edward Austen, Mr. Lyford, of Exeter College, Oxford. My aunt, Miss Austen, is merely enquiring on my behalf. I am keenly interested in natural philosophy, but was too hesitant to disturb your privacy with my questions. My aunt has no such compunction."

"I see." Lyford raised his own hat, and bowed again. "Giles-King Lyford. I am only too happy to respond to inquiries arising from intellect. It is the sensational I wish to avoid. What draws you to the inquest on this tragic loss?"

"No love for the public spectacle, sir," I said. "We are here in support of friends, who are required to stand as witnesses."

He glanced at the Heathcotes, who were pacing the paving in front of the White Hart, their heads close in conversation with Urquhart. The loitering townsfolk gave the party a wide berth.

"Then we have acquaintance in common," Lyford said. "I have been frequently attending the ladies of No. 12, and must be anxious for a speedy resolution to this wretched affair. You wish to know what I should learn from anatomisation? At least a hundred different things about that poor boy. But principally this: whether he went into the water alive or dead."

"You regard the distinction as vital?" I asked.

"I do. Consider the possibilities, Miss Austen. Master Prendergast is struck a blow of punishing force. He may not have died in the instant; he may have been stunned, and overbalanced into the lock. Whosoever wielded the cudgel that fractured his skull may have done so by accident—in the midst of play, or a mock battle. In such an instance, fear of the consequences of his act may have persuaded the assailant to flee the scene, rather than attempt a rescue."

"If the boy was yet alive in the water, then, you regard it as argument for an accidental blow? —But was not the sluicegate opened upon the victim? How else should he have been washed into the culvert?"

Mr. Lyford bowed his acknowledgement.

"An excellent point. I perceive that neither of us credits the notion of accident. Whether Prendergast's assailant left him stunned and drowning in Pot, or waited with troubling sang-froid until life was expired to tip his corpse into the lock, we both of us believe his death the result of deliberate intent. The opening of the sluice confirms it."

"How may anatomisation assist your theories?" Edward asked.

"In two ways." Lyford turned his piercing gaze upon my nephew. "The condition of the brain—from the degree of internal bleeding, I might determine how long life persisted following the breaking of the skull; and the condition of the lungs. If Prendergast was yet breathing when he plunged into Pot, he will have taken water into his lungs. If he was dead when his body entered the lock, the lungs will hold only air."

"Even after death!" Edward exclaimed. "I had not thought it possible."

"The absence of water from the lungs would be decisive for murder," I said thoughtfully, "for in that case, we would know Prendergast's assailant watched and waited until the boy's final breath, before shifting his body into the water and opening the sluice." I shivered involuntarily. "It is unfortunate, Mr. Lyford, that you have been prevented from obtaining your proofs."

The surgeon smiled. "You do not mean to faint at the idea of anatomisation? There are few ladies willing to speak the word. I see Mrs. Heathcote has an excellent support, indeed!"

"Jane," Elizabeth said as she approached us. Her countenance was all agitation. "The panel is returning. Can it be possible they have reached a conclusion, in so brief a period?"

GILES LYFORD'S FLATTERING ESTIMATION of my powers of support were put to a severe test for the balance of the day. I am sorely in doubt that he is justified in his good opinion.

We no sooner resumed our place on the public room's benches—although well to the rear of the coroner's desk on this occasion, being jostled out of position by townsfolk avid to learn the inquest's result—before the panel filed in, their faces alike in gravity.

"Mr. Hickson," Pelham called out sternly to the foreman, from his appearance a prosperous Winchester merchant. "Have you and your fellows reached a decision as to the cause of Master Arthur Prendergast's death?"

"We have."

"And how do you find, sir?"

Death by Misadventure, I thought with the ardent supplication of prayer. I did not for a minute believe that Prendergast had slipped unwittingly into Pot, nor that he had drowned himself. But I could not bear for any other verdict to be pronounced.

"Willful murder," the foreman said without hesitation.

"By persons known, or unknown?"

"Known, sir." Hickson's eyelids flickered, but he did not allow his gaze to stray from the coroner's visage. "We find that Master William Heathcote, with malice aforethought, did strike Master Arthur Prendergast on the head, sending him into Pot, where he was taken up drowned Wednesday morning."

Will surged to his feet. "I n-n-never d-d-did so! U-p-pon my honour, I am innocent!"

Mr. Pelham's gavel struck the deal table, in a vain

attempt to quell the disorder breaking out all around. A pair of rough fellows seated in front of us rose and sprang upon poor William, seizing him by the arms.

"We got him, Coroner, sir!" one bellowed triumphantly, drowning out Elizabeth's desperate entreaties to release her son.

My nephew Edward immediately grappled with the men, attempting to free his friend.

"This is a miscarriage of justice!" Edward shouted.

We were all of us on our feet at this point, being pressed unmercifully by those around us, and I felt suddenly faint. Aware that Elizabeth must be in a worse case, I slipped my arm around her shoulders.

"Jane," she said with difficulty.

Suddenly, two faces swam before us: that of the ginger-haired gentleman whose seat had been next to Edward's; and the parish constable, who had been observing the proceedings from a chair behind Mr. Pelham's table. With a deft movement of his hands, the gentleman broke one of the ruffians' hold on William and then placed himself in front of the boy—an act of selfless courage in the face of what was swiftly becoming a mob.

I know not whether fisticuffs should have ensued—but the gentleman's quick movement afforded the constable an opportunity. He collared the two pugnacious fellows and said, "That's enough, you. I'll take him from here." Without further ceremony he conducted our young friend towards the coroner.

"Clear a path," the unknown gentleman told Edward

commandingly, and with his hand at Elizabeth's elbow, he conveyed her neatly to the aisle. I followed, aware of the unfriendly looks directed at our party from every side. How swift are the mob's passions directed by a word, and how ready are they to condemn!

"Dr. Lyford!" our saviour called out. "You are wanted here, sir!"

Giles Lyford forced his way through the throng, his concerned looks fixed on Elizabeth.

With a nod and word, the Unknown saw her into the surgeon's care, and stepped backward into the crowd.

"Master Heathcote," Pelham declared above the din. "It is my duty to indict you for the willful murder of Master Arthur Prendergast. You will be taken from this place to the Winchester gaol, where you will remain until your case is brought before the Summer Assizes. Have you anything to say?"

"I am innocent!" Will repeated. A look of terror o'respread his features; his thin frame was bent as under a crushing weight. On impulse, Elizabeth started forward as tho' to embrace her son, but Mr. Lyford gently restrained her. She bowed her head and began to weep into her gloved hands.

"Truth preserves the honour of every Englishman, under the Law," I murmured in Elizabeth's ear. "I am convinced it shall be William's salvation."

But Peter Insley, whose testimony differed so markedly from William's, had also sworn to his truth. A grave perjury on one side—or an incalculable confusion of circumstances—was at work. Struck forcibly that a further interview with Insley was of the greatest importance, I craned my head in search of the boy's undistinguished figure—but could not discover it. Had he even returned to the public room when the panel's judgement was announced? Or had the pair of Winchester masters who flanked him, removed him from the premises as soon as his testimony was given?

But the coroner was done his duty; the constable again seized young Heathcote by the arm, and conducted him at speed from the White Hart. We surged after him.

"D-d-do not d-d-despair, M-m-mamma!" William shouted over his shoulder. "Austen w-w-will set all to r-r-rights!"

The front door of the inn swung closed behind the boy's harried form.

Elizabeth, her looks stricken and insensible to the clamour on every side, sank nerveless to the floor.

Giles Lyford bent immediately and lifted her in his arms. "Quickly," he said to us. "We must carry her to safety in the Close."

11

THE POSSIBILITY OF A LEGACY

No. 12, The Close
Winchester
Monday, 31 March 1817, cont'd.

I enjoyed an interval of reflection in a comfortable chair drawn up to the drawing-room fire upon our return to the house. Elizabeth—who recovered from her swoon halfway home—was conveyed directly upstairs by the efficient Lyford, who summoned her maid to attend her. He also dispatched a manservant to his dispensary.

"She requires a draught to calm her nerves," he told me briskly, "for her pulse is tumultuous. I have requested a sleeping draught as well, which you are to see that she swallows before retiring this evening."

I assented to his direction, but was firmly barred from sitting at Elizabeth's bedside—Mr. Lyford offering it as his opinion that I could do with a restorative posset myself, and a hassock at my feet.

"I should be only too happy to offer advice on your health at a later date, Miss Austen," he told me with a searching look at my countenance, "but I am sure we are agreed that

Mrs. Heathcote's circumstance must command all our present anxiety."

Edward stayed only long enough to ascertain that Elizabeth was in no danger, before quitting the house once more for the Winchester gaol, a substantial structure of some three storeys in the Classical stile, that sits in Jewry Street.

I called him back from the threshold, and bade him wait for me to consult my purse, and retrieve a few coins I had secured against vails for the servants at No. 12.[12] "It is not so much as a pound," I said, "but you must present it to the gaoler, to ensure William is adequately fed, and has a blanket to his pallet. Tomorrow, you may wish to bring him a change of clothing, some books, and a letter from his mother."

"I shall certainly do so, Aunt, along with a flagon of ale, and some foolscap for writing," Edward said grimly. Then, softening, he kissed my cheek. "Endeavour to calm yourself. I shall return in good time for dinner."

AN HOUR LATER, WE partook of roast chicken, new peas, and old potatoes in Elizabeth's dining parlour—our hostess having broth sent up to her on a tray. Rain had set in before Edward's return from Jewry Street, and both his coat and hat were damp; I begged him to arrange them before the fire to dry, and dine without ceremony in his waistcoat and shirtsleeves.

---

12 Vails were tips that houseguests were expected to offer their hosts' staff upon concluding a visit.—*Editor's note.*

"Will is blue as megrim," he told me, "as must be expected, and alternates between fiery outrage at what he insists are Urquhart's lies, and terror of his own future. He is agitated for his mother's nerves, and begs that we do all in our power to see his credit restored unblemished."

"Did you ask where he was, between five and seven o'clock last Tuesday?"

"He refuses to tell me, Aunt."

I studied my nephew's countenance. It was suffused with an expression of trouble that was unexceptionable given the circumstances—tho' I suspected deeper concerns underlay Edward's gravity. "Unless we discover the facts of what occurred at Pot on Tuesday last," I said, "William shall languish in prison until the Summer Assizes in July."

"It is a pity that the Lenten Session has only just closed," Edward fretted.

"Not at all!" I exclaimed. "I should not wish William to suffer a too-speedy justice! Reflect, Edward, that his friends are granted several months now to unearth the truth."

"That shall not require more than a few days, surely?"

I lifted my brows. "That depends upon the whim and temper of one Master Peter Insley, and the aid of Master Charles Baigent. The latter must have returned to his people for the Easter leave-out, whereas the former has apparently nowhere to go on such holidays, and is forced to idle in college. Are you at all acquainted with Baigent?"

"He is the third son of a baron," Edward said, "with a family seat in the neighbourhood of Bristol. He will not be returned to Winchester until Monday at the earliest—and if his family has sought travel-leave, perhaps a day later. You believe his account of Monday last should be helpful to Will?"

"—When the two reportedly sailed Heathcote's model frigate? Alas, I fear it is *Tuesday* night that must concern us. If Will is very fortunate, not only Badger but others in Gabell's House may attest to his whereabouts on the evening when Prendergast went missing and apparently died. If but one or more of William's friends swears to his presence in college from the end of Toytime until curfew, there can be no doubt he was incapable of being on St. Catherine's Hill when Prendergast drowned."

"It is indeed unfortunate that most of the Commoners were gone home this week," Edward agreed.

"Not to mention Insley's remaining, and putting the lie to William's evidence. I cannot wonder at the coroner's panel crediting his testimony; did I not have powerful feeling for William's side, I should have done so myself. How well do you know Insley, Edward?"

"Not at all. He is some four years younger than myself. He came to my notice solely because of his Prefect's persecution—it was Insley that Prendergast chose for his horse, in the scob-jumping race I told you of."

"The one with the spurs?" I said, horrified. "It was *Insley* who Prenders sent to Sick House, with gashes in his thighs?"

"When he was but twelve," Edward replied.

"And yet—he spoke with pride of being chosen as *lieutenant.*"

"Even a painful attention is valued, by those accustomed to receiving little praise or notice."

I frowned at him. "You cannot think the same. Nor Urquhart. You are both the objects of general admiration. Surely Urquhart does not condescend to these petty schoolboy battles!"

Despite his anxiety, my nephew smiled. "On the contrary. There is not a boy connected to either house who is not passionately engaged! Thomas Urquhart is a natural leader of men—and I daresay most of Clarke's fellows worship him, so charming and admirable as he is. Unlike Prendergast, who appeared to enjoy humiliating and shaming others, Urquhart was uniformly honourable in his skirmishes."

I conjured in my mind the young Scholar's gentle looks, easy manners, and good humour. "And yet, he befriended Prendergast. I cannot make it out at all!"

"Have you considered, Aunt, that Prendergast, who sorely lacked intimates, may have been at *pains* to cultivate the friendship of a fellow so universally admired?"

"But if Prendergast's character was truly reprehensible," I observed, "that does not explain why Urquhart should welcome his overtures."

"Only if one ignores the importance of self-interest," Edward countered. "Prendergast offered Urquhart the entrée to a noble estate, where he might usefully form connexions during his holidays, and cultivate both habits and friends of a more elevated station than his own. We are not all of us so happy in our fortunes as to spend time with those who have none."

"That is true." I sighed, and set aside my plate, being singularly without appetite this evening. "Even a young man as clearly blessed as Urquhart—with looks, address, and manner—may not be entirely free of mercenary considerations. For a boy such as Insley, who lacks such gifts, the slavish attraction of power must be more severe."

"That is what we must learn, Aunt: Is Insley acting from subtle motives, unsuspected from his youth and general appearance? Is he the sort to deliberately perjure himself, particularly when that perjury should threaten another person's liberty, reputation, and life—as it has threatened Will's? Or does he merely repeat what Prendergast supplied him?"

"And if so—where did Prendergast get such ridiculous ideas, as to accuse Will Heathcote of sordid behaviour?"

"Prendergast was not above lying and besmirching others," Edward said thoughtfully, "nor above using such methods to coerce the support of his juniors."

"Did he invent it, or did he also *believe* it, Edward? —I am inclined to the latter. Why else should he have appeared at Pot, than to confront William?"

"The note William wrote to Badger has a part to play there," Edward added. "How did Prenders come to be in possession of it?"

A doubt assailed me. "Is Badger truly William's friend? Or could he have supplied both the scandal, and the scrap of paper, to Prendergast?"

Edward looked horrified. "Heaven above! If Charles Baigent were to overhear such speculation, you should be called out at dawn, Aunt! He is a loyal friend of Will's and Gabell's House, and none to Prendergast."

"But unless Prenders invented the whole—for no reason we can discern—then you agree that *someone* must have supplied him with both the lies and the evidence to back them up," I mused. "*Who*, Edward? And for what purpose?"

"To lure Prenders to a secluded spot, and watch him drown?" my nephew suggested.

"—And throw guilt quite handily upon William Heathcote."

"William does appear to have placed his neck in a noose." Edward looked sombre. "His unwillingness to divulge his whereabouts Tuesday last cannot help him."

"I do not like this tale of a debauched young woman from town," I admitted. "Insley, too, claims to have seen Will with a girl on Hills, which is testimony independent of Prendergast's stories. Will must be made to explain himself."

"I will try to persuade him again tomorrow. But I have never observed such behaviour, and I was still resident in college as recently as mid-December."

"You would not always have had Will under your eye, however."

"That is true," Edward acknowledged. "But he is far too young to be chasing after the muslin company, Aunt!"

"His uncle Harris begged for my hand at twenty," I pointed out. "And I was six years his senior. Mooning after older women may prove a family failing."

Edward threw back his head and laughed, a welcome sound after such a wretched day.

"Very well," my nephew said. "I shall interrogate Will at the next opportunity. How do you mean to proceed?"

"I should dearly love to subject Insley to similar questioning. I suspect an offer of sweets and hot chocolate at a coffeehouse might lure him. But the Heathcotes have no acquaintance with him; I do not know how to make my attentions *plausible*, without exciting the boy's suspicions."

"Urquhart," Edward said immediately. "He knows Insley far better than we, being also a member of Clarke's House. I shall send round a note to him, first thing in the morning."

"I see now why you figured as a great general of Gabell's," I said admiringly. "Like Wellington, you are a keen strategist . . ."

"As to that—were it not for the danger Will finds himself in, I should regard this as a fine lark, and plunge in with vigour! I might even turn to the study of Law. The work of a solicitor should offer more scope for imagination and variety than that of a clergyman."

"Are those your only alternatives?" I asked gently. "You cannot dedicate yourself to writing?"

Edward laughed brusquely. "I doubt I have the necessary talent to make a success of that."

"Why?" I demanded. "Do you regard me as a frivolous flatterer? I do not offer praise lightly, my dear. When I tell you I enjoy and admire your sketches—so different to my own little bit of ivory, on which I work with so fine a brush—I am sincere, you know. I do not seek to puff you up with nonsense."

He shrugged, with a tinge of despair unusual and thus alarming in so generally sunny a character. "I must earn my bread, Aunt, and cannot depend upon what my father regards as *the vagaries of Fashion*. He intends me for the Church—and most particularly, for the Steventon living, which he expects me to assume once he is done with it."

I swept my eyes over the studied disorder of Edward's locks, the green velvet collar to his coat, and the intricate folds of his snowy cravat; all of these spoke of Town Bronze, not the country life of a clergyman. "But do you wish to be buried in a parish, Edward? Or do you aspire to a broader life—in London, perhaps?"

"A life like Uncle Henry's?" he retorted, with a mordant smile. "For I have heard only too much of it, I assure you! My father is never done preaching about the evils of setting up in Society. He had not the sums invested in my uncle's banking schemes that others had—thank God!—but that does not preclude him from drawing a useful moral from his brother's misfortunes."

"Your Uncle Henry lived very well for a time." I have always detected a similarity of character between my favourite brother and my favourite nephew. "The sad end of his career cannot negate years of success. I do not urge you into banking, of course—but why *not* read Law?"

"Want of coin," he said simply. "I should have to spend a few years apprenticing at some office or other in the Temple—and that requires the sums for room and board, my necessary books, the fees to a solicitor or barrister—"

"None of which your Papa will advance you?"

"I already owe him so much, Aunt. Consider the cost of Exeter, on top of the fees Winchester demanded!"

I bit my tongue. As I have noted before, James's jealous

guarding of his coin against the ambitions of his only son confounds my understanding. He seems to wish to limit Edward to the narrow life he himself enjoyed, in the same house and the confines of a neighbourhood enlarged only by intercourse with The Vyne and its hunt.

"It is possible, you know, that the recent event at Scarlets may afford you greater means."

"Uncle Leigh-Perrot's will, you mean?" Edward's visage lightened. "If he should have left each of us something! Even the smallest legacy should be welcome! I should certainly take up Law, and devote more time to my novel—but I daresay my uncle will have disregarded my generation, in deference to *yours*. I know my father will simply put his bequest into the Funds, against future want; but what will *you* do with your legacy, Aunt? —Follow Miss Alethea, in a tour of the Continent?"

"I should take excellent lodgings in London," I said instantly, "and place myself in the hands of the finest physician available."

It is remarkable how dearly even the most reconciled of creatures will cling to hope—and life. In Cheltenham nearly a year ago, confronted with a physician's grim determination, I had thought myself equal to acceptance of my limited span. But as time passes, and I feel myself weaken—yet rejoice in the warmth of the spring sun, and the continued affection of those dear to me—I wish for more time. I wish for the wisdom of a master physician. I wish to trade base coin for the possibility of a future.

I had not expressed my hope before, even in my most

private thoughts, but I acknowledged the truth of it now: a legacy—even the most modest—should offer me the world.

Edward's lips parted in dismay, and his cajoling expression altered. "Oh, Aunt—do not say so! Indeed, and you ought to go to London this instant, and hang the cost!"

"But as you say, Edward—want of coin." I adopted a rallying tone. "With the entire family's fortunes in desperate case, due to your uncle Henry's losses and your uncle Edward's being sued, I cannot undertake to add to our expence! My last novel did not sell nearly so well as my first; and beggars cannot be chusers. No, I shall remain in Chawton, and learn to be satisfied with Mr. Curtis's laudanum and leeches."

Edward shuddered, and threw off his doldrums with a laugh. "You are braver than I! When do you expect to hear from Aunt Cassandra? Surely she will know the substance of my uncle's will by now!"

"She may be savouring the happy news against her return into Hampshire Monday next," I told him. "Indeed, I believe we ought to bid our hostess adieu on the same date. Our stay here in Winchester cannot be of long duration, particularly now that such trouble has fallen upon Elizabeth's head. She will be wanting her bedchambers for other guests—her brother, I suspect, and possibly Sir William, the third baronet and head of the Heathcote family. They will be sure to descend post-haste upon the Close now that young William is consigned to gaol."

I could not be entirely easy in contemplation of a meeting with Harris Bigg-Wither that must, despite the passage of years, be awkward. But I thought Sir William, or his son and heir Thomas Heathcote, should be more likely to journey south. Thomas was childless, and a widower. Eliza's son was therefore *his* heir.

"We ought to inform Manydown and Hursley Park of what is towards," I said, "by Express, if possible. But I do not like to disturb Elizabeth, and any communication should come from her. Is morning too late to send the intelligence? What is your opinion?"

But Edward's answer was forestalled by a rap at the front door, and the swift answer of Elizabeth's maid. We fell silent, straining to overlisten the words exchanged on the threshold, but in the event, discerned only a deep, male voice and Mariah's deferential assent. In a very few moments she was before us, making her curtsey, to say that a visitor awaited us in the drawing room.

"The Headmaster wished to see Madam," she explained, "only I told him she wasn't equal to visitors at present. He would have gone away again, only that I mentioned Mr. Austen was here, begging your pardon, sir."

"That is perfectly all right," Edward replied, drawing his dry coat from the screen before the fire. "Tell Dr. Gabell I shall attend him in an instant! Do you wish to accompany me, Aunt, or shall I cry off on your behalf?"

I summoned my flagging reserves of energy, and rose from the table. "Lead on, Edward," I said. "I shall certainly support you. I must believe that despite being nearly nineteen, you still quake in your boots at an interview with the Headmaster!"

12

A CALL TO CONDOLE

No. 12, The Close
Winchester
Monday, 31 March 1817, cont'd.

My father, George Austen, was educated at Oxford. That is where he met my mother, Cassandra Leigh, herself the daughter of an Oxford don, my grandfather Thomas, formerly Master of Balliol College. So I have been accustomed all my life to the sort of men who drift about ecclesiastical towns in black academical dress, lost in abstraction. I have been intimate from girlhood with schoolboys as well—my father having taken any number of them into tutelage at Steventon rectory. He was forever cramming young heads with Latin and Greek, while we children harried the boarders by turns on the cricket pitch. Whenever I encounter the illustrious names of those former schoolboys in public accounts of Parliament or the Cabinet, I wonder if they owe their advancement to my father's lessons—or my own in bowling.

All of which is merely to say that I recognised Dr. Gabell's type at an instant.

He stood at the hearth, his hands clasped behind his back and his bespectacled head bent in contemplation of his boots. He was garbed, as I was, in sober black—tho' I assumed from habit rather than the conventions of mourning. His coat was spotted with rain, and his cravat with something darker I suspected was his dinner. I do not think Mrs. Gabell takes over-much care of him; or perhaps he is the sort who defeats every attempt at improvement. He was neither old nor young; fat nor thin; handsome nor ugly. An unassuming and unremarkable man, at what may sadly be termed the zenith of his career—with a tonsure of brownish hair encircling a pink and shining pate.

He turned from the drawing-room fire at our entrance. Edward had allowed me to precede him, and Gabell's countenance evinced a little surprise.

Edward stepped forward and bowed. "Doctor! How very good to see you, sir! May I present my aunt, Miss Austen, to your acquaintance?"

"A pleasure," he returned with a nod. "Henry Gabell. Are you related, ma'am, to Mr. Edward Austen-Knight, of Godmersham Park, in Kent?"

"He is my brother, sir."

"Excellent. We have had the privilege of educating any number of his sons. Indeed, I have quite lost count."

"Four have passed through your hands to date," I supplied, "and a fifth, Charles-Bridges, is at present a Commoner."

The Headmaster glanced around the drawing-room as tho' the boy in question might suddenly appear. "You are staying with Mrs. Heathcote, I perceive?"

"She and I are very old friends," I said, "and, as you no doubt know, Edward is a former schoolfellow of Master William's. Both boys lodged in your House."

"Indeed." His myopic eyes peered narrowly at Edward. "A wretched thing, this business of Heathcote's. I was intimate with his father, you know—we were at Oxford together. A bruising rider to hounds, threw his heart over every ditch and hedgerow. Ought to have ended with a broken neck, but instead, was taken off in his prime by an inflammation of the lung! —Caught, no doubt, while riding out in the rain, neck-or-nothing as usual. He was but thirty."

Gabell came to a full stop, his eyes once more on his boots. "And now this dreadful business. How does Mrs. Heathcote go on? I am charged with my wife's compliments and inquiries after her health."

"You are very good," I said. "We shall certainly inform her of your solicitude, once she is well enough to learn of it."

Edward gestured to a chair. "Won't you sit down, sir? I trust you and Mrs. Gabell are in health?"

"Indifferently so—our minds being sadly oppressed by the calamities in college." He flipped the tails of his black coat and seated himself. "I had hoped for a verdict of misadventure from the inquest into Prendergast's death. The Warden tells me it would have improved the opinion of the Governing Board with regard to my tenure, tho' undoubtedly I should still be subject to a charge of neglect, in failing to learn of the boy's absence from college an *entire night*. I blame Clarke."

"Of course you do," Edward agreed.

If his tone was satiric, Dr. Gabell was impervious.

"Nothing could have been done for Prendergast, however," he persisted, "even had we sent out a search party after dinner—on that point, I must console myself. He was certainly drowned within an hour of leaving college. And as he did so in violation of every accepted rule, entirely without leave, I flatter myself I may claim a certain impunity from general censure."

As a condolence to the family of a student accused and imprisoned on a charge of murder, the doctor's speech must be found wanting. His thoughts were entirely for his own safety, not William Heathcote's. He felt no solicitude for Elizabeth's anxiety. And any concern Gabell might have felt at Arthur Prendergast's shocking end, had long since been put aside by indignation at his own ill-usage.

"Were you present at the White Hart today?" I ventured to ask. "The public room was so full, I did not perfectly notice."

"I was," Gabell said heavily. "The mortification—to observe the outrage of the town on every side—the prospect of gentlemen's sons in the public dock—the indecent nature of some of the accusations . . . I am sure I aged a twelvemonth in a single hour. My own dear wife is naturally too delicate to attend such a sordid proceeding, but spent the interval on her couch, with recourse to smelling-salts, against the dreadful news she was convinced I should bear home."

"Mrs. Gabell was ever a lady of sensibility." Edward endeavoured to conciliate, but his eyes sparkled with ridicule. "The ladies of this household are forced by necessity to greater fortitude. What is your opinion of the circumstances surrounding Prendergast's death, sir?"

Gabell lifted his hands. "I am all bewilderment! Heathcote did himself no favours with his testimony, and as for *Insley Minor*! Who can say which of the boys is truthful, and which the liar? —For certainly their assertions cannot *both* be fact. In such cases, one must rely upon the judgement of those whose calling is Justice." He contemplated this turn of phrase for an instant, his fingers stroking his chin and his gaze on the fire. "Yes, that is the safest course to take. Particularly before the Warden and the Governing Body . . ."

"I have always believed that the truth of a fellow may be determined from his comportment and character," Edward persisted. "Heathcote, for example, I have never found deceitful in all our dealings, over a lifetime of intimacy. I was less well acquainted with Insley Minor during my years in college, however. What is your opinion, Doctor?"

Gabell dragged his gaze back to my nephew. "I confess I have none. The boy is one of Clarke's charges. As was his brother, Insley Major. Sons of a Sussex gentleman. Neither is particularly distinguished; but I know of nothing to reproach in either."

This was to damn with faint praise.

"How did Master Insley come to remain here, Doctor Gabell, during Holy Week?" I asked. "Sussex is not so very far off. My own nephew is gone so far as Canterbury for the leave-out."

"The majority of our boys are absent, it is true. A few whose families are in diplomatic posts abroad, of necessity remain in our care during holidays, although we do our best to see them sent to the homes of particular friends or near-relations."

"Indeed." Edward glanced at the door, where Mariah had appeared with a silver tray of sherry. She moved directly to the Headmaster, who seized a glass. "Thomas Urquhart, for example, ought to have gone into Wiltshire with Prendergast. He has been kicking his heels here without employment; but I for one was most happy to discover him in Winchester, and renew our acquaintance."

"Now, Urquhart," Gabell replied with enthusiasm, "I know very well! A most deserving young man, whom we expect to earn a Scholar's appointment at New College. With his excellent understanding and signal accomplishments, he shall be a great adornment to the 'varsity! I can think of no other boy in the present class so strongly recommended for the honour. There is no limit, I believe, to the heights that young man might attain—regardless of the profession he chuses. One could wish, of course, that he might incline towards the Church—"

Edward's countenance broke into a grin. "With respect, Doctor, I cannot agree. Urks lacks the saintliness to serve as a general example. He should better grace the political sphere."

"Unfortunate that he was denied the visit to Avebury," Gabell mourned. "*There*, he might have benefited from inclusion in the first circles. He might have formed some useful acquaintance. He must feel his friend's loss most acutely."

"Has Urquhart need of connexions?" I asked, puzzled. "I thought Scholars were usually the scions of the Great."

"I am not perfectly acquainted with his background," the Headmaster said austerely, "tho' I believe Clarke was persuaded to propose him for his place by a man of influence and distinction. But by *whom*, or what the gentleman's relation *may be* to the boy, I cannot say."

From the tenor of Dr. Gabell's remarks, delicately phrased before a lady, I suspected a plainer truth: Urquhart was the natural son of one, noble or otherwise, whose identity must remain a strict secret. I was warned off.

"It is unfortunate that so admirable a young man was unable to attest to William Heathcote's character," I mused. "Had he or Charles Baigent—who is away from school— professed something to William's advantage, Insley Minor's remarks should not have held such power with the jury."

"Heathcote ought to have explained where he was Tuesday last," Gabell countered.

"You are inclined to believe Insley, then? —Against the word of one described as the chief of *Gabell's Forces*?"

"As to that—" the Headmaster waved a dismissive hand. "It is all nonsense! A farrago, Miss Austen! There is no more a condition of open warfare at Winchester than there is in this drawing-room, I assure you!"

Edward's brows rose precipitously. "Dr. Gabell, as an erstwhile member of that force—"

"If you are so willing to discount Insley's testimony in *this*, sir," I broke in, "why should you credit any part of it? You have already said—and I must agree—that one cannot accept Insley's account and credit William Heathcote's, too. William has lived these three years past in your House, under your especial care, the son of a cherished tho' lamented friend. You ought to place the utmost confidence in the truth of his testimony; you are intimate with William's character."

"I am." Gabell rubbed reflectively at his nose, his eyes dropping to the embers on the hearth. "I wish I could profess a full confidence in the unimpeachability of his account—but I fear there has not always been plain-dealing, in his relations with the college in the past. There have been incidents . . ."

"To what incidents would you refer, sir?" There was a decided sharpness in Edward's words.

"Heathcote claims incessantly to be the object of spiteful attacks," Gabell returned with asperity, "and would have it that no one is so victimised in the world as he! There is a lack of openness about the boy, a reluctance to confide, that argues a tendency to deceit. And he is forever engaging his Mamma to wage his battles for him! I had hoped that advancing maturity might mitigate these defects, but Heathcote continues to abdicate responsibility; and today's wretched performance before the coroner was of a piece with his usual conduct. That he—a product of Winchester College, as generations of Heathcotes before him—should blemish the school's reputation, by hemming and hawing and gabbling so, in speaking under oath—or should I say, *scribbling?*"

"His stammer and his guilt, in your eyes, would appear to be the same," Edward observed.

Gabell rose abruptly from his seat. My nephew stood as well, his posture stiff with outrage.

"There is not a particle of reason for Insley Minor to

perjure himself, and every reason for Heathcote to do so," the Headmaster declared angrily. "He has not been open. Insley *has*. But my views are neither here nor there, Austen. The decision of the Law is all that matters, in the eyes of God and man."

"We will not debate the relative merits of Law, Doctor, and Justice," Edward replied.

"Indeed we shall not. I am forgetting the principal reason I have waited upon Mrs. Heathcote." He turned to me. "I would beg you to inform the lady that having shamed himself, his name, and his school, William Heathcote is expelled from Winchester forthwith. The college is the sanctum of gentlemen's sons; it ought not to be associated with falsehoods and violence."

"It is only Insley who accuses Will of both," Edward said, but Gabell ignored him.

"How am I to answer the indignant parent, Miss Austen, who demands to know why his blessed child must fraternize with gaol-birds? I fancy your own brother Mr. Knight should be incensed, did he know of our present shame! Indeed, I expect to learn hourly that half the respectable families mean to withdraw their sons from the school."

"My brother Mr. Knight, being acquainted with the Bigg and Heathcote families all his life, is more likely to demand in what way you have supported William's claim to innocence," I retorted. "His dismissal from college, before any determination of the case has been made, is disgraceful."

"No, no, Miss Austen." The Headmaster was impervious. "Heathcote's expulsion is by-the-by. He is to kick his heels in idleness, as a guest of His Majesty's gaol, until July at the earliest; his absence through the remainder of Long Term is therefore ordained. When he does not return for Short Half in September, no one will pay any heed; and if we are very fortunate, the entire matter will soon vanish from the public mind."

I glanced at Edward, and perceived that he was on the point of a regrettable outburst. I understood suddenly a little of what he must have endured, as the observer of so much complaisant hypocrisy during his years in Dr. Gabell's House; it was more than any person of intelligence should be asked to withstand.

I set my jaw and dropped a curtsey to the Headmaster. "No doubt you wish to leave us as soon as may be, to comfort your wife, Doctor. We will extend her compliments and yours to Mrs. Heathcote when she is capable of receiving them."

Gabell bowed, and made immediately for the drawing-room door, where Edward stood, impatient for him to be gone. "Do not bother to beg my indulgence for your hasty words, Austen," he said. "I am sure your loyalty to your young friend, however ill-placed, does you credit. It is quite the conduct one would wish to see in an Old Wykehamist."

"You are too good, sir," Edward returned bitingly.

"No doubt, in view of these sad events, Mrs. Heathcote and Miss Alethea will also wish to consider a change of residence," the Headmaster added, as he turned in the doorway. "There can be no attraction for them to the Close, when such painful memories must obtrude."

13

A MATTER OF WILLS

No. 12, The Close
Winchester
Tuesday, 1 April 1817

Morning saw Elizabeth returned to the breakfast-parlour, a martial light in her eye, and her contempt for such poor creatures as the Headmaster apparent in her refusal to so much as mention his name, once the intelligence of William's expulsion was delivered. She did not weakly dwell on regrets, but turned immediately to the formulation of battle-plans.

Firstly, she despatched Edward to wait upon her son at the Winchester gaol, with strict instructions to set down in writing every detail of William's life Tuesday last—from waking to retiring for the night—to especially include the names of any persons with whom he had spoken, or who might vouch for his presence in school during the interval when Arthur Prendergast met his end.

"And Edward," I added *sotto voce* as I saw him into his coat at the door, "do not neglect to tax your friend for the names of any young women of the town who may form a part of his acquaintance. That accusation must have some scrap of foundation—it should not have been voiced in sworn testimony otherwise."

"I should rather attempt to exonerate him with the fair sex!"

I shook my head. "Depend upon it, you will find some history of intimacy that gave rise to general rumour. Insley's confidence in his statement was too good—he knew it should be supported by others, did the coroner pursue the point. In the event, Mr. Pelham's panel saved him the trouble, by assigning guilt without further investigation."

"You believe it vital that we put a name to the young woman Insley claims to have seen on Hills?"

"As the boy would not—at least before the public—I suspect that we must certainly do so. Pelham will drag it from him."

"Very well." Edward eyed me with respect, quite different from the amused indulgence with which he usually treated me. "I am once again struck by the subtlety of your understanding, Aunt."

"It is a family failing," I assured him, and returned to Elizabeth.

She was drinking her chocolate by the breakfast-parlour fire, her countenance set and disciplined. "It is providential that both you and Edward are here, Jane, for the combined weight of our several intellects shall be more than equal to the present difficulty. If we do but stir ourselves to untangle this coil, I daresay William shall be restored to us by Easter."

"While I admire your faith in our abilities," I demurred

as I resumed my place at the table, "I must believe that you command relations whose interest and support should prove of greater material use. William ought to speak to a solicitor as soon as may be—and engage that solicitor's barrister, in the pleading of his case before the Assizes. As he is a minor, you could enlist the help of your brother, Mr. Bigg-Wither, but upon reflection, I believe your late husband's father, Sir William, is the properest person to act on his grandson's behalf. The weight of the Third Baronet's family name and position ought to convince the courts that your son is far from friendless."

"Sir William?" Elizabeth's brows drew down in consternation. "I am afraid my father-in-law has been most unwell since the death of his beloved wife. He is over seventy years of age, Jane, and much afflicted with the gout—no longer rides to hounds, and has long since given up his lodgings in London. I do not believe he stirs from Hursley House if he can help it."

"What, then, of his heir?"

She hesitated, cup suspended in mid-air. "You would refer to Mr. Thomas Heathcote?"

Elizabeth's late husband William, tho' the baronet's namesake, had been his second son; his first, Thomas, was a gentleman in his late forties, and a Member of Parliament for Hampshire, as well as the presumptive Fourth Baronet. I was not personally acquainted with Thomas Heathcote, but thought it likely that he might do much on William's behalf.

"I apprehend he is at present in London, for the Session,"

I said, "but might he not take a leave of absence, in light of the gravity of your son's circumstances?"

Elizabeth set down her cup. "I doubt that the Distinguished Member for Hampshire would be willing to do anything to help William. He resents and detests his very existence."

I must have stared in wonder at this—Elizabeth's stony expression softened into one of conciliation, and she placed her hand on mine.

"I have never enlarged upon the nature of my husband's elder brother, I collect."

"Not that I recall."

"That is because the subject has long been a painful one. Mr. Thomas Heathcote–or I suppose I should say, Thomas *Freeman*-Heathcote, for that is how he stiles himself—has no child of his own. Freeman is his late wife's surname," Elizabeth supplied. "Thomas appended it to his at their marriage, I presume to secure her inheritance for himself."

"Such things are often done," I attempted. "My own Uncle Leigh-Perrot altered his name from similar motives, as has my brother."[13]

"But neither gentleman was the eldest son and heir to a baronetcy, carrying with it considerable estates," Elizabeth pointed out. "Thomas's alteration of his name certainly wounded old Sir William's pride—but it succeeded in

13 Edward Austen, Jane's elder brother and the third Austen son, was adopted at the age of twelve by a childless cousin, Thomas Knight, who made Edward his heir. The stipulation, however, was that Edward add the name of Knight to his surname once Thomas Knight's widow was deceased. He and his eleven children became Knights in 1812.—*Editor's note.*

gaining him an independence, so that he might conduct his life in complete liberty of family expectations or limits. Having won an heiress, he set up his own establishment; secured a safe seat in Parliament; purchased a string of racehorses; and made a name for himself as a collector of rare antiquities and patron of the Arts."

"He is hardly alone in such pursuits. They have long characterised the gentleman of Fashion. But why should such a career set him against *your son*, pray?"

"Thomas has none of his own. His lady died eight years ago, and he has never seen fit to remarry. William is therefore his presumptive heir, and if he lives—shall be Fifth Baronet, after Thomas."

Presumptive heir, because it was just conceivable that Thomas Heathcote should form a second attachment, in order to secure his succession.

"But that is an even greater reason why he should exert himself on William's behalf, in the present crisis!"

Elizabeth shook her head decisively. "I forfeited any support from that quarter years ago, when I refused Thomas's offer to adopt William."

"Adopt him!" I looked all my bewilderment. "But he has a mother, a number of doting aunts and uncles, and his family name to support him. Why should Thomas adopt him?"

"At the time, I thought it a whim of his wife's. She mourned her lack of children to desperation-point, and longed for a babe of her own. When my own dear husband died fifteen years since, and our child was not yet a year of age, Thomas divined the hand of Providence—and insisted that William should be brought up in his household. *By his wife.* My son should receive every material comfort and benefit, Thomas assured me, as befit the heir to the Heathcote lands and honours—but there was a peculiar stipulation. His real mother," Elizabeth added, "should be wholly unnecessary. Indeed, I should not have been permitted to spend so much as a fortnight with my child, from year to year, lest I confuse William regarding his parentage, and alienate his affections."

"That is monstrous!"

"Naturally, I deplored the idea." Elizabeth reached for a poker and stirred up the fire—a steady rain fell beyond the windows, and despite the promise of spring, the flare of the flames was comforting on the hearth. "But my refusal brought down Thomas's bitterness and wrath. He threatened to set the Law upon me—you will know, Jane, that a mother possesses almost no rights to her children, having sunk her individual rights entirely in her husband at marriage. Even as a widow, I am regarded in some wise as the property of my late husband's family. Thomas meant to have me declared Unfit, and the guardianship of my son conferred upon himself."

"How did you prevent such a calamity?" My mind ran swiftly back over the years, aware that for all the Bigg sisters loved to gossip and canvass each other's business, I had never heard a whisper of this dreadful threat to Elizabeth's peace. She had certainly held her troubles close.

"My late husband did not much care for his elder brother,"

she said drily. "At our son's birth, he possessed the foresight to draw up his Will. He appointed my father the boy's guardian. The document was properly witnessed, signed, and lodged with the Heathcote family's solicitors—it was, in a word, unassailable even to one of Thomas's poor scruples. At my husband's untimely death, I was free to return to Manydown House, with my infant, where Thomas and the Law could not touch me."

"Fifteen years is a considerable period to nurse such a grievance," I mused. "Now that his lady is dead—if the campaign to adopt your son originated with her—perhaps Mr. Freeman-Heathcote has experienced a change of heart?"

Elizabeth cast me a searching glance. "Not at all, my dear Jane. He has found yet another reason to despise William. Thomas abhors my son's speech impediment, and regards it as a fault of my rearing. He believes William's stammer is evidence of a feeble mind, congenital on the maternal side, that ought to bar him from inheritance. Indeed, I know from my various Heathcote relatives—my late husband's married sisters, who remain my friends—that Thomas has lately mounted a campaign to persuade Sir William to cut off the entail. He perceives that his father is ageing and unwell, and wishes the matter settled before Death determines the outcome."

"The entail?" I frowned. "What is his purpose in altering the disposition of a baronet's estate?"

"He means to leave the bulk of his family wealth away from his heir. Thomas cannot deny William the title,"

Elizabeth replied, "unless he remarries and has a son. But he can deprive William of all the income of the estates attached to the baronetcy—all the tenant farms, the great woods that surround Hursley House and supply so much valuable timber; the stables and their contents; Hursley House itself, as well as the furnishings and even the art upon the walls. In his spite, Thomas endeavours to strip William of everything that makes his inheritance meaningful, down to the last farthing."

I sat in stunned silence.

"Do you see now, Jane, why I cannot turn to Thomas Heathcote? He should gladly see William hang, I believe, rather than support his claims of innocence."

"But to whom is all this largess to be conferred?" I cried.

Elizabeth shrugged. "Having no communication with Mr. Freeman-Heathcote, I cannot say. Perhaps he means to expend it all on himself—or upon the *objets d'art* he so delights in."

"Then Mr. Freeman-Heathcote is sadly lacking in family feeling. Does he never think of the respectability of his name? The standing of the Heathcote Baronets in Hampshire society?"

"I cannot speak to the gentleman's motives," Elizabeth sighed. "I will admit that I have written to the Third Baronet, to entreat Sir William to consider of his grandson—whom he continues to see whenever I am in that part of the country—and ignore Thomas's machinations regarding the entail. But I have no notion of whether a woman's argument, when considered alongside that of his rightful heir, will carry any weight in the elderly gentle-man's mind."

"But this is dreadful!" I rose from my place at table and folded my napkin with decision. "You must write to your brother Harris immediately, my dear, and request that he wait upon you as soon as possible, on William's behalf. And then you must assuredly write again to Sir William, and explain in what dire case his grandson finds himself. Surely the baronet will act with force and speed, and despatch his family solicitors to help you in your time of trouble."

"Perhaps," Elizabeth replied. "Or perhaps, Jane, he will decide that Thomas has had the right of it all along—and that William is an unsafe and unreliable future candidate to administer Hursley House and its wealth. I confess, I have no idea how my father-in-law is likely to regard the present crisis, or in what mood he may answer it."

It was indeed possible that an accusation of murder, and the incarceration of young William, should carry shame and indignation to Hursley House as soon as the intel-ligence was generally known. And with so many sons and heirs of Hampshire acquaintance among the schoolboys of Winchester College, news should travel as swift as fire.

I left Elizabeth to compose her letter to Harris, in the privacy of her boudoir, and without alerting anyone of my intentions, donned my cloak and stole out of the house.

14

AN INTERVAL WITH THE TUTOR

No. 12, The Close
Winchester
Tuesday, 1 April 1817, cont'd.

The previous day's rain had left the grounds of the cathedral singularly fresh and brilliant. I determined to fix upon the blowsy daffodils and the delicate leaves of a handsome horse chestnut as I made my way towards College Street, rather than my own dubious strength and unsteadiness. I was always an inveterate walker; one of the griefs of my slow decline has been the diminution of pleasure in exercise. I am sure that Elizabeth must have remarked upon it, during our tour of the Close on Sunday; I noticed that she slowed her pace to accommodate mine. And still, I had been forced to lie down for an hour upon our return to No. 12, after so slight and silly an expedition!

I did not wish my sickness to interfere with my plans today.

I waited for a carthorse and dray to lumber past, then crossed St. Swithun Street at Kings Gate and made my way into College Street. The entrance to Commoners, I knew, was just past Burdon's bookshop where my late father, the Reverend George Austen, was used to keep his account when I was a girl. My footsteps slowed as I passed the shop's vitrine, my gaze lingering on the volumes displayed there; none of my own composition, naturally. Hard by the shadow of the school and the cathedral, such a place must traffic almost entirely in heavy tomes of worth and scholarship; the frivolity of a *novel* should be entirely unknown. Although, I reflected, my father had included works of fiction in his shipments to Steventon rectory—it was from his reading aloud to the whole family by the fire in winter that I first became intimate with *Sir Charles Grandison* and *The Monk*. Poetry, too, fed my early days—but my father had not lived to enjoy the current great age in verse. I wondered for an instant how he should have judged Lord Byron's *Childe Harold*, and settled in my mind that he should certainly have detected the influence of Edmund Spenser on the rakish baron's lines.

I ignored the path leading to Commoners, intent on the quadrangle I purposefully sought: Chamber Court, home to both Scholars and Commoners under the tutelage of Mr. Ruthven Clarke.

It is an imposing and noble edifice of stone, dating from the earliest days of the college in the fourteenth century, I believe—tho' certainly the depredations of time have demanded repairs and changes. I was not perfectly acquainted with the college grounds, despite fully five of my nephews having passed through its cloisters; as a woman in an exclusively male preserve, I ought to have been intimidated. But Chamber Court was largely deserted now, on a Tuesday in Holy Week, with the majority of the boys gone home to their families. My footsteps echoed on the flags as I made my way towards First Chamber, and a raven took flight from a rooftop with a disconcerting clatter of wings.

Scaffolding rose against the stone of the Court's far corner; this would be the result of the fire eighteen months since, and shewed me the location of First Chamber. A heavy oak door, lashed with iron, led to an entryway of stairs, cut from stone; I mounted this, and glanced among the portals at the first landing. *Mr. Clarke* was neatly penned on a stiff card, and affixed to the door opposite. I rapped firmly upon the oak with my gloved fist.

"Come," called the Master's high, rasping voice—and recollecting that he had employed a chair at yesterday's inquest, I reckoned he left the door to his set of rooms unlatched, to save himself the trouble of hobbling to greet every caller.

I thrust myself across the threshold, and paused with my right hand still supporting the open door.

Ruthven Clarke was seated by the fire, with a leather-bound volume in his hands and a pair of spectacles on his nose. A wool rug was laid across his knees, and a glass of what looked like claret was at his left elbow. His expression was of severe irritation, at having been disturbed by a complete stranger.

"Madam," he said without the slightest attempt at salutation, "are you unable to read?"

"I—no, that is—naturally I am able to read," I returned. "You are Mr. Clarke?"

"So you *did* trouble to absorb the name appended to the oak. And yet you forced your way in! You shall not find him here, I assure you. Try the entry next but one. A few boys remain in the attics, I daresay." He returned his glance to the page.

"Find whom?"

With a sigh, and a lifting of his eyes to Heaven, Clarke said, "I have not the slightest notion, nor do I care. Whichever of the benighted brats you pay me to educate. Your *son*, Madam. As you may observe, there are no boys at present in the Master's rooms. Take yourself off!"

"I have no child at Winchester. My business is with you, Mr. Clarke."

"Impossible." He slipped his forefinger between the leaves of his book to mark his place and reached for his glass of wine. "I never have business with females."

Defiantly, I closed the door behind me and approached his chair. There was a companion to it, set on the opposite side of the hearth. "I shall save you the trouble of inviting me in, or rising to acknowledge my presence as any respectable man should do, in deference to your obvious infirmity of body. I hope it does not extend to infirmity of mind."

"It does not," he retorted acidly as I settled myself in the chair. "Who are you, to so outrageously invade my peace? God knows there's little enough to be found within the walls of this Bedlam. Tell me before I shout for my porter, and have you removed."

"I am Miss Austen," I said. "—A guest at present of Mrs. Heathcote, in the Close, whose son is accused of murder."

Confronted with such a dismissive personality, I deemed it wise to be as succinct and clear in my purpose as possible, or the wretched man should certainly have me removed from the premises. My calmness of manner in the face of his abuse must have struck him as singular, however—or at least unique among his usual experience of women— because he troubled to consider my words before setting down his wine and glaring at me.

"Mrs. Heathcote, indeed. I recall, now, your features— you accompanied her at the inquest?"

"I did. And may I say that I found your testimony, sir, to be invaluable."

Ruthven Clarke was intelligent, but exceedingly vain; flattery was a minor sacrifice in the pursuit of justice for young William. Moreover, I suspected Clarke relished the opportunity to trade in information—that he was an avid gossip. He should enjoy extracting what he could from an intimate of No. 12, and dine out on the strength of it for a fortnight.

"I know to my cost," I added, "how troublesome boys of this age may be. No person of knowledge or experience could possibly blame you for the tragedy that befell Arthur Prendergast. He clearly sought misfortune, and brought it upon himself."

Clarke inclined his head in cautious magnanimity. "I regret to say that such was his usual pattern. He rarely met a rule he did not itch to transgress. In this case, he was absent from college without leave, a practice that had become so habitual with him that I wonder his esteemed father, Viscount Beaumont, bothered to pay his attendance fees."

"As Samuel Johnson would have it—the triumph of hope over experience?"

"—Now sadly dashed, and irrevocably." Clarke sighed. "Poor lad. Age might have improved him, had young Heathcote not cut off his life."

"You credit the judgement of the panel, then?"

"The facts admit of no alternative! Prendergast did not die by accident or suicide, for another hand must have opened the sluicegate that sent him into the culvert. But I forget myself, Miss Austen—I should not be discussing this sad business with a stranger. My duties are many and my time short. I trust you will see yourself out."

He made as if to take up his book. I made not the slightest effort to stir.

"I am come on behalf of my brother, Mr. Edward Austen-Knight, of Godmersham Park in Kent," I said. "You may be aware that no less than four of his sons have passed through Winchester College, and a fifth, Charles-Bridges, is lately arrived in Dr. Gabell's House. There is even a sixth son waiting in the wings until he is of an age to be sent away."

"I recollect something of the Knight boys." Clarke's gaze sharpened. "Godmersham is in Kent, did you say?"

Perhaps the wealthiest county in England.

"And in one of the finest neighbourhoods!" I agreed affably. "The park serves as my brother's principal seat—but he possesses considerable estates in Hampshire as well. His broad acquaintance among the first families of this county encouraged him to apply to Dr. Gabell for the tutelage of his sons, as so many Hampshire gentlemen favour Gabell's House. Edward wished his boys to be among friends, you apprehend."

Clarke hummed noncommittally.

"But the intelligence of recent events has lately reached him—I have an idea it has flown rapidly around the entire Kingdom, alas!—and my brother is both shocked and dismayed, that a boy in Gabell's keeping should be suspected of murder. He writes to me only this morning that he plans to withdraw his patronage from Winchester, and send Charles-Bridges to Eton as soon as may be."

A complete fabrication, of course. News of William Heathcote's fate must have had wings, to reach Kent so early; but Clarke did not question the sources of a wealthy gentleman's power.

"That is a pity." His lips pursed in a disapproving bud. "Eton is nothing to Winton."

"I agree. Such a shame, too, as the boy is in his first term, and offers such promise that my brother means to spare no expence." The hint that Mr. Knight should be paying tutors for young Charles-Bridges for the next several years was, I hoped, broad enough. "I intend to suggest, by return of post, that my brother enquire whether his son might instead be offered a place here in Chamber Court, under your careful eye, sir. It must be in every respect superior to the instruction of Gabell's House. And Master Prendergast having left, as it were, a gap in your ranks—"

"Yes, yes, I perceive your delicate intention, Miss Austen." Clarke rose a little in his chair, as tho' every nerve was alive to possibility. My brother's purse must be known as deep and liberal, where his progeny was concerned. "I am all gratitude! And very willing to consider young Knight as a candidate for the select ranks of pupils I supervise, here in Chamber Court."

Did he imagine I had so quickly forgotten his calling those charges "benighted brats?" What a fatuous creature!

"Perhaps when you have had a chance to consider of your many duties and limited time," I suggested, "you will deign to write to my brother yourself, and propose the scheme. You may be assured that I shall convey my complete support. I merely called upon you today to learn whether Prendergast's place was still available . . . ?"

"Many are the distinguished families that have submitted similar enquiries," Clarke replied.

I may be forgiven my doubts on this score; that any gentleman of note should wish his son in the hands of a careless and indolent misanthrope, must confound understanding.

"I am certain my brother should be only too happy to offer an emolument to yourself, equal to the worth of such a prized position for his son."

"Your energy, Miss Austen, on behalf of your nephew does you credit—and I am inclined to relieve your brother's concerns. I have long deplored the laxity of standards in Dr. Gabell's House. Had I been appointed Headmaster, rather than serving in Gabell's shade, affairs in college should be conducted very differently!"

There it was, again—the festering ambition, and the frank resentment, of the man who superseded Clarke in authority.

"I am certain of it," I said soothingly. "There is but one point upon which I cherish anxiety. You may do much to alleviate it, sir, before I write to my brother."

"I am at your service, Madam." He set his spectacles once more upon his nose, and peered at me keenly.

"You referred yesterday to warfare between the ranks of the two houses."

"Alas, I did. Young Heathcote is among the worst offenders—as must be evident to all the world."

"You named him as the leader of Gabell's Gang, in fact."

"Indeed."

"And who, sir, is the leader of yours?"

Clarke started back in his chair. "I beg your pardon?"

I lifted my shoulders with feigned indifference. "It stands to reason that in every war, one general must challenge another. If Heathcote is Gabell's champion, who is Clarke's?"

"I cannot undertake to say. It is an invidious question."

"Was it Prendergast?"

The Master hesitated.

"I should like to be able to reassure my brother on that point. He will wish to know what negative influences remain in college."

"Prendergast was certainly prone to devilry. And his targets were generally among Dr. Gabell's boys."

"Master Heathcote insists that he meant to foment a

rebellion, akin to the Great Rebellion of Winchester's past. William insists that it was Prendergast's aim for the Prefects to revolt: barricade themselves in the halls, interrupt every lesson, and challenge the authority of the Headmaster and Warden. Prendergast abhorred the masters' attempts to limit his behaviour."

"Then Heathcote is a liar," Clarke returned dismissively. "One ought not to speak ill of the dead, but I will confide in you, Miss Austen—Prendergast was a lamentably over-bearing youth, roundly disliked by his peers. He could never command the following necessary to overturn the school. For that, one requires a *leader*—"

He halted in mid-speech.

I smiled at him affably. "Indeed? A young man who may move the hearts and spirit of his fellows, by noble example? You do not refer to Master Insley Minor, I think?"

"He is hardly the most prepossessing of his year," Clarke admitted. "Quite loyal to Prendergast, however—and as such, his testimony must be unequivocal."

A leader. Clarke had a particular boy in mind, among those who lodged in his House. He had very nearly come out with a name—and his easy confidence argued approval of that boy and his aims. But Winchester is known, after all, as a hothouse of tender young Parliamentarians; any number of presently nameless youths might prove a future William Pitt.

Did Clarke expect another rebellion to topple his rival, Dr. Gabell, and place *himself* in the Headmaster's seat?

There must have been many occasions, I judged, when

Winchester boys were the unwitting pawns of their ambitious masters.

But could such a plot extend to *murder*?

If an unprotected and unloved youth belonging to Gabell's House was blamed . . . *perhaps*.

"I shall be most happy to communicate with Mr. Austen-Knight regarding the future of young . . . Charles-Bridges, did you say? . . . at his earliest convenience," Clarke broke into my thoughts. "But now am I afraid, Madam, that my time and attention are demanded elsewhere . . . the duties of a school-master are unremitting, I fear . . ."

I rose from my chair. "Pray, do not exert yourself, Mr. Clarke. I shall disturb your peace no longer. Please accept my thanks for your time and attention."

15

IN PARCHMENT STREET

No. 12, The Close
Winchester
Tuesday, 1 April 1817, cont'd.

The quadrangle of Chamber Court was no longer empty. A trio of liveried footmen bearing trunks and parcels impeded my path to the gate, where two black coaches bearing a coat of arms were drawn up on College Street. The servants bore black armbands and cravats; the gentleman who followed them was arrayed in black from head to toe. He halted abruptly when I appeared, and with a nod, indicated that I should precede him on the path; and out of exceeding interest, I did so.

I had recognised the gentleman's face. It was the same ginger-haired stranger who had been seated next to my nephew Edward at yesterday's inquest, who had extricated Will so efficiently from the ruffians' grasp, and summoned Mr. Lyford to Eliza's aid.

At achieving the pavement, profiting from the interval in which the footmen stowed their trunks in the hindmost of the two carriages, I turned to him on impulse and said, "I beg your pardon, sir, but I believe thanks are due. You most kindly placed yourself in danger at the White Hart yesterday, to help my friend and her son."

The gentleman started, looked more narrowly at my countenance, and then recovered himself to raise his hat. "No thanks are necessary, I assure you. Anyone would have done the same. The lady was clearly distressed, and upon the point of fainting. I trust Lyford was able to assist her?"

"He was."

"And the unfortunate youth? —Forgive me if I am impertinent."

It is true the question surprised me—but I detected only sincere concern and sympathy in his looks. "Master Heathcote is prey to all the evils inherent to his present situation, I suspect. Our anxiety, as you may imagine, is extreme."

"I hope everything that can be done on the boy's behalf, is being done."

His frankness encouraged my own. I glanced at the carriages, and their array of burdened footmen. "Forgive me for detaining you further—but are you perhaps connected to the late Master Arthur Prendergast's family?"

He inclined his head. "I am Beaumont, in fact."

I gasped, and raised my gloved hand to my lips. "Surely not—that is . . ."

"Not the boy's father?" An expression of trouble swept his countenance. "No, indeed. That gentleman—my cousin Frederick—passed from this life but two days ago. I succeeded to the viscount's honours. It has been . . . a heavy period, in the Beaumont household."

I murmured words of assent and condolence. The new viscount acknowledged them with simple grace.

"I ought to be attending to the funeral rites even now, but for the earlier tragedy. News of young Arthur's death reached my cousin last week, precipitating his final illness. I thought my first duty as his successor ought to be attendance at the boy's inquest, and the tidying of his affairs here at school."

"Of course. You have my deepest sympathy, sir."

He smiled faintly. "And yet, I have not the slightest notion to whom I am obliged for it! May I know your name, ma'am?"

"I am Miss Austen."

"Are you a relation to the lad charged with my nephew's murder?"

This was blunt speaking indeed. I shook my head. "An intimate friend of his mother's. I have been staying with Mrs. Heathcote in the Cathedral Close."

"Then she is not without comfort."

The footmen having secured the last of the parcels to the travelling coach, Viscount Beaumont glanced hurriedly around and ordered them to be on their way. I curtseyed, and would have left him, but he held out his hand as tho' to stay my departure.

"I should like to call upon Mrs. Heathcote, if that is not too much of a presumption," he said.

The idea of Elizabeth's being forced to receive and entertain the head of Prendergast's house, while her son sat in gaol for Prendergast's murder, was absurd. I must have looked my amazement, because Lord Beaumont flushed.

"I was once a little acquainted with her. Many years ago, when she was as yet Miss Bigg, of Manydown."

Ah. Nearly two decades since, in fact. My friend was the middle of the six Bigg daughters, but undeniably the prettiest. I wondered if she had danced with a ginger-haired gentleman at Basingstoke, before a handsome clergyman had turned her head, and destroyed Beaumont's hopes.

"I was then known as Mr. Utterson."

There was once a family of that name in Farnham, I recalled; Lord Beaumont must be a Prendergast relation on his mother's side. "I cannot speak for Mrs. Heathcote," I told him. "But you are welcome to send in your card."

"Very well. May I know the lady's direction?"

"Number 12, The Close."

He bowed, and mounted into his carriage.

I returned to Elizabeth with as much energy as I could command, the sooner to prepare her.

"GOOD MORNING, AUNT! THERE is a letter from Berkshire for you, in Aunt Cassandra's fist."

My nephew Edward was established before the dining-room fire, with a healthy nuncheon disposed on a platter before him: cold ham, dried apples, half a loaf of country bread, and a wedge of cheese. A tankard of ale stood at his elbow. Visiting a prisoner in his cell must stir the appetite.

"Have you heard anything from your father?" I enquired, as I sifted through the post laid on a side table.

Edward shook his head around a mouthful of bread. "He believes me to be right and tight at Grandmamma's. No doubt she is collecting my correspondence for me, but sees no cause to send it on here."

It could not matter; anything James might communicate regarding my uncle's will, should be repeated in Cassandra's letter. I reached for a silver file to open it. "What have you learned this morning?"

"Mrs. Heathcote despatched a summons to her brother at Manydown by Express not an hour ago," he supplied, reaching for the ale-pitcher, "and I spent only a quarter-hour with young Will, as he refused to tell me anything about his acquaintance among the young women of the town. But I have received some peculiar intelligence from another quarter."

Edward paid strict attention to replenishing his tankard, so that I was unable to read his meaning in his countenance.

"Do not teaze me." I set down the letter-opener. I was feeling greatly fatigued, and was looking forward to an interval of peace and rest in my bedroom, with the comfort of Cassandra's news.

"Very well." My nephew sat back in his chair. "I confess I have been confounded by Heathcote's silence on the charge of *meddling with tradesmen's daughters.* That he remains obdurately mum, despite the salutary influence of a night spent in gaol, is cause for anxiety. I reasoned that if William chuses to guard his secrets, others might prove more enlightening—and so, upon quitting his cell in Jewry Street, I made my way to the George, in the hope of discovering my friend Urquhart there. You will know he has been keeping body and soul together during the Easter leave-out by taking his meals in the local taverns. Urks is a prefect, which must command Heathcote's confidence and respect; and tho' not as intimate with him as a member of Gabell's House should be, is undoubtedly Will's friend. If anyone should know of Will's pursuit of the muslin company, I thought it must be Urquhart."

"And did you find him in the public house?"

"I did not." Edward pushed aside his plate. Not for him the pot-luck of a Winchester tavern; Elizabeth's cook is too good. "I did, however, find a collection of familiar faces breakfasting at a table by the fire—fully four of the respected members of Mr. Pelham's inquest jury. Replete with fried eggs and rashers of bacon, the burghers of Winchester were in heated discussion of Heathcote's guilt. So naturally, I ordered a pot of coffee from the barmaid, the better to overlisten their conversation."

I sank down in the chair opposite my nephew. "Did you learn anything to the purpose?"

"I hardly know." Edward's looks were a study in abstraction. "You will recall the foreman—a fellow named Hickson?"

I attempted to summon the man to mind, and succeeded in conjuring only a prosperous, if unremarkable, merchant of middling years and comfortable aspect.

"It was he who was holding forth. I do not know the names of the other three," Edward added, "but they appeared to credit every assertion the foreman made. It was Hickson's view that young Will is naturally bad, 'like so many of the nobs's sons,' and that lacking a father—'and who knows how he died?'—was doomed to go astray. After all, 'a fellow that can't speak for himself, can't be trusted, when all's said and done.'"

"That wretched stutter," I murmured thoughtfully.

"Yes. One of Hickson's fellows observed that it was no doubt the dead boy's threat to expose Will's wenching, that got him murdered—"

"Insley Minor's testimony."

"—And then the whole party agreed that the young woman in question had enjoyed a merciful escape—bastard on the way, or no."

"Will has been tried and hanged in the court of public opinion," I said.

"Or at least, in the public room of the George. But there is more, Aunt."

I glanced at Edward enquiringly.

"Hickson sighed that it was right confounding, the girl in question being a quiet, well-behaved creature, but certain it was that the Devil was in all women from birth, and only wanted time to reveal himself."

"You cannot be serious!" Until this moment, I had been certain the rumour of skirt-chasing was merely that—a *rumour.* "He put a name to the young woman?"

"He did not," Edward replied. "When one of his mates demanded that Hickson voice his suspicions, the foreman merely replied that he was not the sort to cast stones—but he reckoned *the surgeon* knew enough to see Heathcote hang, and had cause enough, too."

"The surgeon?" I repeated. "Can that be Mr. Giles Lyford?"

"I should think so." Edward met my gaze, his own grim. "He is the only surgeon who appeared at the inquest, Aunt—and it was there we first heard of Heathcote's interest in the muslin company. Moreover, he is known professionally as Surgeon-in-Ordinary, of the County Hospital. In effect, he is the surgeon required to care for the indigent of Winchester, and must be the most notable surgeon in town. Hickson and his friends had no need to be explicit."

Surgeon-in-Ordinary was only a part of Lyford's duties, to be sure—he looked a well-to-do man whose private attendance upon the genteel of Winchester was vouchsafed by the Bigg sisters' reliance upon him. Moreover, I knew him to descend from a long line of similar professional men; his uncle and grandfather had both worked as surgeons in Basingstoke. He was not the sort to procure young women on behalf of minors. What, then, could Lyford know of Will Heathcote's "meddling" with tradesmen's daughters?

I sighed heavily, my certainties confounded. The idea that Will's dalliance among the muslin company was generally known, and the subject of tavern gossip, was too lowering. If Will had deceived his mother about this—and indeed, had denied it under oath—what else might he have concealed?

"We must call upon Lyford," I said aloud, "and beg him to reveal what he knows. Only Lyford, certainly, may put the lie to Hickson's words."

"At this time of day"—it was just past one o'clock by Elizabeth's handsome case clock, that rang the hours in her front hall—"the surgeon will no doubt be among the sick at the hospital," Edward said. "That sits in Parchment Street, if memory serves. But I am not sure, Aunt, that you ought to risk your health in calling there. Even were it respectable for a lady to enter such a place, God knows what contagion you might take! Lyford is bound to wait upon Mrs. Heathcote here in any case, to see how she goes on after yesterday's swoon. We have only to wait!"

"And waste precious hours in the process," I countered. "Any discussion with Lyford in Mrs. Heathcote's drawing room is bound to involve Mrs. Heathcote—and I cannot like canvassing William's vices before his mother. It is cruel; it can only distress her. If you do not wish to venture into Parchment Street, Edward, I shall certainly go alone—but your escort should be most welcome."

Edward sighed dubiously, but reached for his coat. "I ought not to risk your health. If my mother were to hear of it—! However, Aunt, I live to serve you."

ONE OF THE SINGULAR advantages of a good-sized town like Winchester is the abundance of conveniences one should never encounter in my neighbourhood of Alton, and certainly not in Chawton. Among these was the prevalence of sedan chairs for hire. We had only passed through the Priors Gate, the main exit from the Close, when three of these presented themselves—awaiting the custom of such visitors to the Cathedral as might require transport back to the town's coaching inns. I stayed Edward with my hand on his arm. "Good Lord, the very thing!"

"You mean to hire a chair?" he blinked at me.

"You may walk beside me if you chuse." I raised my hand to the nearest bearer. "You, sirrah! I wish to be taken to the county hospital in Parchment Street. This gentleman will supply the exact direction."

I briskly settled myself within the black leather chair, received a decent rug to my knees, and heard the door latch home. An instant later, a pair of bearers lifted the chair's poles, and off we swayed.

I trusted that Edward ambled alongside.

The sedan chair, by the by, has far more to recommend it than the average donkey. My Aunt Leigh-Perrot was forever employing them in Bath to pay calls on acquaintance and conduct her errands, her stoutness and the city's hills being ill-suited the one to the other. I was used to regard the conveyance as the resort of self-indulgent old ladies.

Apparently, I am now become one.

I enjoyed my privileged position at head-height with Winchester's foot-traffic, free of jostling from strangers, shielded from draughts, and treated to a leisurely survey of shopfronts and bow windows through the chair's side-glass.

It was not above ten minutes before the chair swayed to a halt, and was set down with care; the door was swung open; and I was handed out by my nephew—who also franked my journey. When I protested that he should not be bearing my charges, and would have drawn out my purse, he dismissed me with a charming diffidence.

"You already spent enough on young Will," he said, "who

is benefiting from a far warmer blanket than he should otherwise have won."

"Elizabeth will repay me, I am sure, when she has time to consider of such things."

"When once she does, we shall settle our accounts between us," Edward replied. "Now, hasten within doors, Aunt, or you shall catch your death. For all it is spring, the wind is sharp!"

THE HOSPITAL, LIKE MANY edifices in Winchester, was a handsome, modern building erected in the last half-century. The old medieval town within the ancient Roman walls has gradually given way to broader thoroughfares better able to accommodate carriage traffic, and neater rows of shops catering to their trade. Parchment Street was in such a quarter; and any fear I might have felt, of contagion or exposure to the indigent or insane, was tempered by the place's appearance of order and propriety.

Edward, however, drew a kerchief from his pocket, and held it against his nose. "There is a strong smell of damp. Have you a square of linen in your reticule, Aunt? I suggest, if so, you employ it in a similar manner."

Reflecting that my nephew had acquired some sense in later years, I did so; then allowed him to conduct me into the foyer, where a porter enquired our business.

"Mr. Lyford is attending to his rounds," we were informed, but at both of us producing our cards, the porter assured us that the Surgeon-in-Ordinary would wait upon us as soon as he was able. We were obliged to seat ourselves on a bench set against one wall, and compose ourselves in patience.

Above twenty minutes wore away, before Lyford's sturdy figure, in a black cloth coat, pantaloons, and a disciplined cravat appeared before us; but I whiled away the interval in observing the persons who came and went in the hospital foyer. There was a serving-girl, in the extremes of labour, borne in on the arm of an older matron, possibly a parent; few are the girls retained in service in such a condition, and she must either have been thrown on the parish or the mercy of her relations when cast out of her employer's household. An elderly man, his face hideously disfigured with pox, was dragged in on a pallet and summarily deposited in front of the porter, who appeared not at all discomfited by the occurrence, but only pulled on a bell-rope, and was answered within minutes by a pair of men, who lifted the groaning figure and bore him away into the hospital's interior.

Lyford, as he approached, tossed a word to these two; he was chafing his hands in a cloth, then handed it to a serving-boy who followed behind him, wordless yet vigilant. The hall-porter bowed to the surgeon, and received a nod in return. Lyford, I concluded, was a demi-god in this peculiar world.

"Miss Austen, Mr. Austen," he said as we rose from our bench. "I trust Mrs. Heathcote is not in immediate danger? You are not come hither in an extreme of anxiety?"

"Indeed, she is well enough," I assured him. "We seek you, sir, on another matter."

"I am relieved. I intend to call upon Mrs. Heathcote once my duties here are done, but that will be several more hours at least. How may I serve you?"

"Is there somewhere we could converse in private?" Edward asked.

"There is the dispensary. Pray, if you will follow me—"

We obediently fell in behind the surgeon, who led us down the hospital's broad central passage to a door at the very end. Beyond this was what appeared to be an apothecary's shop, lined from waist-height to ceiling with jars scrawled in Latin. Two young men in aprons toiled there at compounds.

"My son, Henry," Lyford said, with a gesture to the younger of these. "And his fellow apprentice, Mr. Jerrold."

The two young men bowed.

"Pray, leave us," the surgeon ordered, and without hesitation, the two apprentices set aside their mortar and pestles, wiped their hands on their aprons, and quitted the room.

"We shall not detain you overly long," I told Lyford. "We are come because my nephew overheard a damaging conversation in the George's public room this morning. The foreman of the coroner's panel, one Mr. Hickson, held forth among his cronies there—and spoke of William Heathcote's scandalous relations with a young woman of the town. He suggested, indeed, that *the surgeon* knew her name—and had cause to wish Heathcote hanged. Could he possibly have referred to *you*, Mr. Lyford?"

The surgeon looked searchingly first at Edward and then at me. "That is possible, of course. But I am uncertain why you ask the question, Miss Austen. Would you interfere in the coroner's business?"

"We would see William Heathcote acquitted," Edward interjected, "and his good name restored. If we identify the young woman whose reputation was sullied during the inquest, and secure her testimony—we might establish Will's innocence."

Lyford's grey brows drew together in consternation. "Admirable goals, Mr. Austen, but they come at considerable cost. You would implicate my daughter in young Heathcote's affairs."

16

THE ARTIST AND HER METHODS

No. 12, The Close
Winchester
Tuesday, 1 April 1817, cont'd.

"Your daughter!" I exclaimed.

"Pray sit down, Miss Austen." Lyford drew forth a straight-backed wooden chair from its position against the wall, and gestured with his hand. "If you will forgive me for saying it, you look far from well. Your solicitude for your friend Mrs. Heathcote, I fear, has required too much of you."

After an instant's hesitation, I sank onto the seat, for in truth my legs would barely support me. The gentlemen remained standing—although Edward adopted a leaning position against the apothecaries' bench. Lyford folded his arms across his chest and fixed his gaze earnestly on my countenance.

"You have a daughter?" I enquired.

"I have five, in fact. The lady Mr. Hickson would indicate in his public hints is my eldest child, Charlotte, who is one-and-twenty years of age."

Older by roughly five years than William Heathcote.

"But far from being a creature of loose habits, she is one of considerable skill. Charlotte is what is known as a speech artist," Lyford continued.

"What is that, when it's at home?" Edward demanded.

"My daughter employs her skills to cure speech defects."

"Is it possible, then to cure them?" I asked, astonished. Surely, if a remedy for stammering were to be found, Harris Bigg-Wither and his sisters should have sought it long since.

Lyford inclined his head. "It is Charlotte's passion to *attempt* to do so. She receives such sufferers of oral impedimenta as she consents to treat, in a consulting room reserved for that purpose, at our home in Middle Brook Street."

"Yet she calls herself an artist?" Edward frowned. I discerned the sceptic in his looks; and indeed, all manner of quackery and charlatanerie were implied in the lady's description.

Lyford sighed. "My daughter would assert that her work is a calling, Mr. Austen, akin to that of my own here at the hospital. Indeed, were she a man—" He paused, appearing to debate within himself, then lifted his shoulders in resignation. "Charlotte began to stammer at the age of fifteen, directly after my first wife, her mother, passed from this life. I was greatly grieved by the change in her conversation—and at the time of life, too, when a young lady is most desirous of shining in social circles. Her defect caused her much anxiety and distress. As a grieving parent, I determined to aid her in any way I could."

"Naturally," I murmured.

"I sought the help of colleagues in Edinburgh—which

university, you will know, is a great institution of medical learning—and was directed to consult Dr. Charles Angier. He is the fourth generation of his family to practice the methods of speech artistry. His father, who bore the same name, made a specialty of it, tho' never a learned man himself. Doctor Angier has been keen to separate his career from his father's, and at first was loath even to discuss the nature of it; but upon meeting my daughter, and recognising her plight, he consented to treat her."

Edward's brows rose. "The doctor is no longer in Edinburgh, I collect?"

"He resides in Bath. Charlotte removed to lodgings there under the chaperonage of her aunt, and within a year—eight months, to be exact—her impediment was cured."

"Remarkable!" I said. "And the young lady then determined to treat others, as she herself was treated?"

"Indeed." Lyford inclined his head. "She had learned much from Dr. Angier about the nature of oral affliction, and with his blessing, undertook to share what she might of his methods with others. Being then still quite young—not above seventeen years of age—she embarked upon a course of study, of such works as Angier believed might enlarge the female mind without exposing her to danger."

"Then she is fortunate," I murmured. Too many gentlemen of my acquaintance are determined to prevent women from learning anything, lest excessive knowledge lead to strong hysterics; but in my experience, it is ignorance that is more likely to drive us all mad.

"At nineteen, when other young women's heads are filled

with romance and the delights of the social whirl, my Charlotte received her first pupil—here in Winchester—and soon found that she had all the applications she could wish for, among the families of the Great."

"It should not be remarkable that men in positions of power seek to improve their public speeches," Edward observed, "or feel anxiety when their sons and heirs suffer from defects. Some, I imagine, are patrons of Winchester College?"

"I am often consulted by such gentlemen," Lyford acknowledged, "and it has become my practice to introduce them to Charlotte."

"Was it Elizabeth Heathcote who solicited your help with young Will?" I asked.

Lyford shook his head. "It was her brother, Mr. Harris Bigg-Wither."

I was all astonishment. "He, too, suffers from a pronounced stutter."

"Such things, I find, run in families. You will know, Miss Austen, that I am a great friend of the ladies at No. 12, who generally seek my advice over trifling matters of health. It was in their dining-parlour that I met their brother—and when the ladies had retired, leaving us to our port, I happened to enlarge upon my daughter's ability to amend defects of speech."

"—Being unable to ignore Mr. Bigg-Wither's."

"He was unperturbed at my hints, but deemed himself too old to benefit from Charlotte's art. He wished most passionately, however, that his nephew be introduced to her. Youth is everything, in the correction of defects. He was required to quit Winton the following morning, but determined to write a letter of introduction for his nephew to Charlotte."

"And William consented to meet with her," I said.

"Master Heathcote was overjoyed to do so—having believed he was doomed to go through life marked by an encumbrance that must shame even the most sanguine of persons! He waited upon Charlotte in Middle Brook Street but a few days later, and has been under her weekly tutelage since late last Michaelmas term."

I did a swift mental calculation. "Above six months? That seems a lengthy period without—forgive me, sir, for my frankness—significant audible improvement."

An expression of pity suffused the surgeon's countenance. "Young Will experienced considerable relief from his defect, prior to the events of this past week. I suspect that apprehension and dismay are at the root of his apparent relapse at the inquest yesterday. But I shall not defend my daughter further; it is for Charlotte to explain her methods to you."

"We must wait upon her, then, as soon as may be."

"I shall not delay you a moment longer. Stay only while I pen an introduction for you to Middle Brook Street."

Mr. Lyford quitted the room in haste, and I turned in amazement to my nephew Edward.

"A speech artist!" I cried. "Whatever shall we meet with next?"

"She must be a bluestocking," he returned grimly, "or

worse yet, the sort of young woman who is determined to quack herself or her friends. I wonder at Will submitting to it!"

Mr. Lyford returned, bearing a folded slip of paper. "It is nearly two o'clock, and I know that Charlotte has no fixed engagements until four. I have instructed her to receive you, and to speak as fully as may be."

"Thank you." I rose and held out my hand. The surgeon bowed over it. We left him to his labours among the deserving poor, and set off for Middle Brook Street.

THE DISTANCE BETWEEN HOSPITAL and house was not far, and my seated interval had restored my fleeting strength. Edward escorted me to the Lyford home on foot, therefore, supporting me along the uneven paving-stones where necessary. A neat maid greeted our knock at the glossy black door, and at being presented with Mr. Lyford's instruction, led us immediately along a passage to a room on the ground floor where a lady clad in sober grey was seated at a writing table. An oil lamp was already lit against the dismal weather beyond the single window. She glanced up from what appeared to be a ledger, and set down her pen. "What is it, Nance?"

The maid bobbed, wordlessly handed her the note, and awaited Miss Lyford's response.

"Very well." The young woman glanced over our faces, and smiled encouragingly. "Pray bring us some tea. Mr. Austen, Miss Austen, won't you sit down?"

Two armchairs were set close to the hearth, and there

was a small fire burning against the chill of spring. We each availed ourselves of a place, and Edward removed his hat, resting it on the knee of one crossed leg. The expression of doubt with which he had entered the house was entirely absent now from his countenance; only dignified respect suffused it. Miss Lyford's quiet demeanour and tidy dress might account for the change in Edward; certainly the practicality of her rooms underlined her good sense. There were no little tables scattered about, as might befit an artist; no lace doilies or silk flowers to suggest a feminine frivolity. I felt the warmth of the hearth's flames, however, and realised how sharply the hospital's damp had penetrated my clothing. This consulting room was warmer and more comforting in both fact and spirt, and I felt my tension ease.

"You have questions regarding Master William Heathcote," Miss Lyford said, folding her hands in her lap as she faced us. "My father urges me to answer you freely, and as fully as I may."

"You are aware that William is presently in gaol?" I enquired.

She inclined her head. "Poor fellow. Father informed me of the whole upon his return from the inquest yesterday. You are intimate with the family, I collect?"

"We are—and most desirous to see William's innocence established, and his good name restored."

Edward leaned a little forward. "Mr. Lyford tells us that Will has been meeting you in the hope of improving his stutter?"

"Twice each week—since September."

"And has he obtained leave from college to do so?" Edward asked.

"I do not know," she acknowledged. "Such leave would require that William's mother approve his absences, and she was not meant to be in on the secret."

"The secret?"

"William wished to correct his impediment in solitude, Mr. Austen—and reveal his improvements to his mother only when he judged himself cured. To add to her happiness, and relieve her mind, were great objects with him. He is a most devoted son."

A troubled line creased my nephew's brow. "The meetings could be described as clandestine, then."

"That is possible." Miss Lyford appeared untroubled. "But William is hardly alone in demanding privacy to pursue his instruction. Most of my students do so. Afflictions of the tongue are an embarrassment many prefer to bury in silence. My sufferers attempt, at least, to change their lot, but they do not wish any failures to occur under the gaze of the world."

A little interruption then ensued, as the housemaid reappeared with a pot of tea, and set it down near her mistress, who poured out a dish of Bohea for each of us. After we had settled ourselves, and I basked with relief in both the warmth of the fire and the tea, Edward resumed, "But you apprehend that if William stole out of college to meet with you, Miss Lyford—and was observed by the malicious—that an indelicate presumption might be placed on such meetings?"

She straightened in her chair and studied my nephew gravely. "I rely upon my respectability, and that of my father, to protect me from such stuff!"

"Did William always consult you here in Middle Brook Street?" I interjected.

"Often he did," she said, "tho' in mild weather, I consented to meet him at the foot of St. Catherine's Hill, so that we might practice his exercises as we walked out-of-doors. Boys of that age require fresh air, as I have learnt from my brothers."

"You met with Heathcote when he was released to Hills? In the company of all his fellows?" Edward looked his consternation. "It is no wonder the pair of you were the subject of rumour!"

"Were we?" Miss Lyford retorted tartly. "No such scandal has come to *my* ears. I will thank you, Mr. Austen, to reserve your indignation for such ladies as have little learning and less skill; I have been at pains for many years to acquire both."

"These exercises," I interjected. "Could you explain a little of your methods, Miss Lyford? We had not been aware of a cure for stammering, before your father referred to it."

"I am only too happy." She rose, and crossing to an easel that stood folded against one wall, turned it round to face us. Revealed were a series of ink illustrations, of what appeared to be the mouth, tongue, lips, teeth, and an extraordinary study of the throat and jaw. This last was coloured in crayon and charcoal, and featured whorls of material I could not at first interpret.

"Good Lord!" Edward peered at it narrowly. "Is that taken from an anatomisation?"

"It is," Miss Lyford said. "It is a representation of the bones and muscles underlying the skin of the neck and skull. I drew it from life—or rather, death—myself."

She had observed *post mortems*, then. At the hands of Dr. Charles Angier, or her own father? Aware of the benefit of such practices tho' I am, I felt myself shrink with distaste. That a *lady* should . . .

But no. I was acting the Poor Honey. I despised such creatures and their die-away airs.

"Difficulties in speech are bodily impediments," Miss Lyford said. "The tongue, too short or too large, may fumble within the mouth cavity and against the palate. The lips may contort or suffer paralysis when we would have them form syllables. The throat may constrict, forbidding the passage of air, and strangle speech at its birth. Such obstructions may be eased and eventually eradicated by careful methods. Firstly, I observe and record the specific speech contortions peculiar to the individual patient. Secondly, I design and prescribe exercises intended to ameliorate the defects. Thirdly, I insist upon the repetition of the regimen, with corrections and amplification as necessary, over many months of effort."

"And in William's case?" I asked.

"He demonstrates two impedimenta." She turned away from her easel and resumed her seat at the desk. "He chokes on his words at their formation, trapping them in his throat; and he repeats the initial consonants, both hard and soft, of many common words. This is not unusual. Indeed, I suspect that his maternal uncle suffers from similar defects."

This aligned with my own experience of the boy and his conversation. "And how does one attack such problems?"

"The choking sensation and resultant noise is a problem of constricted air." She reached a delicate hand to her throat. "I recommend a vigorous chafing of the muscles *here* to relieve constriction and render the throat *supple*. I also abjure William to practice the forceful inhalation and expulsion of his breath for intervals at a time." She demonstrated a vigorous *huff.* "The stammer over consonants arises chiefly from haste—William rushes into speech out of fear. He wishes to spend as little time mangling his words as possible; he is often unintelligible as a result. I require him to practice the most troublesome words, by pronouncing them with exaggerated slowness. We recite them together, so often that I imagine William may now repeat them in his sleep! His instructions are to do so at whatever moment of the day he finds himself alone. From words, we progress to whole passages of recitation and oral reading."

"If I may—" Edward began, then hesitated, with an expression of consciousness. "I cannot pretend to know anything of speech artistry, having never heard of it before this morning, but—"

"*But?*" Miss Lyford repeated, smilingly. I suspect she has often met with gentlemen eager to instruct her in an art of which they know nothing.

"Is there not a distortion of the nerves as well, in such

cases? I have known William as boy and young man. And I have observed, only so recently as yesterday, how the agitation of his mind and spirit will immediately destroy his powers of speech. When among those he trusts, and relieved of care, Will is as capable of conversing as anyone—or very nearly. But threaten his composure, and you will swiftly have him hind-legs foremost."

"That may be very true," she conceded. "But I am not a philosopher, nor yet a spiritual counsellor. Certainly William had cause for agitation at yesterday's inquest, and certainly my methods then deserted him. Father tells me he resorted to writing down his testimony, and offering it to the coroner."

"That may have prejudiced the coroner's panel," Edward said.

She sighed. "It is unfortunate he lost command of himself so completely. I have urged Will to resist the temptation to silence himself."

"But he had no alternative! His garbled words suggested the kind of feeble-mindedness that—"

"—Argues for violence and murder?" She lifted her hands in a gesture of resignation. "By this, you make his defect and his guilt the same."

"I am very certain the jury did so," Edward returned, nettled.

He had a point; but I had rarely seen him so quick to spar with a young lady, and wondered at it. Miss Charlotte Lyford had put all my nephew's charm to flight.

"When did you last meet with William?" I asked.

She reached for the ledger we had noticed upon entering the consulting-room, and glanced at the page. "Exactly a week ago. In the normal way, I should also have seen him this Saturday, but for the Easter leave-out."

"Then you met last Tuesday?" It was the very day of Prendergast's death. "At what hour?"

"Half-past four o'clock. Master Heathcote was generally at his lessons until four. My father never dines until seven, being consumed by his duties, so there is ample time for me to receive a patient."

"Then Will was with *you*, when he would not tell us where he had gone!" Edward cried. "Did you meet here, Miss Lyford, or at St. Catherine's Hill?"

"The weather being inclement Tuesday last, William came to this consulting-room."

"Did anyone observe him to do so, beside yourself?"

"Nance will have received him at the door, and conveyed him hither."

Edward sank back in his seat, satisfied, his fingers crushing the brim of his hat.

"How long would he have remained here?" I asked.

She considered the question. "An hour, perhaps an hour and a quarter. I will consult my notes." She returned her gaze to her ledger. "I see that I am incorrect. William remained with me until a quarter before the hour of six, so absorbed were we in the exercises—and at the tolling of the clock, he started in dismay, being aware that he might well be missed in college at the dinner hour. He took himself off, and no doubt ran all the way back to Gabell's House."

The college porter, I thought, might well have a record of Will's return—unless it had been effected clandestinely, through a side-window.

"Did your father tell you," I continued, "that William was accused at the inquest of consorting with women of the town?"

Miss Lyford frowned, and looked from my countenance to Edward's. "He did not."

"You never heard a rumour that he meddled with tradesmen's daughters?"

"How should I? My connexion with the boy was entirely of a private nature. None of my acquaintance should find occasion to speak of him to me, much less comment upon his way of life."

"But the judgement of the coroner's panel turned upon the scurrilous idea." Edward's tone was biting. "The witness asserted that William murdered Master Prendergast, because he would have exposed William's vicious propensities to the college, almost certainly resulting in his dismissal."

"But that is absurd! Will is the merest boy, and exceedingly shy. What young woman could ensnare him?"

"We think it probable," Edward added, "that the lady implicated is yourself."

17

NEWS OUT OF BERKSHIRE

In the briefest terms, Edward related the jury gossip overheard in the George tavern.

Miss Lyford's complexion paled, and she emitted a faint gasp as she listened. "But this is outrageous! Is all of Winchester talking of it?"

"Perhaps not," I soothed. "A few people only may know of your connexion to the boy, such as chanced to observe you walking with him on St. Catherine's Hill. One of these may have circulated a rumour. Pray, how many persons form a part of this household?"

"There are eight of us—my father and his children, of which I am eldest."

"Your mother died some years since, I think."

"Yes—as did my father's second wife. Childbed, in both cases."

And not even a surgeon husband could save them.

"Servants?" I enquired.

An expression of asperity suffused her countenance.

"There are four. A cook, two maids, and a manservant. All have been with us some years, and none, I am sure, would so insult our household by trafficking in scandal of this kind."

My gaze strayed to Edward's. I read a question in his looks. Miss Lyford's loyalty to her people did her credit, but *someone* had circulated the intelligence of her meetings with William Heathcote. Prendergast, also, must have known Miss Lyford's name—tho' his supposition that the young lady was pregnant, and was to be drowned at dusk by her schoolboy suitor, seemed now a fantastickal notion. How had he come by it?

"Tell me the name of the witness who would so impugn my character, and William's," Miss Lyford said fiercely.

Edward lifted his shoulders. "There is no great secret as to his identity. He acknowledged it to all within the White Hart. It is another Winchester boy, one Master Peter Insley."

"He is a stranger to me." Miss Lyford was indignant. "Why should he utter such falsehoods about me and my art?"

"Were you at all acquainted with Master Arthur Prendergast?" I asked.

"The drowned boy?" She shook her head. "Not that I recall."

"Perhaps he and Insley observed you in company with William Heathcote at Hills," Edward explained. "Hickson may have done so, as well. Any number of townsfolk take their airings near the Itchen; a perfectly innocent promenade on your part may be the sole root of this whole rumour."

"We must task your friend Urquhart to find out," I reminded my nephew. "As a prefect in Clarke's House, he is perfectly suited to the interrogation of Insley Minor."

"Urquhart? Do you refer to Mr. Thomas Urquhart?"

Miss Lyford's cheeks were faintly tinged with pink.

"The same. You are acquainted with the young man?" I asked.

Her gaze slid away. "I have that honour. *He* at least will not credit such insults. *He* will silence the malicious." She rose abruptly and reached for a bell, summoning the housemaid. "And now I am afraid that the hour is much advanced, and my duties call. I must beg you both to leave me."

THE RETURN TO ELIZABETH'S home was effected slowly, owing to an unfortunate weakness in my limbs.

"You must lie down upon your bed, Aunt, once we regain the Close," Edward said anxiously. "You have over-tired yourself."

"I shall agree to do so," I said, "if you will seek out Urquhart with the utmost haste. The sooner he interrogates that wretched boy, the sooner we may put an end to William's troubles. If only Insley Minor has not left Winchester for his family in Sussex, now that the inquest is done!"

When we achieved the foyer of No. 12, however, we discovered that Urquhart had called in our absence—and left a scribbled card for Edward.

"I am commanded to draw a tankard with him at the

George," Edward read out. "I shall nip over there directly, Aunt, while you rest."

"Ask Urquhart for his frank opinion of his Master, Mr. Clarke. I spoke with him this morning—and was much struck that he nurses a grievance against Dr. Gabell. Is it possible, Edward, that Clarke conspired to excite another rebellion, in order to have *himself* appointed Headmaster?"

Edward whistled his admiration. "I cannot see how drowning Prendergast should advance that aim, but—"

"Clarke told me outright that the Honourable Arthur could not sway enough of his fellows to rebel, being too despised by most of them. He referred, instead, to a *true leader*. I have an idea your friend Urquhart might name such a boy—or perhaps wring the name from Insley Minor."

"Urks is such a fellow himself," Edward returned. "I know of no one so capable at swaying the general opinion of Winchester boys."

"But for Clarke's ambition to succeed, your friend ought to have been allied with Prendergast's anarchic aims—and that *cannot* be likely. Urquhart has too much sense, I think, to overthrow authority."

"Turning rebel is hardly the way to go about winning a scholar's place at New College," my nephew agreed. "Never fear, Aunt. Urks and I shall talk strategy in all the privacy of a snug, and dispose of your enquiries in a trice."

I saw him go, then went in search of Elizabeth—whom I found in her boudoir, at work on a letter.

"I have received an Express from Sir William, at Hursley," she explained, "that must be answered this moment."

"He has learned of his grandson's incarceration?" I asked.

"—and informs me that he is now determined to cut off the entail, in accord with his heir's wishes, as my William is unlikely to escape hanging," she returned bitterly. "Age and infirmity must bear the blame for such unfeeling words, Jane; but I had hoped for better. My late husband was Sir William's favourite child. That he should cast off that favourite's son—"

"Perhaps he wrote in haste, and in the first flush of mortification." I adjusted the cashmere shawl on Eliza's shoulders; beneath my hands, her frame felt huddled and frail. "He shall recover himself—perhaps has done so already—and will write again to offer his utmost aid."

She set down her pen and put her head in her hands. "Was there ever anyone so wretched as I, Jane? But a year hence, Will should have been gone up to Oriel—it was his father's college, and the most brilliant of academies at the present hour. The scholarly nature of the place should have suited William's inclination for quiet and solitude; the sobriety of his peers should have strengthened him. And *now*—"

"I am certain Oriel will answer all William's wants and hopes, entirely."

"But Jane," she wailed. "—If he should be found guilty of this hideous charge! How am I to bear it?"

"Hush," I soothed. "That cannot be possible; we know William to be incapable of evil."

"If he should be wrongly judged—if he should be hanged, or *transported*, even!" She pressed a hand to her lips, as tho' to stop the words.

"Eliza," I said gently. "You cannot help Will from weakness. You must evince your utter belief in his innocence and goodness, and so comport yourself that the entire world cannot but fall in with you."

I said nothing of William's meetings with Miss Lyford or his effort to cure his defect; Elizabeth was in no fit state to consider them.

Her brimming eyes fixed on my own. I allowed her to weep, consoling her with murmurs and what comfort a steadying arm might offer. But I felt excessively tired, and not a little discouraged regarding Will Heathcote's future. True, the propriety of his connexion with Miss Lyford erased any scandalous motive for murdering Prendergast. But Miss Lyford could vouch for William's whereabouts for only a portion of the period in question. He had appeared at her door at half-past four Tuesday last, and left it at a run an hour and a half later—but we had no witness to vouch for William's return to school, or his presence at dinner. Insley had last seen Prendergast at a quarter to *five*. The Honourable Arthur might have been killed at any moment in between, or thereafter.

I longed to close my eyes and rest. Reinforcements were required if I was to fight on for the Heathcotes' peace.

"You have written to your brother?" I asked.

She drew back, dashing tears from her eyes. "Only this morning. If we are fortunate—if Harris is not *from* home, when the letter arrives—we may see him here so soon as tomorrow dinner. My desire is that he should bring a solicitor to William's aide by Thursday morning, or Friday at the latest."

I hoped for it fervently. "Then there is only the rest of today to be got through. Finish your letter to Sir William with as much grace as possible—and then recruit your strength. I have been told we may expect a gentleman caller, and would not have you meet him with red and swollen eyes!"

"Of whom are you speaking, Jane?"

"Cast your mind back to our Basingstoke assemblies, Eliza. Did you ever dance with a ginger-haired fellow by the name of Utterson?"

A faint line creased her brow. "Do you refer to *Gideon* Utterson? Of the Farnham family? —He was used to hunt with The Vyne."

"He is the new Viscount Beaumont," I said quietly. "And he means to wait upon you before the week is out."

IT WAS ONLY AS I disposed myself on the coverlet of my four-poster that I recollected the letter received that morning from Cassandra. It seemed an age ago that I had thrust it, unread, into my reticule. I retrieved it from the chair where I had discarded my outer garments and broke the seal. Foolish tho' it must be, I felt my pulse to increase, for she had certainly written from my Aunt Leigh-Perrot's home in Berkshire. What news of a legacy might the letter contain? Was it barely conceivable that I might be able to pay the fees of a London physician, much less the sums that a period of treatment and recovery in the Metropolis should entail? I ought not to allow myself to hope—but it is an unruly emotion, surging in the blood despite strict injunctions to the contrary, and the mere whisper of salvation sent a wave of heat to my head.

Expecting a full account of Uncle Leigh-Perrot's funeral rites, melancholy episodes of grief at Scarlets, and ridicule of my brothers' mercenary behaviour, I was astonished to find that Cassandra had penned barely a page.

My dear Jane—

Forgive the brevity of this letter. I write in haste, that I might catch the post before my brother James, who intends a more fulsome missive to Chawton in his usual sermonic stile. You must prepare my Mother for the intelligence: Uncle Leigh-Perrot leaves everything of which he was possessed, to the sole use and enjoyment of his widow. Only upon Aunt Leigh-Perrot's death does the residue of the estate, such as it may be, pass to his relations—and then, only to my brother James and his heirs. To his sister and the rest of her children, Uncle Leigh-Perrot leaves nothing at all.

My Aunt is in such robust health, as shall long outlast the rest of us; but James exerts himself to flatter and cajole her at every turn, lest she ignore his virtues, and find a way to alter my Uncle's disposition with time.

I feel for each of us in this hour; but may I say that it is Charles who is uppermost in my sympathy. His life has been an unhappy and unfortunate one of late, and a bit of security against being turned onshore, should have meant much.

*It will be a bitter blow for my mother, I know.
Console her as best you can. I pray the shock does not
bring on apoplexy.*

I remain, etc.
Cassandra

A bitter blow for my mother!

I ought to fly to Chawton as soon as possible—but how, then, should William and Elizabeth Heathcote suffer?

"Oh, that I knew what to do!" I said aloud.

The throb of blood in my ears was so strident it seemed my heart must burst from my chest. I sank down on the bed, Cassandra's letter slipping from my nerveless fingers. Chimeric spots swam blackly before my eyes. I had not understood how ardently I hoped for a legacy, until the sum was denied me—how much faith I had pinned on future schemes of recovery, in the hands of the learned. But all hope for myself must be at an end. Given the current privations cheerfully borne at Chawton Cottage, and the tangled affairs of my harassed brothers, it must be impossible for me to cause further financial strain.

I curled into myself and drew a shawl over my frail form. But it was some time before I slept.

18

A CONVERSATION AT THE GEORGE

No. 12, The Close
Winchester
Wednesday, 2 April 1817

I must have fallen into a semi-swoon, or suffered a relapse of the symptoms that had troubled me throughout the winter, for when I awoke darkness filled the bedchamber and Elizabeth's housemaid, Mariah, was seated in a corner with a single candle, the light shielded by a shade.

When I sat up—discovering as I did so, that I had been placed beneath the bedclothes, although not undressed—Mariah rose from her chair and carried a basin and cloth to my bedside. Without a word of leave, she placed a compress on my brow, her lips pursed in disapproval.

"Have I a fever?" I asked.

"Aye, and you do, ma'am, as should not be remarkable when you *will* go chasing about town with Master Edward in the rain. We shall be fortunate if you have not caught your death."

An unholy bubble of mirth rose in my chest; Mariah could hardly intend a mordant humour, but achieved it all the same. I touched my temples with my fingers. I did not feel overly-warm; Elizabeth was perhaps over-vigilant. But when I thrust myself higher against the pillows, my head swam. I closed my eyes.

"A bilious attack," I whispered. "They have been coming on for some time."

"And did you take a nuncheon today?" Mariah asked severely.

I shook my head. I rarely ate between breakfast and dinner.

"Maudling your insides with tea, I'll be bound. A nice, warm, gruel is what you need, ma'am, and I've got just the sort warming on the fire even now."

She soaked her compress once more in the cooling water, and applied it to my forehead. "You lie quiet, and I'll fetch some from the kitchen directly."

"Mariah," I said as she reached the door, "what is the hour?"

"Nigh on eight o'clock."

"Has Mr. Austen returned?"

"He is dining with the mistress."

"Is Master Urquhart with him?"

The maid's brows furled. "The mistress is not like to entertain at present, ma'am, given the cloud over the house, as I'm sure you collect."

I hoped she imputed my solecism to fever, and closed my eyes.

When next I opened them, the darkness in the room was akin to velvet, and the compress plastered to my brow, stickily warm. Mariah had returned, and was seated at my bedside, a bowl of gruel and a spoon in her hands.

I did as she bade me, and swallowed at least half of the wholesome stuff, grateful that I was required to stomach nothing else. When she declared herself satisfied, and had straightened my sheets, I begged one more indulgence.

"If Mr. Austen is not otherwise occupied, Mariah, I should like to see him now."

"I MEAN TO SUMMON Lyford to you tomorrow," Edward said. He had drawn a chair close to my bedside, and the candlelight threw his features into flickering relief. "I should not have allowed you to visit that den of pestilence in Parchment Street. Mamma will have my head when she hears of it."

"Then we shall take care never to tell her. I believe it is merely a return of my old complaint." I covered his hand with mine. "A good night's sleep shall set me up, and you will have no occasion to blame yourself. Indeed, I suspect it was the sad news I received of Cassandra, and nothing else, that overset me so."

"What news?"

"The paper is sure to be lying on the floor somewhere. I dropped it when the faintness first came on. I give you leave to read it."

I lay still while Edward retrieved the letter, and waited in silence. After a brief interval, he refolded the sheet with sharp movements of his fingers, and set it carefully on the bedside table.

"So we are not to each frivol away our futures in writing satiric accounts of the human condition," he said drily. "It seems I am destined for Holy Orders after all. Uncle Leigh-Perrot has ordained it."

I smiled feebly at his pun. And to prevent him from touching upon a wound—my own disappointed hopes—I hurried into speech. "I understand that Urquhart declined your invitation to dine here this evening."

"He pled an earlier engagement." Edward rose to stir up the fire, and added more wood to the flames. One of the comforts of staying in other people's houses is the profligacy with which one may waste their fuel. "But in truth, he was loath to meet Mrs. Heathcote."

"Why?" I was all astonishment. "There was no difficulty before. Is Urquhart jealous of his reputation now that poor Will is charged and gaoled?"

"Jealous, certainly, but not of that. Urquhart needed no urging from us, Aunt. He has already spoken to the wretched Insley Minor on his own initiative—and pressed him to disclose the name of William's young woman. Urks is held in such high regard by the juniors of Clarke's House, that Insley was eager to talk of the scandal and his sordid rumours; it raised his worth before his prefect, so naturally he shared everything Prendergast told him."

"Insley named Miss Lyford?"

Edward met my gaze soberly. "Miss Lyford is twice wronged, I fear. When I met with Urquhart at the George, I discovered him in his cups—both incensed and maudlin over the betrayal of his lady-love. He has lost his heart to Miss Lyford, Aunt, and is vowing vengeance against William Heathcote, for having ruined her before all of Winchester!"

"Oh, Lord," I murmured. "You assured him of the

unimpeachable nature of their connexion? You explained the idea of speech artistry?"

My nephew lifted his shoulders. "I *tried*. It may have been the ale talking, but Urks would have it I am in league against him, and shielding Will by putting out a Banbury tale. It was all I could do to prevent him from slapping my cheek with a glove, and demanding satisfaction!"

I sighed with frustration. "He will come to his senses, however aching and clouded they may be, in the morning. You were unable, I collect, to enquire about Mr. Clarke and the rebellion—or which boys Urquhart might regard as *true leaders?*"

"On the contrary. I was fortunate to have another topic at hand, to divert the interest of my sodden friend—rather as one might wave off a bull with a scrap of red!" Edward replied. "Being in his cups, Urks was less guarded and charitable than he might have been in Mrs. Heathcote's dining parlour. He insists that Winchester has had a narrow escape. The Honourable Arthur was leader enough to foment rebellion within college, according to Urquhart— and intended to unleash his forces a fortnight after the return from the Easter leave-out."

"Was there a particular provocation your friend could name? A punishment or stricture to which the fellow objected?"

My nephew shook his head in the negative. "Prendergast detested the overlordship of men he regarded as of inferior birth. He believed he ought to be immune from their attempts to restrict his behaviour, and meant, as Urquhart put it, to *teach them a lesson*. Doctor Gabell was to be held hostage in his rooms, along with the Warden, until certain conditions were met."

"And these?"

"The abdication of Gabell for Clarke—whom, evidently, Prendergast regarded as more amenable to the rule of wellborn-boys. Urquhart told me that his friend had secretly trained a militia of his followers, in the techniques of rock-throwing and barricade building, while his House was at liberty on Hills."

"And Urquhart did nothing to stop it?"

Edward shrugged. "He assured me he did not like the trend of the plotting, and meant to inform Dr. Gabell at the very hour the rebellion was to unfold. Do so before time, Urquhart said, and he should lose Prendergast's confidence; he should then lose all means of averting disaster. But it is clear he deplored his friend's intentions, and had no interest in furthering them. Urquhart is too careful of his prospects and reputation to risk embracing anarchy. It is Gabell who shall propose him for New College, after all—not Clarke."

This intelligence was of absorbing interest; it offered a decided motive for Prendergast's enmity towards the leader of Gabell's Forces. "William Heathcote's knowledge of the planned rebellion, and determination to stop it, must have loomed in Prendergast's mind as a significant threat. Was he afraid, I wonder, that Will might lay proofs of the rebellion before Dr. Gabell—and cause Prendergast's dismissal from school?"

"Reason enough to smear William's reputation first, with rumours of wenching," Edward agreed.

19

THE VISCOUNT PAYS A CALL

No. 12, The Close
Winchester
Wednesday, 2 April 1817, cont'd.

I had just finished writing the account of last evening's events in my journal this morning when Dr. Lyford was announced.

He had come to assure himself that Elizabeth was recovered from the distress of Monday's inquest. He found her enough in command of her senses to receive him in the drawing-room, with my nephew to hand; and no sooner had the pair greeted the surgeon, than they entreated him to examine *me*. I was afforded no opportunity to weigh or reject the visit. A knock on the door, a word from Edward, and Lyford was revealed as awaiting my pleasure on the bedchamber threshold.

Elizabeth kindly remained to support me while the surgeon peered into my eyes and mouth, took the measure of my pulse, and interrogated me as to my complaint. I divulged the whole: fevers, weakness, broken sleep; discolouration of the skin and eyes; wasting of my person, due to want of appetite and a bilious complaint. Excessive pain in my lower back.

"An ailment of the liver, or perhaps the kidneys," he murmured to himself, his gaze abstracted as one who sails far on inner seas. "Bile is at the root of it, to be sure."

Being disinclined to conceal anything from Eliza at this juncture in our long history, I spoke frankly before her and Lyford of my rest cure at Cheltenham spa last May.

"The doctor I *then* consulted told me I suffered from a malady common to spinsters. That having failed to employ my body as God intended—*for procreation*—I now reap the result: a decay, deep and fixed, at the root of my life-force. He told me death was inevitable, and not far distant."[14]

The surgeon halted his private ruminations and stared at me. "Indeed! Now, that is an excessively intriguing supposition. It has long been agreed, of course, that the influence of the uterus governs female health, its appetites and courses being a hysterick and weakening force that sap the female mind and body. Coupled with an excessive influence of bile . . ."

I glanced at Elizabeth sardonically. Her countenance was suffused with doubt. We were both of the sort of bookish disposition to have drawn the censure of illiberal minds; but I had not thought Lyford to possess one. He paced in philosophick agitation before the fire, hands clasped behind his back, while declaiming his theories to himself alone; but of a sudden, he stopped short, and threw up his hands.

---

14 A 2003 NIH study found that women who experience early-onset meno-pause—defined as before or at age forty—are three hundred times more likely to subsequently develop Addison's Disease. Some Austen scholars believe Jane died of Addison's, although others suggest liver or pancreatic cancer might have been the cause.—*Editor's note.*

"You will give me the Cheltenham physician's direction, Miss Austen. I shall write to him, and receive his full analysis of your case."

I lifted my chin and vouchsafed no response.

"But in the meanwhile," Lyford said, "we will try what extract of *lycopodium* and *chelidonium majus* may do. I have known both to work excellently well against an excess of bile. I shall send over draughts directly I am returned to the dispensary in Parchment Street."

"Thank you, Mr. Lyford." Draughts I would swallow with a vengeance, if they might buy me time. Lacking the funds now to consult a London physician, I was willing to make do with Winchester's preeminent surgeon. He should outstrip poor Mr. Curtis of Alton and his despairing looks, in any case.

LYFORD QUITTED NO. 12 not long thereafter. Mariah insisted that I break my fast with a pot of weak tea and fingers of dry toast. Within the hour I felt so much improved, as to put on my dressing-gown and descend the stairs to sit by the drawing-room fire. I intended to compose a letter for my mother—far too late to supersede brother James's ill communications from Scarlets, but hopefully of a propitiatory nature. I meant to comfort her with reflections of Uncle Leigh-Perrot's benign intent, of benefiting her eldest son in time; and with the consoling thought that the shattered Aunt Leigh-Perrot's life could not endure above a twelvemonth.[15]

---

15 In fact, Jane Leigh-Perrot survived nearly two decades after her husband.— *Editor's note.*

I had just completed this instructive missive when the front door knocker sounded, and Mariah bustled to answer it. Conscious of my dressing-gown, I made to quit the chair by the fire, but Elizabeth said calmly, "Do not disturb yourself, Jane. It will be the boy with the dispensary draughts."

I regained my seat, only to be disconcerted by the sudden advent of a visitor in the drawing-room doorway, trailing in Mariah's dignified wake.

"Viscount Beaumont," she intoned regally, "for Mrs. Heathcote."

There, in considerable splendour of dress, was the handsome ginger-haired cousin who had acceded to the honours of the Prendergasts. He glanced at me, inclined his head, then fixed his gaze on Elizabeth.

"Madam," he said, and doffed his hat. "I may be better recalled to your memory as Mr. Gideon Utterson, tho' I cannot flatter myself you retain the slightest impression of our former acquaintance. Having recognised Miss Elizabeth Bigg, however, in the Mrs. Heathcote so unfortunately circumstanced by Monday's inquest, I resolved to send in my card. I confess I did not expect your maid to receive me."

I stole a glance at Eliza; her countenance was flushed, and as I watched she dropped a curtsey. "Of course I remember you, sir. You hunted with my late husband, I believe."

Lord Beaumont smiled, and the expression transformed his sober countenance into something more closely resembling the young man he must once have been. "I *followed* William Heathcote in the field, ma'am, and was spattered with his mount's mud, for my pains! There were few capable of keeping to *his* pace."

"I am sure you are very welcome, my lord, tho' I rather wonder at your willingness to speak with me, given the judgement of the inquest."

Eliza remained standing, a look of doubt in her eyes. The viscount's gaze strayed to me. With as much dignity as my dressing-gown afforded, I inclined my head.

"My friend Miss Austen is a trifle indisposed this morning. I trust you will excuse her informality of dress."

"I was so happy as to make Miss Austen's acquaintance yesterday," Beaumont said. "Please accept my best wishes, ma'am, for your health."

Elizabeth gestured. "Pray, be seated, and tell me how I may serve you."

Beaumont adopted a chair at a little remove from ours, and dangled his hat against his crossed knee. "What a very comfortable home this is, to be sure! I was formerly unacquainted with the Cathedral Close, and must declare it to be a minor Arcadia, upon inspection."

"I removed hither in order to be close to my son, who as you know has been a Commoner of Winchester."

"Then he has been fortunate, indeed—whatever difficulties he presently faces."

As with my first impression of Gideon, Lord Beaumont, I remained astonished at his want of acrimony, and his freedom from reproach for those so nearly associated with a boy accused of murder. I must wonder at such magnanimity; and where wonder led, suspicion must follow. Mr.

Utterson had come into considerable rank, wealth, and property at the death of his Prendergast cousins! Did he regard young Will Heathcote as his dearest benefactor? Or had he somehow contrived the family tragedy, and was relieved that another should shoulder his guilt? —Would he dare to befriend the accused's parent, in such a case? Or was the reason for his presence merely a tender memory of Elizabeth Bigg, cherished for two decades?

"I must offer my deepest sympathy, my lord," Eliza said, "in double measure, for both your cousin the Fifth Viscount and his son Master Prendergast. I have no words that may console such a loss, and I confess I cannot account for the honour of seeing you here."

"You are dismayed, in fact, at being confronted with a bereaved and injured party," Beaumont returned with an anxious look. "I apprehend the world regards me as such. But pray believe, Madam, that I do not hold you responsible for the calamity that has befallen both our houses. Indeed, it is in an effort to penetrate the matter that I have prolonged my time in Winchester, and sought an interview with you today."

I gathered the folds of my gown together and began to rise from my chair.

"Stay, Jane," Elizabeth commanded. "There is nothing we can say to each other in this room that you may not hear. My lord, in speaking before my friend, you speak to me."

"Very well," Beaumont replied.

Obediently, I reseated myself.

"The only matter I care to *penetrate*," Elizabeth continued, "is the mystery of my son's unjust imprisonment. However ardent his participation may have been in the schoolboy pranks and mischief that obtained between Mr. Clarke and Dr. Gabell's houses, he is incapable of injuring another human being. *He is incapable of murder.* I say this as one who has known his every breath, from the instant I gave him life."

"I do not doubt your words. Having observed your son at the inquest yesterday, I thought his testimony—both written and spoken—to have the ring of truth."

"Your kindness in coming to William's aid at the last—and to my own—is deeply felt," she said in a lowered tone. "I am astounded you could bear to attend the inquest at all."

"It was imperative, as head of my family. Reflect that but for his sudden death, Master Arthur should still have been the Fifth Viscount's heir—and the Fifth Viscount, saved the shock of losing his son, should presumably be fit as a fiddle! I have stepped into dead men's shoes twice over."

The viscount leaned forward in his chair, his gaze intent upon Eliza's visage. "I am not merely come to offer sympathy, Mrs. Heathcote. I am come to canvass this entire matter, regardless of how it may wound either of our sensibilities. We *must* determine how and why it happened."

"The cynical might suspect you of having a hand in it, my lord," I interjected diffidently. "You might be acutely in want of funds and a title—and determined to remove the schoolboy obstacle in your path. Tho' I acquit you of the Fifth Viscount's end; you cannot have foreseen apoplexy."

"No, indeed, tho' my predecessor was aged—and had

got his son only on his third wife, who died giving birth to the child. I suppose if I were a gambling man, I should say that with the dispatch of young Arthur, the odds that his father should not long survive, were in my favour."

"*Are* you a gambling man, my lord?"

"Jane," Elizabeth murmured in reproof.

But Viscount Beaumont smiled. "Do not check your friend, Mrs. Heathcote. She has put her finger on the crux of the dilemma! I recognise in myself the ideal object of prosecution, now that young Arthur's death is adjudged a murder. I ought to be chief suspect, indeed, but for the fact that your good son languishes in gaol!"

"He does so, in part, because of the rumours of wenching," I said deliberately. I had not broached the matter with Elizabeth since the inquest, and I observed her to bridle at my words. "The judgement of the coroner's panel went hard against Will, once the idea of his meddling with tradesmen's daughters was broached."

"I perceived it," Beaumont said.

"I have accounted for one young woman, at least." I looked at Elizabeth rather than her visitor. "According to William, she is the only person from town with whom he consorted. He has been meeting with Dr. Lyford's eldest daughter at least twice each week, since the start of the Michaelmas term. They have met at Lyford's house in Middle Brook Street, and while Will was at liberty on Hills. They met Tuesday last, while Prendergast and Insley Minor kept vigil by the lock-keeper's hut. I speak of Charlotte Lyford."

"The speech artist?" Elizabeth enquired.

"You know of her avocation?"

"The entire world has been informed of it! —Or at least, so much of the world as is bound by Hampshire. My brother has been urging me to consult her regarding William's stammer . . . Good Lord, Jane! Do not say that William has been *subjecting* himself to her quackery!"

"With a vengeance," I said. "I have interviewed Miss Lyford; she believes your son to have benefited from her methods."

"He did not demonstrate so much before the panel yesterday," Eliza retorted grimly. "When I think of the *fees* she must have wrung from the boy—!"

"He wished to conceal his activity from you, in the hope that any improvement would be a gratifying surprize."

"It has been that and more, to be sure." She met my eyes, her own swimming. "Poor lad! He so desperately wished to be rid of his affliction! That Charlotte Lyford should *prey* upon his hopes—"

"Acquit her of that, at least," I soothed. "However imperfect her results, she sincerely wished to help your son. As dearly, perhaps, as he wished to mend his defect. But the construction that has been put on their meetings—the twisted imputation of vice—"

"I for one do not believe it," Viscount Beaumont broke in. "Your son, Mrs. Heathcote, appears too retiring—too scholarly—too fastidious, in his nature, to be lost to the muslin company."

"You are alone in your opinion, sir, among the worthies of Winchester!" Eliza said bitterly.

"Because someone means for your son to hang." It was an extraordinary statement—and yet Beaumont's tone was merely thoughtful. "The vital question before us, is *why*. Why has someone decided that William Heathcote must be guilty of murder? Only once we have determined that, may we understand how and why young Arthur Prendergast died."

A perplexed silence, on Elizabeth's part; a fearful one, on mine. At the viscount's words, I had experienced the oddest sensation—as tho' a lens had been placed before my eyes, sharpening my sight. My suppositions had been turned upon their heads.

"Would you suggest, my lord, that your cousin was never the murderer's principal object? Do you in fact believe that the point of this entire episode—the death of Master Prendergast, and the subsequent investigation by the coroner and its result—was merely a *means* to destroy William Heathcote?"

Viscount Beaumont lifted himself from his inner contemplation. He regarded first Eliza, and then me.

"Yes, Miss Austen. That is exactly what I would suggest. And if William is cleared of guilt before the Assizes—if he is released too soon from his present gaol—I should judge that his life is not worth a ha'penny."

20
A CLANDESTINE COURTSHIP

No. 12, The Close
Winchester
Wednesday, 2 April 1817, cont'd.

"My lord," I ventured, "were you at all acquainted with your cousin, the late viscount, and his heir?"

"I was," Beaumont said. "You must not be thinking me the long-lost relation, emigrated to the colonies, who is thunderstruck upon learning of his sudden accession to an estate he never anticipated. Indeed, for much of my youth I was Beaumont's heir-presumptive, his first two wives producing only daughters. I was raised as much at Avebury Court as in my own country of Hertfordshire."

"What was your experience of Master Arthur? Having learnt of him only with his death, I hear such varying opinions of him as puzzle me exceedingly."

The viscount did not hesitate. "The Prendergasts are very different people to my own. My mother was the late Beaumont's first cousin; my father, tho' of less elevated breeding, a far more admirable man than he. Arthur, being the longed-for heir, was his father's spoilt darling. He was reared from infancy to look meanly upon others, and to take pleasure in ruling them."

"Among his schoolfellows, that tendency won few intimates. You cousin was not universally beloved," I pointed out. "I have heard him described as *cruel.*"

"—Hence the general acceptance of his likely murder." His lordship viscount betrayed no more grief at his loss, than he had at the inquest. "I think it fortuitous, indeed, that Avebury Court and its dependents are spared the illiberal tyranny of Arthur's viscountcy. My own shall be far more enlightened."

"Master Prendergast had few friends, it is true," Elizabeth countered, "but one is Thomas Urquhart, an admirable young Scholar of Winchester College. His judgement and principles are all that are correct; he should never embrace a character so irredeemable as you describe. He has often been staying with your young cousin at Avebury Court, and I believe hoped his example should work for good upon Arthur."

"Has he, indeed?" Beaumont's eyes were sharp with interest. "My intimacy with my young cousin did not extend to his schoolfellows. Certainly the one who appeared before the coroner—young Insley—impressed me little. But I must regard your opinion, Mrs. Heathcote, as paramount. You live in the midst of these young men, and may measure them with a mother's acute perception."

"Of Insley Minor, I know nothing, for he was no friend to William. But I have welcomed Master Urquhart as almost another son," Eliza continued, "for he has no relations of his own."

"The world seems to embrace him at an instant," I observed. "We may impute it to his charm, Lord Beaumont, which is considerable. He exerts it among masters and pupils, gentlemen and ladies alike. My nephew, another of Urquhart's intimates, believes he shall go far in *politics*."

"That is to judge him harshly, Jane," Eliza protested. "Thomas Urquhart depends for his future upon his excellent understanding and his wits—not to mention the benevolence of Winchester College, in awarding him a Scholar's place. I could wish he had spoken on William's behalf before the coroner; no one should have been more eloquent in defence of my son's character and motives."

"The lad is a Scholar?" Beaumont enquired. "I had thought such places awarded to gentlemen of influence, as a mark of a son's distinction. It has been centuries, indeed, since Scholarships were offered to those who truly require them."

"And Ruthven Clarke was the boy's sponsor," I supplied. "I doubt that *he* should confer anything upon a fellow who lacked what my nephew calls *pull*."

"Then we may account for Master Urquhart's attentions to my young cousin." Beaumont's brows lifted. "He will have enjoyed the notice he received, and the useful connexions formed, at Avebury Court."

"What interests me exceedingly," I mused, "is *Prendergast's* embrace of *Urquhart*. Insley Minor I understand; he is the sort who will slavishly follow a bully, to save his own skin, and your young cousin should take his adulation as his due. But if, as you claim, Arthur Prendergast despised the less fortunate and humbly-born, why should he—or his father the haughty viscount—cultivate Thomas Urquhart's friendship and attentions?"

"Perhaps he admired what he *was not*, and *could never attain*," Lord Beaumont said quietly, his eyes on Elizabeth. She coloured, and dropped her own gaze. "But I agree, Miss Austen, there is some mystery here. Will Dr. Gabell know of the boy's antecedents?"

"If so, he has not deigned to publicise his knowledge. Mr. Clarke, too, is evasive on the subject."

"One cannot wonder at the discretion of both," Eliza attempted. "They should be poor safeguards of Urquhart's privacy, did they proclaim his birth to the world."

I noticed that Viscount Beaumont seemed almost not to attend to my friend's speech. His expression was abstracted in thought, and as a little silence fell among us, he rose abruptly and bowed.

"Forgive me, Mrs. Heathcote, for taking up so much of your time. There will be many demands upon your energy, I know, in coming days. For my part, I must return into Wiltshire within the hour, to attend the late viscount's funeral at Avebury Court."

"Of course," Elizabeth murmured.

"May I impose upon you further, however—or do I demand too much?—by sending my solicitor to wait upon you? I should like young William to be afforded the most adept counsel possible in the weeks before the Assizes. Mr. Judford should be of essential use."

Eliza looked a little shocked. "You are very kind, my

lord, but I believe my brother, Mr. Harris Bigg-Wither, of Manydown Park, will do all that is necessary. We expect him every hour."

Beaumont frowned a little. "But—forgive me, if I am impertinent—will not Sir William Heathcote, of Hursley House, do all in his power to aid his grandson in the present crisis?"

The viscount gazed at Elizabeth keenly; she merely inclined her head. Her reserve must have spoken volumes, however, for his lordship did not persist in his interrogation.

"Please believe, Madam, that if such near relations, upon whom you have far greater claims, somehow fail you—you should not hesitate to apply to *me*." He bowed, then, and left us.

I SUCCEEDED IN SWALLOWING a bit of clear beef broth and some tea, into which I dipped half a piece of dry toast, and felt well enough to dress an hour later. I descended the steps in time to discover Edward removing his cloak in the front hall; it was beaded with the fine misting rain that had descended once more upon Winchester. We are close enough to the coast in this town—Portsmouth is not above thirty miles distant—that the weather must often be influenced by the whims of the Solent.

"You have been to visit William?"

"I have." My nephew's countenance was grave. "I bear a message for his mother."

"Elizabeth is working her embroidery in her boudoir. I shall take you up to her."

Edward followed me along the passage to the small room Eliza had fitted out as a pleasant area of repose, where she and Alethea might linger over dress-patterns, periodicals, and needlework when no obligation to receive or entertain in the principal rooms below was demanded of them. Fitted out in blue, it held serviceable branches of work-candles and a table where lengths of stuff might be draped and cut. On brighter days, sunlight should stream through the north window; at the moment all that was visible beyond the panes was a dispiritingly grey sky, fingered by a bough of tentative hawthorn. Eliza had a small fire burning in the grate. For an instant, I regretted disturbing her peace; from Edward's expression, I guessed his communication was not a happy one. He stood awkwardly in the doorway, as tho' loath to enter such a private realm.

"You are returned from my son?" she said without preamble. "You saw my letter to him, delivered into his hands?"

"I did. He read it before me, ma'am, and I may say that it afforded him considerable comfort. To know that you were not prostrate under the weight of his misfortunes, and that so many friends are active on his behalf, much relieved his mind."

"Pray, sit down and tell me the whole."

She gestured to the chair beside her.

"Aunt Jane must have precedence. I am well enough where I am."

There was, indeed, only one other chair in the room— the sort of armless, low-seated piece ideal for a lady engaged in needlework. I slipped into it, and gazed at my nephew.

"Is William well? Is he getting enough food? Did you pay out to the gaoler the coins I gave you? I doubt Will shall have anything hot, or any meat indeed, without the rogue is liberally bribed."

"I did all in my power to do," Edward said, "but I will not deny that I found William to be low in spirits. Yesterday, he was all defiance; today, he is more sensible of the weight of evidence against him, and the need to bring greater proofs to his defence. Consequently, perhaps, he was the more willing to discuss his condition."

"Oh, God, that I could alleviate his distress!" Elizabeth set aside her embroidery with finality and knotted her fingers in her lap.

"I have one item at least that demands your energy: Will begs that you will write to his friend Baigent's people, and implore them to return their son to Winchester as soon as may be. Baigent may swear to Will's being in House Tuesday last from the time he returned from his appointment in Middle Brook Street—which he believes was at about six o'clock—until they were all of them in their beds, and their lights put out."

"That does not preclude him from hitting Prendergast over the head with a cricket bat and tipping him into Pot, in the interval between leaving Miss Lyford's consulting room and arriving back at college," I ruthlessly observed.

Elizabeth drew a sharp breath. "Jane—"

"It does not," Edward agreed. "The distance between Middle Brook Street and Hills is considerable, however, and even a betting man would hesitate to back Will to do it, complete his murderous deed, and be safely in Gabell's House for his friend Baigent's edification in so short a period as a quarter-hour. I would remind you, Aunt, that is the interval in question."

"Provided Miss Lyford is correct in her estimation that William remained with her until a quarter before six. A betting man—or a judge—could pick holes in the certainty of either."

Edward's shoulders lifted. "Nonetheless, Baigent should be summoned. He might prove useful in other ways."

"I shall write to his mother, immediately you leave me," Elizabeth said crisply. "William could do with a steadfast friend."

Edward inclined his head, but made no move to leave. "I told William we knew of his visits to Miss Lyford. He was most displeased. He wished to astound you, Mrs. Heathcote, with his progress, when more of it should have been made. He insisted that Miss Lyford's name not be dragged into this business. When I informed him, however, that Insley had already disclosed it to the coroner, he was dismayed. I did not *dare* refer, then, to Urquhart's fury!"

Elizabeth stared at my nephew. "What do you speak of, Edward?"

"Urquhart nurses a *tendre* for the young woman. When he learned from Insley Minor that it is Miss Lyford young Will has been meeting, he appeared to credit Prendergast's lies."

"Miss Lyford, and Urquhart!" Eliza cried. "But he is not above eighteen! And she is nearly one-and-twenty!"

"Recollect that there were six years between your brother Harris and me," I observed, "and he offered *marriage*."

"But what will Miss Lyford see in a mere schoolboy, Jane, without family or prospects?"

"Everything that you perceive, my dear, in enumerating Thomas Urquhart's gifts. He is handsome, well-made, charming, and has considerable address. She is something of a bluestocking, and bashful of Society. It is not to be wondered at, that having once met Urquhart, she should regard him as superior to every other creature she has yet encountered. Her sphere cannot extend very far beyond her father's hospital, after all."

"The real question," Edward said quietly, "is what Urquhart sees to cultivate in Miss Lyford. She is pretty enough, I daresay, but nothing out of the ordinary way; and by many, she would be regarded as a tradesman's daughter. She possesses neither fortune nor connexions, which Urquhart badly needs. I should have thought him too careful to entangle himself, where there was not great benefit to earn."

"That is very true." I considered the point. "Perhaps he trifled with the girl, as so many young men do, in a test of his power."

"I cannot believe that," Elizabeth objected. "Being not perfectly acquainted with him, Jane, you misjudge Urquhart's sincerity. He has been mistaken, perhaps, in his valuation of Miss Lyford, as he clearly was in Prendergast."

Any further argument Eliza might have offered was suspended at that moment by a bustle below-stairs. A carriage had pulled to a halt before the door of No. 12, and a hound was heard to be baying before the door. As I rose from my chair, Mariah's heavy tread hastened along the passage.

Harris Bigg-Wither had arrived—and brought his hunting dog with him.

21

A PRAYER TO OUR LADY

No. 12, The Close
Winchester
Wednesday, 2 April 1817, cont'd.

Harris Bigg-Wither at five-and-thirty was a very different gentleman from the one whose offer of marriage I had refused at the age of twenty. A rather tall and inelegant youth, he had added a substantial weight to his frame. Hair that had once been Elizabeth's chestnut brown, was now silvered at the temples. His demeanour was one of quiet confidence, and his gaze direct. He looked what he was: a prosperous man of influence in his sphere, in the prime of his life, and content with the riches afforded him. Chief among these, I am certain, was his wife—the unobjectionable Anne-Howe Frith, with whom he was the parent of ten hopeful children.

Good lord, I thought suddenly. *Had I accepted him, should I have had ten children?* —And shuddered at the thought.

My admiration for the improvement time had wrought in Mr. Bigg-Wither was not mirrored in his countenance when he greeted me. *A happy escape*, I am sure was the phrase uppermost in his mind, the Jane Austen of one-and-forty being nothing like the bewitching siren who had apparently robbed young Harris of his wits. I curtseyed to him circumspectly, and he bowed without a word; in this much, at least, he was unchanged from the youth I had once known. A martyr to his defect, Harris avoided speaking whenever possible.

The dog was a blithe-looking spaniel named Mudge, who followed his master's every step. In the drawing-room, he flung himself down on the hearth-rug and placed his head on his paws, his brown eyes fixed ecstatically on Mr. Bigg-Wither.

"I shall not intrude upon your privacy," I said. "You will have much to discuss and plan. I shall take a turn about the Close."

"I have arranged to meet a friend," Edward informed us significantly, "and shall hope to speak further with you, Mr. Bigg-Wither, over dinner."

Edward and I donned our cloaks.

"Are you bound for the George?" I asked him, "and another tankard with Thomas Urquhart?"

"For Chamber Court, rather. I mean to collar Insley Minor."

"I shall come with you," I said.

WINCHESTER COLLEGE WAS DESERTED at this hour on Spy Wednesday. Our footfalls echoed on the stone passage beneath the fourteenth-century Middle Gate, and neither of us spoke until we emerged into Chamber Court. The College chapel was immediately opposite, across the quadrangle. First and Second Chambers were still masked by a forest of scaffolding. I half-expected to glimpse Ruthven Clarke's querulous visage framed in a first-floor casement; but the windows were blank.

"Insley will be housed in Sixth Chamber, with the rest of Clarke's Commoners," Edward said. "That is the last stairway immediately to our right."

"We may not find him within. He may have gone into Sussex and his family, now that his testimony is given."

"He was here so recently as yesterday, when Urquhart spoke with him."

Edward led me to the heavy oak door and pulled it open. A lanthorn suspended from an iron hook cast a flickering light. A small foyer on the ground level revealed a portal; unlike in Clarke's chamber, there was no descriptive card pinned to its door. As we halted before it, Edward whispered, "This is the dormitory. There are normally twelve boys in such a room, Aunt. Above are masters' sets."

"Prendergast lodged here as well?"

He nodded. "Urquhart is in Fifth, with the other Scholars." He lifted the latch.

The large room beyond the door was lit mainly by weak daylight, seeping through leaded panes that were clouded with damp and weather. Six bedsteads flanked each side of a central aisle, most of them neatly made up, with large trunks at their feet. A fireplace was at the room's far end, and a few coals still glowed in its grate. Someone had been toasting crumpets on the fender.

In the fourth bed on our right, a humped shape beneath

the quilts snored audibly, tho' it was well after two o'clock. I espied tufts of mouse-brown hair and a flushed cheek.

Edward strode to the slumbering form. In an instant he seized the bedclothes and tossed them in a heap on the floor. "Oi there, Insley! You have guests!"

The boy snorted loudly, his head turning on the pillow, and struggled to sit upright. Edward reached for a jug on the small table that sat between two beds, and dashed a quantity of water in Insley's face. I suspected it was cold, because the boy shrieked and knuckled his eyes. Rough treatment, perhaps, but Edward had not been many months removed from the school's careless methods, and Insley apprehended them immediately.

"What's amiss?" he demanded. "Is there a fire?"

"Not yet." Edward restored the jug. "But there will be, if I must drag you to the hearth and set your toes to the coals. Get up, Insley!"

"You're Heathcote's friend," he declared, thrusting himself to his feet. He flushed as he met my indifferent gaze and attempted to straighten his linen—which, in addition to a set of nankeen breeches, was all he wore. "Ma'am."

"I am indeed Heathcote's friend. You will address me as Mr. Austen. This is my aunt, *Miss* Austen. We have questions that require your answers, Insley. And as the room is chill and you are wet, I suggest we repair to those chairs by the fire."

My nephew is not a great, tall fellow such as might cause a lesser boy to quail. His manner, however—and the four years' seniority he possessed over Peter Insley—were sufficiently daunting. Insley glowered, but he moved to the hearth tamely enough and stirred the flames as Edward saw me handsomely seated in a heavy armchair.

"You shall have the Prefect's place," he said, "as by right." He bent to the fender and retrieved the iron toasting fork, tossing a stale bit of crumpet in the hearth, where it flared brightly. Edward held the fork's tines under Insley's nose.

"Now, then. I happen to know that you are responsible, Insley, for throttling a blameless stray dog that William Heathcote befriended, during the last Short Term—and that you placed it in his bed, when you ought to have been with your Latin tutor."

The boy's protuberant eyes bulged wildly. "I never did! Who says so!"

"Thomas Urquhart. Would you give him the lie? Is your life worth so little?"

Insley shook his head frantically and slumped on the fender, breathing heavily through his mouth.

"What have you to say?"

The boy swallowed hard. "Nothing *to* say. Must take the blame like a stout one."

"You heard that, Aunt? He has admitted guilt before two witnesses. I shall inform both Mr. Clarke and Dr. Gabell, of course," Edward continued, "but if you contrive to answer my questions as truthfully as you know how, it may go easier; you may avoid expulsion."

Insley nodded wordlessly.

"Was it you who gave Prendergast the note William Heathcote wrote?"

"No need. Prenders had it in his purse. Showed it me himself, as we went down to the river."

"Did he say where he'd got it?"

"Didn't have to. Heathcote gave it to him."

"Let us suppose, Insley," Edward suggested, "that Heathcote passed it to Charles Baigent instead, the previous day, exactly as he claims. We expect Baigent any hour, by-the-by, and he shall give the lie to your testimony, I reckon, so perhaps you will consider carefully of your answer: Did Prendergast *tell you* for a fact that he'd received the note from Heathcote? —Or did you simply assume as much, and testify to it, *under oath*?"

The expressions moving swiftly across Insley Minor's visage as he weighed this tortuous thought might have been amusing, had Will Heathcote's future not been at stake. The boy's mouth abruptly closed and his eyes shifted about the corners of the room as tho' in search of an exit. "Dunno what you're on about."

"It's quite simple, Insley. Whoever lured Prendergast to Pot, did so in order to kill him," Edward explained patiently. "My Aunt and I mean to find out who that was."

Insley rubbed his nose with a dubious air. "Seems hare-witted to me. Likely kill you next."

"Answer the question."

"Very well. Prenders never said where he got the note. But stands to reason it was from Heathcote! I mean to say—he wrote it, didn't he?"

I expelled a long breath. "Master Insley, why do you hate William Heathcote?"

"*Hate* him?" The boy stared at me uncomprehendingly. "No particular feeling for the fellow, one way or t'other."

"Indeed? Then why persecute him? I assume it was also you who hung his gown in a noose from the rafters of his dormitory, and tossed his lexicon in a privy."

Insley's expression cleared. "As to that, nothing in it. Most of Gabell's House are treated to the same."

"Did you also steal William's watch? —and leave it near Mr. Clarke's chamber when you set fire to the Court?"

The boy shot to his feet. "I never did! He won't place the guilt for that on *me*! I was not yet a Commoner when the fire was set—I only came to Winton a year since! And as for *stealing*—"

"*Who* will not place the guilt?" I asked. "William? —Prendergast? —Mr. Clarke?"

Insley struck out with both hands and pushed his way between Edward and me, hurtling towards the dormitory's entrance. Edward fell back, then would have gone in pursuit, but that I called out.

"Let him go, Edward. He is half-mad with fear."

My nephew stopped short. "I was not *that* severe with him, Aunt."

"No," I agreed. "Someone else, however, was—and has struck terror in the boy."

EDWARD AND I PARTED company on the gravel before No. 12, he bound for a tankard with Urquhart at the George, and I for the cathedral. It seemed to me that prayers, on behalf of all of us, were in order.

I entered the great church by the south portal, hard by the arched slype, and made my way quietly through the chilly south transept to the south choir aisle. My hands were joined loosely at my waist, hidden by my cloak but devout from habit; my head I kept tilted well back, the better to scan the soaring interior spaces. Lacking a tower, Winchester Cathedral is curiously unremarkable when viewed from the exterior, but once inside, it is a place that robs the lungs of breath. When one is accustomed to an intimate family church like St. Nicholas, which sits just off the sweep of Chawton Great House as it has for some five centuries, the grandeur of stone pillars and vaults, the magnificence of stained glass and lead veins, the weight of tombs and the sharp smell of countless epochs, impose a sombre reverence.

Or so I felt, at least; there were any number of persons roaming the various sectors of the church in animated conversation, as tho' awaiting the display of fire-works at Vauxhall. Cathedrals are for many the equivalent of a town square, and behaviour is accordingly as raucous. I have not yet learnt the habit, and at this rate, never shall.

The Gothick choir stalls are magnificently carved, and I allowed my eye to roam freely over them as I proceeded east, past the presbytery and the feretory. I hurried my steps a little through the retro-choir and came at last to the peace and privacy I sought—the Lady Chapel, at the extreme east end of the massive edifice. Passersby and enthusiasts were fewer here. I dipped my finger in the stoup, crossed myself, and entered the magnificent carved wooden stall on the chapel's south side. There, I bent my knees to prayer.

Dear Mary, I prayed, *You who were a mother of an unjustly imprisoned son, deliver William from his enemies, unless it be that he bears true guilt. In that case, give him strength to face his culpability, and his judgement. Help his mother Elizabeth to bear any sorrow that may come, and to greet joy with equanimity. Help each of us to meet adversity with calm, loss with peace, and the future with hope. Amen.*

I did not pray for myself specifically. I did not pray for healing. I did not pray for more energy, more health, more time with those I loved, and who loved me. I knew that such things were already in God's hands—already determined, no doubt—and that any supplication of mine should influence the humours of my body not a single whit. The Virgin could neither extend nor shorten my time on earth; but speaking with her might render it more peaceful.

My prayer concluded, I sat back with folded hands and permitted myself to study the glorious arched window, its blues and reds and purples scintillating even in the pale spring light; then I glanced towards the north wall, where painted wood panels depicted the many miracles of the Virgin Mary. We Austens are good Church of England folk, and steeped in Holy Orders; but my father had a fondness for Our Lady, and I liked the old stories well enough.

As I lingered in the hard wooden stall, I became conscious of two things: the ache in my lower back, exacerbated by kneeling; and the muffled sobbing of the only other person the Lady Chapel held.

She knelt at the stall's far end, an abject figure. In the usual way, I should never intrude upon those who seek privacy in trouble, and especially when privacy is sought in prayer. I studied the bent head, knew at once that the person was female, and young; and further comprehended at a glance the figure, dress, and styling of the hair.

Miss Charlotte Lyford.

And in considerable distress.

I rose from my place, drew breath to steady my swimming head—I was not yet fully recovered from my fever of yesterday—and then exchanged my position in the stall for one directly next to Miss Lyford.

She shifted slightly as I knelt beside her, probably astonished that with the freedom of the Lady Chapel at my disposal, I should chuse to deposit myself so near. I forestalled her predictable flight by placing one gloved hand on her shoulder.

"My dear Miss Lyford," I whispered. "I will not disturb your distress. But know that I am a friend, however brief our acquaintance. You have my sympathy."

She turned her veiled head, and I caught a glimpse of eyes wild and desolate as an orphaned fawn's. She drew breath, rose abruptly, and with a swirl of grey muslin, quitted the stall and the chapel.

I forced myself to my feet, and made my way after her. She was hurrying down the north aisle, her youth allowing her greater speed and freedom. I am not the sort to call out and disturb a sacred atmosphere; I hastened my steps as much as I was able; and was thankful that fewer townsfolk and gawkers populated the north side of the cathedral than the south.

Fortune favoured me a moment later, when Miss Lyford was halted by a party of clerics garbed in black, wading upstream, as it were, against her direction. They were in preparation for the Spy Wednesday *Tenebrae* service, no doubt. Miss Lyford effaced herself against a Romanesque pillar so that the clergy might pass, their steps measured and serene in dignity. In the interval, I diverted my course to the centre aisle running the length of the nave, keeping the veiled young woman in parallel.

There is, I should explain, no north portal to balance the south one. To quit the cathedral, she must turn towards the nave and progress through the main west entrance.

And it was there I came up with her, directly in front of the pair of beautiful, red-painted Gothick arched doors, slim and tall, studded at intervals with iron. The veil over her face trembled a little with the rapidity of her breath.

"Please, Miss Lyford," I said in an undertone. "Walk with me a little."

WE PACED SEDATELY TOWARDS town, her intended direction. The publicity of the familiar streets should deter her from taking flight, I thought, should my questions prove too distressing.

"When we first met yesterday, Miss Lyford, you were serene," I began. "Yet by the end of our interview, you were uneasy. Today you are equally so, and bent in prayer.

I believe I apprehend the source of your trouble—it is to do with Master Thomas Urquhart, is it not?"

I expected her to deny it, and affect ignorance of my meaning. She surprised me, however, by hesitating only an instant, before ducking her head in acknowledgement. "I am a little acquainted with the gentleman, as you perceive; and had thought him to hold me in esteem. —Or in enough respect, at least, to preserve my reputation. I was mistaken."

"I am sorry for it. You did not appear to think so yesterday."

"I had not yet been visited by the coroner, Mr. Pelham," she returned quietly. "He called upon me in Middle Brook Street this morning."

"Ah."

She darted at me a quick look through her veil. "The boy Insley has indeed told him that *I* am the young woman from town Master Heathcote met in secret these many months past. A scandalous and illicit imputation was attached to a connexion that existed solely for Master Heathcote's benefit. I informed Mr. Pelham of the salutary nature of my meetings with Heathcote, and further revealed that my maid was present for the entirety of every such meeting—including those conducted in the open air, on St. Catherine's Hill. He swore me to the testimony, and then swore my maid. Mr. Pelham knows, now, that there was nothing improper in our activities; that indeed, I attended Will as a healer should tend a patient."

"The coroner accepted your assurances?"

"He did. He had my oath." She sighed. "Being aware

that the courts are likely to accord the word of a woman less weight than that of a man, I did not scruple to involve my father in my business. He, too, testified to the truth of all I had told Pelham. I believe the coroner was satisfied."

"Then what is the source of your distress?"

She drew a ragged breath, as tho' stifling a sob. "Urquhart has written me *such* a letter—! Full of anger and rebuke! He entirely believes the lies told about Heathcote and me, at Monday's inquest."

"Urquhart wrote to you? —You are on such terms, then, as to accept the missive?" It is regarded as unseemly, indeed, for an unmarried lady to correspond with a gentleman to whom she is not affianced.

Miss Lyford pressed her gloved hand to her lips. "It is wrong of me to do so, I know. In truth, we have been corresponding some weeks."

"If your father finds nothing to dismay him in this, it is not for me to condemn you."

"My father knows nothing of it." A second swift, sidelong glance. "The letters we exchange are left in the pew at the Lady Chapel, where you just discovered me."

"I see." A private post. There was so much that was romantickal in the arrangement, as should capture the heart of any devotee of Gothick novels. "And you secured Urquhart's communication only now?"

She shook her head. "I entered the chapel for the purpose of leaving my final reply to him. It is a definite end to our attachment. He has employed such language as must alienate any affection he once inspired. To think, Miss

Austen, that I regarded him as the partner of my future life!" she concluded in a trembling accent.

I looked all my sympathy.

She came to a halt in the street, and turned towards me. "He accused me of falsity. Of double-dealing. Of trifling with the sentiments of an honest man. In short, he believed the lies his friend Prendergast told, and declared himself incensed by the wrongs I had done him."

"My poor dear. You have not deserved such treatment, I am sure."

"What hurts me the most is that he believed me capable, as he said, of spurning a self-made man for one of higher birth. When I showed him nothing but kindness," she said in a bewildered tone.

I began to walk onward; Winchester is too busy a town for blocking the passage of others along the thoroughfares. "How did you come to meet? He did not consult you as a speech artist, I collect?"

"Not at all—tho' having known me a little, he expressed a decided interest in my work. We met when he sought out my father's services in Middle Brook Street. Urquhart rang the bell of the consulting room, whilst my father was attending patients at the hospital. As is usual in such cases, I requested that Urquhart pen a note for the boy my father employs as messenger—but he insisted that the matter was trifling enough, that he should merely leave his name, and consult the surgeon at his convenience. From that simple beginning, our acquaintance sprang."

I had a ready idea of it: the handsome young man, blessed

with easy address, and the retiring young woman who had dedicated her girlhood to study. Urquhart's charm should be a heady dose. "There must have been difficulties. He was tied to Winchester College, after all, and its obligations."

"As a senior and a Prefect, he enjoyed unusual freedoms. Then, too, he is held in such regard by the masters that he is often granted absolution when others might earn punishment. Soon, we were not merely leaving letters in the Lady Chapel but walking together about the grounds, exchanging ideas. Urquhart has an excellent brain, Miss Austen, and he appeared genuinely interested in my work."

"Did he, indeed?"

"He went so far as to make a study of it! I was astonished, at first—for you will know that there are few men, particularly those barely out of boyhood, who will credit a woman as possessing anything like an education. In time, however, as Urquhart continued in his enthusiasm for my efforts, I warmed to his praise. What began as a circumspect acquaintance deepened to mutual regard—or so I believed. I must now consider myself a dupe, and his attentions the grossest flattery."

"He is merely hotheaded, perhaps—being but eighteen. You will be his first attachment, and in such travail, youth is not always wise." I considered an instant. "To what do you impute his interest in speech artistry? Did you ever mention your work with William Heathcote? —For I know they are good friends."

"I did. Thomas was most sympathetic to Heathcote's troubles, and I thought the case of a young man roughly his age, and of his particular sphere, should be of interest. That is why it is so mortifying that Urquhart should *now* throw my connexion to Heathcote at my head!"

"It is surpassing strange!" I agreed.

"I shall burn the letter," she added bitterly, "as I shall every one he sent me. I have merely suffered what so many ladies may claim—the duplicity of a charming young man, whose object was frivolous, and whose mendacity is happily discovered before too great a harm was effected."

Wise words, I thought; and with time she might even believe them. She had been imprudent, perhaps, and easily won—but how many of us might say the same? I placed my gloved hand over her own.

"Do not destroy the correspondence, my dear. I daresay a little time will put all to rights. He will regret of his harshness, and beg your pardon a thousand times! In the meanwhile, pray believe that you have my discretion, Miss Lyford, and my sincere regard. You may soon be serene again."

Unless, I thought as the young woman parted from me, my nephew Edward was correct—and the *self-made* Thomas Urquhart should never ally himself with one who could not bring him both fortune, and an illustrious name.

22

DEFECTION OF AN ARDENT SUITOR

No. 12, The Close
Winchester
Wednesday, 2 April 1817, cont'd.

"Harris is gone out," Elizabeth informed me upon my return to the Close, "in search of a solicitor, to whom he bears an introduction. His own attorneys are in Basingstoke, and thought a Winchester man should serve us best; it is they who provided my brother with this fellow's direction. A Mr. Irving, apparently, who is familiar with the Winchester courts. He shall bring in the best barrister of his acquaintance, Harris assures me, and do all he can for William."

"That is excellent news!" I cried. "And have you written, yet, to Master Baigent's people, requesting the boy's early return?"

Elizabeth pressed a hand to her forehead. "The duty entirely fled my mind. I shall sit down at my desk directly, Jane. There will be just time enough—we are not to wait dinner on my brother's account, as he may be detained some time. He means to visit William once he has secured Mr. Irving's interest."

She hurried away.

Edward had not yet returned from the George. I mounted the stairs slowly to my bedchamber, my strength of this morning already depleted by the short walk from Close to cathedral. I paused at the top of the stairs, one hand clutching the newel post, until my swimming sight steadied. Whether dinner waited for Harris or no, I did not think I should be likely to eat it. The enforced activity and strain of recent days was telling upon my condition, and to weakness was coupled now a persistent nausea.

I moved slowly down the passage to my room, thankful for my comfortable bed, and laid down upon it.

"AUNT!"

Edward, of course, scratching at my door.

I sat up against the pillow, and bade him enter.

He slipped into the room bearing a teapot and two cups on a tray. These he carefully set down on a table near the fire, before turning to scrutinize my face. "You've been going the pace again too hard. Are you well?"

"Perfectly," I lied. "I shall be thankful for that tea."

He took the hint, and dutifully poured out my cup, carrying it to my bedside. "I have had a letter from my father. Grandmamma forwarded it here, no doubt recognising Papa's fist."

"And what does James say?"

"That the rooms at Scarlets are entirely too warm, Mrs. Leigh-Perrot having no idea of economy, but building up her fires to an excessive and wasteful degree. He has been obliged to sleep with his windows thrown open, and consequently has taken a severe cold, which he expects will shortly prove to be an inflammation of the lung."

"He is faring splendidly, then," I mused, "and could not well be happier. The situation in which he finds himself, that of overlooked and suffering heir, shall justify him in denying every luxury that might make his wife and children's situation bearable, and provide him the satisfaction of regarding himself a true Christian."

Edward's lips quirked. "Did you read the letter before I opened it?"

"Many times, throughout my life—or at least, I have had joy of similar missives. Is he very bitter about the want of a legacy?"

"Not at all." Edward was brisk. "As you suspected, the injustice of leaving so much property to the use of a frivolous and possibly-mad old woman has strengthened his belief that material pleasures are fleeting, and true wealth is only to be obtained in Heaven. He is the same dear old Papa."

"He has no notion you are in Winchester?"

Edward shook his head. "I expect he shall hear of it by tomorrow, however, as Grandmamma will have written to the Scarlets party. I fear we shall have to undertake to return to Chawton so soon as Friday, Aunt, or Saturday at the latest. My father informs me he means to quit Berkshire in good enough time to take the Easter Sunday service at Steventon."

"Now that Mr. Bigg-Wither is arrived to aid his sister,

we may have no qualm at leaving," I agreed, "tho' it goes sorely against the grain to do so without having learnt the truth of this affair. How was Urquhart? Recovered from his agonies of yesterday?"

"I cannot tell you." Edward disposed himself in the chair before the fire and poured out his own tea. "I was met at the George by a message from the publican, who informed me that Master Urquhart was unavoidably detained. He is mortified by his display at our previous meeting, I collect, and nursing both his head and his grievance in private."

"—Or has gone to *Tenebrae* service, to retrieve his post from the Lady Chapel." I related Miss Lyford's confidences to my nephew, and received a low whistle of surprise as my reward.

"Fancy Urquhart having led the girl to believe he intended *marriage*! —When we all *know* he is meant for a scholar's place at New College."

"Love is responsible for any number of stupidities," I mused, "and perhaps Miss Lyford imputed more than was said."

"To have been writing to her, however!" Edward took a turn about the room. "There is a want of delicacy in such behaviour—an exposing of the young woman to general censure—that I cannot like. And you say he cast her off with an angry note?"

"He must truly believe Prendergast's scandal."

"Then he is more of a simpleton than he appears. To know Miss Lyford as Urquhart did, is to know that she was treating Heathcote for his defect—not dangling after an eligible *parti*. I wonder if he tired of her, and saw in Insley's slander a welcome expedient?"

"I am intrigued," I admitted, "by his striking up the acquaintance in the first place. Miss Lyford, as you have said, is not the figure to inspire a grand passion! And while there is no accounting for tastes, you have suggested that Urquhart does not hold himself cheap. He seems, however, to have shewn great interest in speech artistry, Edward."

My nephew stared. "Speech artistry?"

"He spent a good deal of his courtship, it seems, in talking of it. Perhaps he intended only to flatter Miss Lyford with his interest—to affect a passion for all that she held dear. But she tells me she spoke to him of *William Heathcote's* defect. Now, is it not odd that he should listen to so much regarding a friend whom he now charges the lady, with treating as a *rival*?"

"Are you suggesting, Aunt, that Urquhart sought out Charlotte Lyford *because* she was treating William?"

I lifted my brows. "Neither her station nor her wiles ought to have won Urquhart's interest; therefore, it must be her unusual profession. And reflect, Edward: William is the only person, so far as we know, that the two have in common."

"But *why*? There is some mystery, here."

I frowned, following my stray thoughts. "If Insley Minor or Prendergast saw William meet Miss Lyford on Hills, during the boys' Remedy hours, surely Urquhart did so? What if the sight gave rise to a useful idea in his mind—of impugning William's reputation, because he *meddled with tradesmen's daughters?*"

Edward frowned, and ran his fingers through his disordered mop of hair. "Would you mean, Aunt, that Urquhart planned Prenders' drowning at Pot, and intended William to hang in his place? Impossible! Leaving aside his obvious friendship for Will, *why* should Urquhart kill Prendergast? The fellow was his entrée to Avebury Court—to wealth, ease, and useful connexions. Prendergast dead, should be of no value to Urquhart at all!"

"Have you considered, Edward, that Urquhart is undoubtedly the natural son of a powerful man? Dr. Gabell implied as much; and how else may we account for his having won a place as Scholar? Such preferment is not offered to *nobodies*. What if Urquhart cultivated Prendergast because he suspects, or even *knows*, himself to be the Honourable Arthur's brother?"

"Beaumont's by-blow, you mean?" Edward looked thunderstruck. "And hoped, with Prendergast dead, that he should succeed as heir? —But he must know, Aunt, that illegitimate sons cannot inherit titles!"

"Perhaps the title is immaterial. Perhaps Urquhart thought to persuade the late viscount—whom he could not have known would be immediately taken off by apoplexy— to cut off any entail on his property. Being a viscount is nothing, Edward, to being master of Avebury Court and possessor of all it brings! Moreover, the present Lord Beaumont has never met Thomas Urquhart. It is possible Urquhart was ignorant of the presumptive heir."

But Edward shook his head. "Again, I say, *Impossible*! You do not know Urks as I do, Aunt. He is uniformly agreeable, ruefully accepting of his condition, and happy in the gifts that have made his advancement by merit possible. And if all you suggest were true, then he should knowingly have slipped a noose around Heathcote's throat. But he is not half so cold-blooded, I assure you—and has no reason on earth to harm Will, who has shown him nothing but kindness. Even believing the worst of Miss Lyford yesterday, Urquhart still spoke of the Heathcotes with sorrowing affection."

"Everything about the affair puzzles me exceedingly," I admitted with a sigh. "But perhaps Mr. Bigg-Wither, or his solicitor, will apprehend more than we do—and all may be resolved by the time we sit down to dinner!"

23

WHAT THE WARDEN KNEW

No. 12, The Close
Winchester
Thursday, 3 April 1817

A ll was not resolved by dinner. It was an excellent
haunch of venison brought from Manydown, with
stewed apples and a macaroni, but I could not enjoy above
a few mouthfuls. Elizabeth was so taken up with her son's
troubles, that she thankfully paid no attention to my lack
of appetite. Her brother Harris had not returned, as pre-
dicted, and his absence exacerbated Elizabeth's strained
nerves. She was every moment imagining further impediments to be strewn in William's path.

I retired to bed early, and had some warm milk brought
up to me, unasked, by Mariah. There was also a draught
delivered from Mr. Lyford, with express instructions that it
be drunk at bedtime. I swallowed the foul stuff, and hoped
that its use was superior to its taste. As Mariah closed
the bedroom draperies, I caught a glimpse of the moon,
just on the wane. It had not yet been full when I quitted
Chawton. By this time, I reflected, my mother should have
received both James's letter and mine, and know all of her

brother's neglect in the matter of legacies. I could not leave Cassandra to bear the brunt of her lamentations alone; I must be wanted at home. And yet I quailed from the prospect. A strong sentiment urged me to remain here, in a kind of suspense between the ill-health of the winter months and the further ill-health to come. I had snatched an interval of diversion from my wearying decline, a few days that recalled the vigour of the past, and I was loath to give it up.

I do not recall what I dreamt of, last night, except for the figure of a man, seen from behind. He walked purposefully away from me, the length of a churchyard. I attempted to call out for him, but my voice was stifled in my throat. I discerned nothing telling in his features. Was it Raphael West? My brother Henry? Lord Harold Trowbridge? My father, perhaps?

Then he turned at last to look at me, and I recognised Elizabeth's dead husband, William Heathcote the elder. As I stared at him in bafflement—still barely thirty in death, as he was when life deserted him—his features altered subtly, and it was Thomas Urquhart who challenged my gaze.

I am certain I should have understood what the vision meant, had I been afforded more time. But Mariah awoke me by rapping at the door, with the intelligence that Mr. Lyford waited upon me.

"YOUR PULSE IS TUMULTUOUS," he said gravely as he fingered my right wrist. "Let me see your tongue."

Obediently, I stuck it out at him.

"I cannot like the colour." He peered closely into my eyes. "Have you suffered further pains in the back?"

"They are perpetual." I indicated the region just below my waist.

"I may offer you laudanum."

I hesitated. Relief should be welcome, but I knew the tincture, even diffused in water, should blanket my mind in lethargy. I would be of no use to William Heathcote. And then, there was the spectre of the future: if I deadened the pain I *now* endured, how should I bear the greater suffering that might come?

"Not yet," I said.

His eyes narrowed a trifle, and then he nodded once. "Very well. I shall send over another draught from my dispensary—take it before meals, and before retiring. And see that you actually eat something, Miss Austen."

"I shall try."

With this, the surgeon was forced to be satisfied.

I FOUND ELIZA SEATED at the breakfast-table with her brother and my nephew. Harris Bigg-Wither rose at my entrance and bowed solemnly, but did not utter a word. I was reminded of his chusing never to speak when a look or gesture should suffice, and apprehended how strongly young Will must have wished to be rid of his similar defect. I found myself hoping that if the boy should be acquitted, and freed, that he continue his work with Miss Lyford. Lacking any proofs of the utility of her methods, I must nonetheless support Will's exertions. Any effort must be preferable to the silence Harris adopted.

"There is a letter for you, Jane," Eliza said.

I glanced at the post laid by my place. "It will be from my mother, I do not doubt, urging me immediately home."

But the hand was one I did not recognise. It had been franked with a scrawled signature that was similarly unknown to me, and the wax sealed with an unfamiliar crest.[16] Curious, I sank into my seat and opened the missive while Elizabeth poured out my chocolate.

"It is from Lord Beaumont," I said. "Penned yesterday, from his seat in Wiltshire."

> *"Miss Austen:*
>
> *"I write to you in haste from Avebury Court. Pray forgive the impertinence of my addressing you privately as I have done, and regard this correspondence as a matter of business—importuning Mrs. Heathcote seemed indelicate under the circumstances, and I thought it preferable to inform her friend, who might more ably judge if and when the intelligence could safely be shared.*
>
> *"When I took my leave of you Tuesday, I went immediately to the Warden of Winchester College—"*

---

16 In Austen's day, postage was usually paid by the individual who *received* a letter, rather than the one who sent it. The exception to this was when a letter was franked—which means, the envelope was signed and dated by a member of parliament or under the authority of certain public offices, waiving postage altogether. The practice ended in 1840 with the introduction of the penny postage stamp.—*Editor's note.*

"Good God!" my nephew Edward exclaimed, breaking off my recitation of the letter's contents.

I glanced at him over the page, a tiny frown between my eyes. "What is it?"

"The *Warden*, Aunt Jane! This fellow Beaumont disturbed the peace of the Double Bishop!"

"What can you possibly mean?" I looked to Eliza.

"Mr. Huntingford has lately been elevated to the bishopric of Hereford," she explained. "Before that, he was Bishop of Gloucester. Hence the nickname to which Edward alludes."

"A prince of the church is also Warden of Winchester?"

"Indeed! And he has been so long in the office, he is the only Warden I have ever known. Generations of boys have come and gone, and the Double Bishop continues in his comfortable lodgings above Middle Gate."[17]

"—Not finding it necessary to reside, it seems, as chief cleric of either Gloucester or Herefordshire."

"Fellow's a Master, too. Tutored me in Greek." Edward had the grace to look abashed. "Or at any rate, he *tried*. But what I mean to say is, Aunt, he's not the sort of crony you just hunt up on a whim. Very high in the instep, is George Huntingford. I rather wonder Lord Beaumont had sufficient courage."

From his chair at the breakfast table, Harris Bigg-Wither coughed discreetly. I took the sound as an abjuration to

---

17 The Warden of Winchester College presides over the Fellows, up to fourteen appointees who form the governing authority of the school. The office is independent of that of Headmaster.—*Editor's note.*

continue reading, and looked down at the paper I still clutched in my hand.

> "—I went immediately to the Warden of Winchester College, and was so happy as to find him in residence. Mr. George Huntingford is an indolent man, but he has reason to receive any Lord Beaumont, as it is thanks to my late predecessor, the Fifth Viscount, and his great friend Henry Addington (later Lord Sidmouth), that Huntingford retained his office after the college's Great Rebellion of 1793."

"Sidmouth!" Edward cried. "The Home Secretary?"

"You must know it was *he* who first made Huntingford a bishop," Elizabeth broke in, "when he was prime minister. That was in 1802, or thereabouts—not long before my dear husband died."

Harris coughed once more, less discreetly this time.

"If you will not be quiet," I told them all severely, "we shall never get to the end of this letter." I resumed reading.

> "Your reference to Thomas Urquhart's unknown parentage, and his being a frequent visitor at Avebury Court as a guest of my nephew, interested me exceedingly. My late cousin was uncompromising on the importance of birth; he should never have countenanced his son and heir's association with any boy outside his proper sphere; I deemed it probable therefore that Urquhart's condition was better than is generally assumed.

"I thought it possible, in short, that Urquhart is the late viscount's natural son."

I gave Edward a significant look. Elizabeth uttered an exclamation of surprise.

"In the belief that knowledge of his antecedents might shed light on my young cousin's murder, I determined to petition the Warden to share whatever intelligence he might possess.

"Huntingford received me with some surprize, but I did not sport with his patience. I put the question to him baldly, as one who was acting now in loco parentis, *and had a right to know all that concerned Arthur Prendergast's death.*

"The Warden presented no impediments. He explained with alacrity that Thomas Urquhart had been put up for the place of Scholar by his former pupil Henry Addington, Viscount Sidmouth, as a gesture of goodwill to Addington's intimate friend, a neighbour in his home county of Berkshire. The boy, according to this friend, was the son of his butler, although Addington suspected a far closer tie. He believed that Urquhart was in fact his neighbour's natural son, owing to a resemblance he detected in the features of both.

"And this neighbour's name? I demanded.

"One Thomas Freeman-Heathcote, heir to Sir William Heathcote, baronet, of Hursley Hall, Hampshire."

24

SPARE THE ROD

No. 12, The Close
Winchester
Thursday, 3 April 1817, cont'd.

"Thomas!" Elizabeth cried. "My brother-in-law! But what can he have to do with Urquhart? Why should he solicit Sidmouth's help in gaining a Scholar's place for the boy here at Winchester? Most of his family are Old Wykehamists already! He need not have sought the influence of a comparative stranger, on Urquhart's behalf. And why should he advance that young man's interests, in any case?"

I set down the viscount's letter, my mind in a whirl. "These are only questions that Thomas Heathcote may answer. But did you not say, Eliza, that he was childless, and a widower?"

"Yes—and my William his presumptive heir. When old Sir William is gone, and Thomas after him, William may be the Fifth Baronet—tho' we have never regarded the prospect as likely, Thomas being perfectly capable of marrying again, and getting a son of his own."

"What if he has already done so?" Edward asked quietly.

I met his eyes over the breakfast table, and nodded slightly. "Eliza, I believe you said that Mr. Freeman-Heathcote had set his face against young William, in part because you refused to give up your son into his care, and in part due to Will's stammer. You told me that your brother-in-law meant to persuade old Sir William to break off the entail of Hursley, so that he might leave the wealth—if not the title—away from the family line."

"B-b-blackguard!" Harris Bigg-Wither burst out. "I n-n-never liked the f-f-fellow! Ram-sh-sh-shackle and loose in the haft! S-s-so he'd s-s-see Will hang, and p-p-put his c-c-cuckoo in the nest? I'll c-c-call him out!"

He sprang to his feet, followed immediately by his sister, who placed her hand imploringly on his arm.

"You shall do no good by firing your duelling pistol at Freeman-Heathcote's head," she declared. "You will do much by setting your solicitor to learn what is towards at Hursley—and putting the facts to Sir William, before he is very much older."

Harris's lips worked on a heated rebuttal, but tho' red in the face, he consented to sit down.

"If, as we surmise, Mr. Heathcote's interests are tied up in Thomas Urquhart," I mused, "we are a long way towards understanding why Urquhart should wish to see young William put out of the way. The lack of a legitimate heir, and time to dissolve the Hursley entailment, should offer Freeman-Heathcote and his son a period of peace in which to establish their relation legitimately—and pass any amount of William's rightful property, to the child of your brother-in-law's blood."

"He shall not be able to convey the baronetcy," Eliza said. "If William did not exist, the title should fall to one of his younger male cousins. But Hursley House itself—its contents—its considerable land and tenants—all might be alienated, if Freeman-Heathcote has his way with Sir William."

"Making the title a hollow gift indeed." I looked at Eliza compassionately. "That is nothing, however, compared to the unjust conviction of your son for the murder of Arthur Prendergast."

Her face went white. In all the complications of wills and parentage, Elizabeth had for a moment lost sight of the threat to William. "The coroner, Mr. Pelham, is unlikely to think this discovery has any bearing on Prendergast's death," she said. "It is not evidence of a blow to the head, a drowning in the sluicegate, of one life snuffed out to incriminate another."

"Of all that, we have not the slightest evidence indeed. There is no crime in being born a bastard, or accepting the assistance of a putative father, as apparently Thomas Urquhart has done. But we suspect that Urquhart killed his friend, supplied the fatuous Insley with much of his testimony, and meant to destroy the heir whose shoes he plotted to fill."

"S-s-solicitor," Harris said, rising from the table.

Eliza looked to me. "Jane, what are we to do?"

"Let me think a while," I told her. "I shall not desert you. We shall all of us find a way out of this coil."

THE SUN SHONE THIS Maundy Thursday morning, but the light was of a quality that suggested rain to come. I determined, therefore, to think in the open air—and put on my cloak to pace about the Close's square of indifferent lawn. The air was damp and gentle, coming up from the south. At a plaintive call overhead, I glanced up to discover a herring gull dipping its wings above the trees, far from its Solent home. I, too, was out of place—roaming here where vanished nuns and monks once walked. I was reminded suddenly of another abbey, long since ruined, whose tumbled rocks were backdrop to intrigue—across the Solent, at Netley. It was there I had watched my beloved Lord Harold breathe his last, the victim of an intimate betrayal. A little over a decade since—but it seemed another age. What would the Gentleman Rogue think of me, were he to glimpse me now?

I shook myself a little. Such wanderings in thought, far afield from Winchester, were of little use to my friend or her son. I had an idea of how Arthur Prendergast had died—another intimate betrayal—at the hands of his good friend Thomas Urquhart. Charm, an easiness of manner, and good looks may hide any number of sins, as I knew to my cost. How many heroines had I thrown in the way of such men—the Willoughbys, the Wickhams, the William Elliots? A young man of ambition and ruthless self-regard, as I now judged Urquhart to be, had decided last week that only one person stood between himself and a sizeable inheritance. Urquhart might simply have murdered Will Heathcote, of course, rather than Prendergast; but how much more satisfying to a cunning mind, to appear blameless in the loss of a beloved friend, and to throw suspicion on the *true* object of one's malice! Better that the Law should put an end to William Heathcote's life, and mortify his family name; all the more likely that Thomas Urquhart, with time, should be accepted as his father's heir.

I had an idea of how it was worked. Urquhart had chanced upon Will's note to Baigent, which Badger had carelessly discarded; the existence of the meeting put an idea in his head; he shared his notion with Prendergast—yes! The rumour involving poor Charlotte Lyford had been of *Urquhart's* construction, not his friend's—and having succeeded in luring Prendergast to Pot, he had only to wait a little until dusk fell, and the place was deserted of the obliging Insley, to bludgeon his friend and dispose of his body. The timing of the murder, a few days before the Easter leave-out when any witnesses to William Heathcote's movements should be gone home and unlikely to support him at the inquest, was ideal to Urquhart's purposes.

He would have known, perhaps, from Miss Lyford that William Heathcote was absent from college during the crucial interval that Tuesday afternoon—studying to heal his stammer in her consulting room. Urquhart might guess at Will's reticence about appointments with the speech artist. He could certainly count on William to garble his testimony, and defend himself ill, before the coroner. Indeed, the plan was not an unlikely one, and might still succeed—for we had little in the way of proofs against Urquhart, and the judgement of the coroner's panel weighing against Will.

Proofs.

If, as I suspected, the murder of Prendergast was pre-meditated rather than the act of a moment, Urquhart should have been careful to get rid of his bludgeon. He should never have carried it away with him in case he should be seen and remembered. Similarly, he would be unlikely to discard it carelessly on Hills, lest it be found and somehow linked to him rather than Heathcote. What had he done with his weapon, therefore?

Cast it into Pot, along with the stunned Prendergast.

The sluicegate opened; the water roaring through its channel and filling the lock, then churning through the tunnel below—where the body of his unfortunate friend came up against a blockage, and fixed there, out of sight for a night and much of the following day, until the lock-keeper's boy had been sent into the culvert to investigate.

Something nagged at my mind: there was a difference in the culvert as described at the inquest, from the one Edward knew during his years of bathing in the Itchen lock. Edward had laughed with William at the way their friends shot out of the tunnel the previous summer, due to the force of the sluice's water. And yet when Prendergast was cast down the culvert, he had stopped up the tunnel and failed to exit at all.

My pulse began to throb a little, quickening with excitement. I turned in my tracks, and almost ran in search of Edward.

AT SHOCKING COST, WE persuaded a pair of chairmen to carry me the considerable distance—my nephew striding alongside—down what is called College Walk, across the river and to the base of St. Catherine's Hill. There, I was obliged to step out of my comfortable sedan chair and traverse the uneven ground to the particular lock the boys call Pot. Any number of persons were taking the air on this subtle spring day; I was unremarkable as I toiled through the grass with my arm secured in Edward's. Despite the most acute interest in the proceedings, my nephew could not forebear from reminiscence—and treated me the entire way with an account of his schoolboy exploits, in which the chase of various wild animals figured largely. He became brisk and purposeful, however, once the lockkeeper's hut was achieved.

The man himself was sitting near the sluicegate, a small knife and a bit of wood in his hands, whittling what looked to be a model barge. Edward bade him good-day, passed a comment on the weather, and being respectfully answered, imposed upon the lockkeeper's patience without further waste of time.

"You are Matthew Harper, I think," he said. "You gave testimony at Monday's inquest."

"Aye, and I did." A shaving of wood curled at the man's feet. He glanced up at Edward's face. "You were the one as begged Coroner to let the lad write out his words. Friend to a murderer, are ye?"

"We are endeavouring to clear his name." I stepped forward. "We merely wish to ask you a question."

The lockkeeper's eyes shifted from my face to Edward's. "Already answered Coroner's. That's good enough for me."

"And lost valuable time from your work to do so," my nephew said smoothly. He produced a coin from his pocket and offered it to the keeper. "We will not cost you more."

The man palmed the coin. "What would you know?"

"Is there a grate or grille of some kind, within the lock culvert, where the body of the drowned boy fetched up?" I asked.

"Aye," Harper nodded. "Navigation put it in, to keep the boys from shooting the culvert. Too dangerous, the Navigation said, and once the grate was put in, 'twould keep the boys out of Pot."

"When was this done?" Edward demanded. "I swam here countless times, in summer terms past."

"Then you did not go down the culvert," Harper said wisely, "for the grate was placed last June. Boys still swim in Pot, but they don't venture the tunnel, nor sluice their fellows down it neither. To my mind, Navigation made Pot worse, for 'tis terrible hard to climb back out, once you've struck the grate. Against the flow of water it is, you see."

"I do see." I saw a great deal, in fact. Edward was ignorant of the grate's installation. But Urquhart must have known of it—and counted on Prendergast's body being found at William Heathcote's appointed meeting place. Otherwise, he ought to have expected Prendergast to flow with the Itchen all the way downriver to the next lock. That would never do; it should make his careful framing of the murder, meaningless.

"Were the Winchester boys told of the grate's existence?" I asked.

"Navigation warned Headmaster. 'Twas for the boys' good."

"And Gabell would have informed the prefects," Edward mused, "of which I was never one. No doubt the Head regarded affairs on Hills as the prefects' province, not his own. It is not *Gabell* who would pull anyone out of Pot, after all."

"Is your son about?" I asked the lockkeeper. "The brave lad who went in after the unfortunate victim?"

"What do you want with him?"

I untied my reticule strings. "A reward. For risking the culvert once again."

The lockkeeper frowned. "And for why? Dead boy's long gone."

"I should like to find his cricket bat," I said, and presented the man with a shilling.

THE LOCKKEEPER'S SON WAS named Jed. He was small for his age, which he informed us was ten. When told that he should earn a shilling for climbing again down the wooden gate of the lock, and into the culvert—which was dry, the sluicegate being closed under the careful eye of his father—Jed clambered swift as a monkey into Pot. I was reminded of the powder boys I had often observed clinging like limpets to the gunwales of Navy ships. Wiry, fearless, and at home in water, they became hardened sailors, old before their time.

We asked Jed to pry apart such refuse as he found collected against the culvert grate, and retrieve anything that might look like a useful implement of wood. Surmising there might be a good deal of flotsam, I resigned myself to waiting some time; but in the event, the boy reappeared at the culvert mouth within minutes of his disappearance. His trousers and hair were damp, and his hands reddened with cold; but he bore two waterlogged and scarred lengths of wood in his hands, each nearly a yard in length.

"T'ain't no bat," he called out, in his boyish treble, "but I found these."

I looked to Edward.

"They are rods," he said grimly, "for the beating of schoolboys. The kind only Prefects are permitted to carry."

25

AN IMPROVISED CONFESSIONAL

No. 12, The Close
Winchester
Thursday, 3 April 1817, cont'd.

"Do you mean to tell me that *this* is what you were flogged with, for so many years in school?" I demanded, aghast.

"Not exactly, Aunt." Edward scrutinized the rods narrowly, looking for I knew not what. "Observe the four grooves at the end of this handle? They normally have inserted in them an apple-twig each, which are the true instruments of torture. It is those twigs, no doubt torn off by the force of the water and lost in a tangle at the culvert's grille, that inflict the true damage."

"That is barbaric."

He shrugged. "It is nonetheless an intriguing find, and we must carry it to the coroner, Mr. Pelham, without delay."

"You say that only prefects are allowed to command such things?"

"Yes—and being proud of their privilege, they are rarely found without them. Ash rods are the sceptres of a prefect's office. It is extraordinary that two of these should be in the culvert. Prendergast's ought to have been found on the ground where he went into Pot. If the second is Urquhart's, I have an idea why he disposed of it—in the most expedient fashion possible, by tossing it into the lock. There may have been blood, even hair, on the end that smashed his friend's skull."

I winced at the vision that swam before my eyes: two young men, jousting and fencing with the rods accorded them as a right. And then one lunged forward with deadly intent—and the other, plummeted broken into Pot.

The attack should have been swift, silent, and in the falling dusk, as little noted as the flick of a bird's wing.

"William Heathcote would never have walked about Winchester with one of these."

"Any more than I should," Edward agreed. "To parade with the privilege of a prefect, absent the title, is punishable by a severe beating—one a Master administers. Upon prefects' privileges, the entire system of authority rests. No schoolboy should dream of transgressing it."

"Pelham is unlikely to apprehend the rod's significance."

Edward smiled thinly. "Because he lacks the benefit of a *public school* education? Perhaps we shall be forced to compel Mr. Clarke to explain that our discovery exonerates William Heathcote from murder."

"We should have to show that one of these struck Arthur Prendergast a fatal blow. And that must impossible—no trace of blood remains."

"True." Edward looked thoughtful. "Mr. Lyford might prove of use in that regard."

"How so?"

"If he were able to compare the impact in Prendergast's skull, with the rods we have found, he ought to be able to judge if the one was caused by the other."

"But we are too late," I said, "for Viscount Beaumont will have conveyed his young cousin's body back to Avebury Court, for interment with his ancestors."

My nephew sighed heavily. "All the world conspires against us, Aunt! Nonetheless, having found these ash rods, we must turn them over to Pelham."

"Let us employ a useful proxy," I replied. "Place these in the keeping of Mr. Irving, the solicitor employed by Mr. Bigg-Wither. He is the properest person to handle evidence, and shall best know how to persuade the coroner."

THE EXPEDITION TO ST. Catherine's Hill, sedan chair notwithstanding, taxed my limited strength. I retired therefore to my bedchamber, where Elizabeth very kindly ordered a fire to be kindled and Mariah succoured me with broth. There I rested a period in brooding over the facts of William's case, as I now conceived them to be.

I suspected that by the time the unfortunate young man came before the Assizes in July, his uncle Harris should have contrived to mount such a defence, as should see William acquitted. But the lapse of months in gaol should break his spirit, if not his health, and might ruin forever the sanguine hopes of a promising scholar. I felt most strongly that our object should be William's immediate release, with all charges of murder dropped. The only way such an end might be affected, was if the true killer were named in William's place.

I roused myself from my couch, and sat down at the little writing table in the room's far corner. The note I penned to Miss Lyford was brief. It demanded her aid. And it was phrased in such terms as I am sure must appeal to her sense of justice. I thought it likely that Thomas Urquhart had cultivated her interest, so that he could monitor William Heathcote's speech. Will must have confided in Urquhart his desire to be rid of his stammer. Urquhart must be aware that his patron, Thomas Freeman-Heathcote, despised William's impediment. If Will ceased to stutter, Heathcote might look more kindly on him, and dash Urquhart's hopes of inheritance. Miss Lyford's confidence that Will's stammer had improved had signed Prendergast's death warrant. Urquhart determined to do away with a prefect universally disliked by Winchester's schoolboys, and throw the guilt on William.

Nothing could erase Charlotte Lyford's mortification at being used by Thomas Urquhart; but helping to free Will might ease her conscience.

I begged her to meet me in the Lady Chapel at three o'clock. Then I signed the missive with a flourish, and handed it to Edward to take round to Middle Brook Street.

SHE CAME AGAIN VEILED, and wearing her grey muslin, looking for all the world like a shade determined to haunt the cathedral. I was already kneeling at her preferred end of the south stall. She glided in beside me, and dropped to her knees.

"Miss Austen," she breathed.

"Miss Lyford."

I afforded her a moment to pray, if she felt the need to do so, then ventured: "You are kind to meet me here."

"I am not sure that what you contemplate is wise. Or indeed, to the purpose. Urquhart is unlikely ever to look for a letter from me again—much less, in this place. He is done with me entirely."

"And you, I hope, with him." Knees and back aching, I eased onto the stall's seat. "Are you familiar at all with Chamber Court, where Urquhart is quartered?"

She shook her head.

"Then I shall take the liberty of delivering your note to Fifth Chamber. I am grateful enough that you have written it; your hand shall certainly be one he recognises; and if we are fortunate, you shall succeed in summoning him hither."

She rose from the kneeler in turn, and sank down beside me. "I shudder to contemplate a meeting."

"If you wear your veil, you shall feel safe. And you shall not be alone."

She was silent, head bowed.

"What is a brief period of unease and embarrassment," I said softly, "to the hanging of William Heathcote, who ought never to have been accused? Consider the relief you shall feel when this business is entirely over!"

She nodded once, then reached into her reticule. She handed me the sealed note to Urquhart and rose immediately from her place, as tho' afraid she might snatch her letter back if she lingered longer.

"Until eight o'clock," I said, and watched her hurry from the cathedral.

I made my way more slowly back to No. 12. And sent my nephew on one more errand as post-boy. There were a number of people to collect, and admit to our plans.

WE ATTENDED THE MAUNDY Thursday service as a family party, dining early so as obtain our preferred seats not far from the south portal. I made certain to consume very little of Elizabeth's admirable repast, for the sake of greater plausibility when I should fall into a swoon halfway through the account of the Last Supper.

Once I pretended to faint, Edward bore me gallantly from the south aisle out into the starlit night and the chill air of the lawn. He had succeeded in dissuading Harris and Eliza from attending me; he was equal to the revival of his aunt, he assured them, and would return with her as soon as he was able.

We did not want too many to overlisten the encounter between Miss Lyford and Thomas Urquhart. Mr. Pelham the coroner and Mr. Irving the solicitor were more than enough.

We discovered them lurking already in the neighbour-hood of the slype, where Miss Lyford had set her meeting. At such an hour, in the midst of Divine Service, it was entirely deserted—and deliciously Gothick in atmosphere, the waning moon casting oblique shadows through the succession of curved arches. We greeted one another in whispers, and as silently as we were able, hid ourselves behind the columns midway down the passage, each of us taking position in the shadow of a separate mass of stone. We had only to wait.

I had instructed Charlotte to set her meeting for immediately before the elevation of the Host, when the attention of all within the cathedral should be fixed upon the celebrant. I hoped devoutly that her message to Urquhart had proved persuasive—and that he had attended Maundy Thursday. If his sins were as black as I expected, he had need of shriving.

The sound of footsteps echoed in the slype. I peered discreetly around my pillar, and espied a frail silhouette that must be Miss Lyford. She was heavily cloaked and veiled, and I should certainly not have known her identity, had I not ordained her presence. She kept her hands in a muff, and turned a little about the passage. I longed to indicate that I was present, in order to lend support, but at the very moment I might have whispered to her, the sound of iron-shod hooves resounded against the stone.

On horseback—not at all what I had expected—Thomas Urquhart was approaching.

Charlotte turned towards the opening in the passage, her feet rooted to the slype's flags. The horse whickered; I heard the jingle of tack and harness as the rider dismounted; and then the ring of booted feet on the passage. Miss Lyford wavered slightly, as tho' strong emotion coursed like a current through her frame; then she recovered enough to gaze steadily at the young man who came to a halt before her.

"Miss Lyford," Urquhart said coldly. A shaft of moonlight glinted on his blond hair, turning it to silver.

"Thomas," she replied. "Was not I once Charlotte to you?"

"Before I knew you for a whore," he said impatiently. "Say what you must, and let us be done. I leave Winchester within the hour."

She took a step towards him, her tone suddenly urgent. "I do not deserve such calumny! You know I was never unfaithful. You *know* why I met Will Heathcote—to help him in his difficulty, and cure his defect. To pretend otherwise is the grossest duplicity!"

I tensed a little behind my pillar. This had not been a part of the lines Miss Lyford was meant to recite; her indignation had got the best of her. And as I feared, Urquhart turned on his heel with a dismissive gesture, and would have gone.

"Stay!" Charlotte cried. "I must warn you! The Law is hard on your heels!"

He stopped short, his back still turned. "What do you mean? Of what are you speaking?"

"The coroner has been to speak with my father." She took another step towards him, and lifted her hand to his rigid back. "I overlistened their conversation. Thomas, they have found your prefect's rod! It has been retrieved from the lock. They mean to compare it to the wound in Prendergast's head . . . My father declares that the proofs shall be conclusive."

He wheeled around, looming over the girl with a sudden air of menace. Gone was the ready charm, the self-command, the unstudied willingness to please. "That cannot be possible, damn you!"

Charlotte shrank back. "Why would I lie? I am come at great risk—stealing out of my house on a pretext—to warn you, Thomas! I cannot bear that you should hang!"

He advanced on her, and seized her shoulders. "If that is so, then do what you may. Go to Lyford and *tell him* I was never near Pot that day—that I was with you, all the afternoon, and your appointment with Heathcote was a blind! For my part, I shall confess the same, to Pelham the coroner. If we admit our sin to separate parties, our story will have the ring of truth."

"But that is a lie," she retorted in a bewildered tone. "You were not with me. You were with Prendergast. And I know, now, that you did indeed kill him."

He raised his hand as tho' he would strike her, and she wriggled free of his grasp. She might have run from him then—through the gap between the slype's arches—and as if perceiving it before Charlotte did, Urquhart gathered her swiftly into an embrace. "Oh, Charlotte, my darling—do you not see? Everything depends upon your support for my story. To inherit the wealth destined for me—to redress the myriad wrongs visited upon me by my birth—I *must* remove the obstacle of Heathcote! Only then shall I be able to live—and *marry*—as I ought! Can you not do your utmost to aid us both? —When I have done so much, already, in order to deserve you?"

She stood still in his arms for an instant, her veiled face against his shoulder. "Are you saying, Thomas, that you killed Arthur Prendergast *for me*?"

"Of course, my dear girl," he said distinctly. "Everything

I have done—my hopes and plans—are for you. I should never have struck the fatal blow, did I not believe it necessary to win our future. I should kill a hundred Prendergasts for one Charlotte Lyford."

Lies, I thought. It was all lies. He had failed to win his object with threats, and thought to cajole her with caresses. *Do not believe him, Charlotte*, I pled with her silently. *He is a devilish killer.*

She thrust Urquhart suddenly back—so sharply and without warning that he stumbled a trifle in his surprize.

"You disgust me," she said bitterly. "A liar and murderer, incapable of remorse."

He lunged at her then, his hands at her throat.

"Charlotte!" I cried out—but Pelham and Edward were already upon him, each grappling with Urquhart's arms, until his hold on Miss Lyford's neck was freed. I supported her as she slipped to the flags, a huddled and stunned figure.

"You are all right," I soothed. "He shall not hurt you anymore."

"To think, I loved him!" she whispered hoarsely, an expression of horror on her face.

At that moment, Edward cried out—and doubled to the ground. I glanced up from his writhing form—he had been kicked sharply in the groin—and saw Urquhart break Pelham's grasp. He pelted back down the slype to his tethered horse and worked frantically at the reins. In hot pursuit, Pelham nearly reached him when Urquhart threw himself up into the saddle, turned his mount's head, and kicked hard at the flanks. The horse sprang off into the darkness, the coroner running flat out behind.

"Edward," I said faintly.

Mr. Irving, the solicitor, helped my nephew to his feet. "Walk a little," he advised. "It eases the pain."

Edward stumbled about the passage, breathing deep. "The swine," he muttered, then glanced at me. "Is Miss Lyford badly injured?"

"I am not," Charlotte replied, in something like her normal voice, and with my help, contrived to stand. "I hope I have done all that is required, to bring that villain to justice."

"You have, my dear," Mr. Irving replied, "and more."

26

GOOD FRIDAY

No. 12, The Close
Winchester
Friday, 4 April 1817

Iawoke to a quiet scratching at my door, and raised my head from the pillow to find Edward peering around it.

"Urquhart was overtaken by Pelham's constables on the Southampton road," he said without preamble, "and is being brought back to Winchester gaol. With any luck, he shall be placed in William's cell, and the lad restored to us by noon."

"That is a relief!" I cried. "We may return to Chawton with our minds easy."

"Not until tomorrow, I'm afraid." Edward's countenance was suffused with indignation. "The horse Urquhart rode on his wild flight was stolen, Aunt—from the Close's stables! My own pony, Shadow, in point of fact."

"I did ask myself where a penniless schoolboy obtained a mount," I admitted, "but did not like to distract the authorities with the question last evening. I hope Shadow is unharmed?"

"He'll be badly fagged," Edward said dubiously, "if not a complete break-down. I'm told a constable will bring him back at a walk; but we shall surely be unable to leave for Chawton today."

"I shall enjoy the reprieve," I told him, "and rejoice at William's reunion with his mother."

I DESCENDED TO THE breakfast-parlour to find Eliza in high spirits, and her brother Harris relieved of his burdens; he intended to quit Winchester for Manydown so soon as William was discharged to the Close. We had barely sat down to our tea and toast when there was a ring at the front bell, and Mariah threw open the door to a jubilant young man of almost sixteen, Mr. Pelham at his elbow.

"Mamma!" he shouted, and threw his cap in the air. He looked none the worse for captivity, and his cheeks were becomingly flushed with joy and excitement.

"William!" Elizabeth cried, and rose from her chair to throw her arms around her son. She drew back rather swiftly however; stared searchingly into his face; and commanded, "Draw a bath, Mariah. Master William is decidedly in need of one."

"We shall have to inform Dr. Gabell that all charges against Master Heathcote have been dropped," I murmured to Edward, "so that William may finish out his studies at Winchester."

Mr. Pelham cleared his throat. "If indeed his mother wishes it," he said, "I shall undertake to communicate with the Headmaster so soon as I leave you."

"That is very kind in you, sir," Elizabeth said. "Indeed, I do wish it. I believe that Winchester shall be the better for certain influences being removed, and the remainder of the term shall be easy."

I hoped, for William's sake, she was correct.

I SPENT MY REMAINING hours in Winchester in folding my few gowns; consuming a little broth; and commanding a sedan chair—without Edward's escort—to carry me to the hospital in Parchment Street.

As I expected, I found Mr. Lyford absorbed by his business there.

I proffered my card to the porter and sat down to wait in the hospital foyer. Lyford was so kind as to keep me idle barely a quarter-hour.

"Miss Austen," he said. "I rejoice to see you abroad in the world. I trust my draughts have restored your strength?"

"They have worked wonders," I said firmly, "as has an excellent piece of news I wished to share with you. William Heathcote is freed, and Thomas Urquhart remanded in his place, and a great wrong righted."

I said nothing of his daughter's activity in pursuit of justice, having no wish to betray her confidences. I thought it likely, however, that the surgeon would impart the news of William's release upon his return to Middle Brook Street this evening, and greatly relieve her mind. Whether the knowledge of her former lover's capture should bring peace or misery, I could not say, but hoped Miss Lyford should recover with time.

I rose from my bench and curtseyed. "I must offer my thanks, sir, and take leave of you. My nephew and I journey north tomorrow."

"Not for *too* long, I hope," he said in an accent of concern. "I should not like your frame wearied with travel."

"We are bound for my home in Chawton. It is only a mile or so from Alton—perhaps you know it?"

"Alton!" His expression lightened. "Mr. Curtis is apothecary there. An excellent fellow."

"I have been his patient," I said quietly. "Although of late, I have brought him to despair."

Mr. Lyford met my gaze with one of compassion. "I do not despair of you, Miss Austen. Indeed, I am confident that if I could have you under my care for a necessary interval, I might effect a complete cure."

A wave of faintness swept over me—the faintness of *hope*, not illness. But I could not bring myself to speak; I was fearful, perhaps, of dispelling the illusion.

Mr. Lyford bowed. "I hope, if your indisposition returns, you will undertake to consider what a removal to Winchester might do. I shall always, I need not say, be at your disposal."

It is not the London physician I had hoped to consult, when the prospect of a legacy remained to me; but it is something, indeed, to have a man of science back me.

Who knows, after all, what the future may hold?

AFTERWORD

On Tuesday, 27 May 1817, Jane Austen wrote a letter to her nephew Edward from "Mrs. Davids, College St Winton."

> *Mr. Lyford says he will cure me, & if he fails I shall draw up a Memorial & lay it before the Dean & Chapter, & have no doubt of redress from that Pious, Learned & disinterested Body. —Our Lodgings are very comfortable. We have a neat little Drawing-room with a Bow-window overlooking Dr. Gabell's Garden . . . We see Mrs. Heathcote every day, & William is to call upon us soon.*

She had travelled south from Chawton with Cassandra three days earlier in the carriage belonging to Edward's father, James, in order to place herself in Giles-King Lyford's care. Elizabeth Heathcote arranged for the Austens to rent the first floor of what is believed to be No. 8

College Street (a blue historical marker now marks the building's exterior) while Jane underwent Lyford's treatment. She wrote to her London friend Frances Tilson a few days later that:

> *My attendant is encouraging, and talks of making me quite well. I live chiefly on the sofa, but am allowed to walk from one room to the other. I have been out once in a sedan-chair, and am to repeat it, and be promoted to a wheel-chair as the weather serves.*

This appears, however, to have been the final letter she was able to write. Her condition varied but continuously declined over the next month and a half, and early in the morning on Friday, 18 July 1817, she died. The following Thursday she was laid to rest in Winchester Cathedral, with her nephew Edward and her brothers Henry, Edward, and Frank as mourners.

She was unable to finish the novel she called *The Brothers*, which has come down to us as *Sanditon*, but her brother Henry ensured that *The Elliots*, renamed *Persuasion*, was posthumously published in 1817 along with *Northanger Abbey*—a book she had written decades before, sold for ten pounds, and been forced to buy back from the publisher when he refused to print it.

IN EARLY MAY, 1818, Winchester College endured a Rebellion at the hands of its students. Wielding axes, they held the Warden, Bishop George Huntingford, hostage overnight in his set of rooms, and a number of boys were expelled when eventually the revolt was put down. Elizabeth Heathcote wrote an account of it to her son William, who had left the previous month for Oriel College, Oxford; she refers to the culprits only by their initials, but one is C.K. (Charles Knight?) who has "behaved very ill," and is to be fetched home by his uncle, Mr. A. (Henry Austen?). Dr. Gabell remained headmaster regardless, until 1823.

William is described by his biographer, F. Awdry, as a student who, though never strong physically, had a significant influence on the tone of Winchester Commoners and the school in general. Gabell trusted him, the writer adds, because William "made a stand, almost at peril of his life, against the evils of a brutal day." A subsequent headmaster of Winchester, Dr. Moberly, credited William Heathcote from preventing the 1818 rebellion from occurring earlier.

Thomas Freeman-Heathcote became the Fourth Baronet at the death of his father, Sir William, in 1819. He had succeeded in breaking the entail on the Hursley estate, and at his death in 1825, William Heathcote inherited only the title of Fifth Baronet. Will was forced to expend over £80,000 (a huge sum for the period) in order to buy back Hursley House, its contents, and surrounding acres. All these had been left to the son of Thomas Freeman-Heathcote's steward, for reasons that remain unexplained. The vast expense crippled subsequent generations of Heathcotes, and at William's death, Hursley House was sold. For more on William, see *A Country Gentleman of*

296 · STEPHANIE BARRON

the Nineteenth Century, by F. Awdry (Warren and Son, Winchester, 1906).

In researching the town of Winchester and Winchester College's Regency period, I found these sources most useful: *Winchester: Its History, Buildings and People*, by The Winchester College Archaeological Society, Third Edition (P. and G. Wells Ltd., Winchester, 1933); *School-Life at Winchester College; Or, the Reminiscences of a Winchester Junior Under the Old Regime*, by Robert Blachford Mansfield (P. & G. Wells, Winchester, 1893); *Winchester*, by J. D'E. Firth (Blackie & Son Ltd., London, 1936); *The Old Boys: The Decline and Rise of the Public School*, by David Turner (Yale University Press, New Haven and London, 2015); and *The Wainscot Book: The Houses of Winchester Cathedral Close and Their Interior Decoration, 1660–A.D. 1800*, John Cook, ed. (Hampshire Record Office, Hampshire County Council, 1984).

JAMES AUSTEN SURVIVED HIS sister Jane by only two years and five months, dying in December 1819. His hopes of a legacy from Jane Leigh-Perrot, who lived on until 1836, went unrealized. Jane's nephew Edward inherited the residue of the Leigh-Perrot estate at his great-aunt's death, and by stipulation of the Will, added Leigh to his name. He took Holy Orders in 1823 and married Miss Emma Smith, niece of the Chute family of The Vyne, in 1828. They had ten children, and Edward enlarged Scarlets to accommodate them, before selling the property in 1863. James Edward Austen-Leigh published the *Memoir* of Jane Austen in 1869, and his descendants collaborated on *Jane Austen, her Life and Letters, a Family Record* in 1913.

SO MUCH FOR FACT. What about fiction?

I have spent nearly thirty years adrift in the sea of Jane Austen's mind: reading her letters, absorbing her novels, studying her encounters with people she loved and the strangers who darkly amused her. In 1994, plagued with a peculiar but engaging voice in my head, I wrote *Jane and the Unpleasantness at Scargrave Manor.* Pregnant with my first child, I had been rereading Austen's novels that winter, as I generally do during the bleaker seasons. For whatever reason, Jane became the internal voice-over of my life. Simply to silence her, I sat down and transcribed what she told me. That she was a detective seemed obvious—her great gift as a writer was a profound understanding of the human heart, and no skill is more vital to exposing truth, deceit, and motivation.

I picked up Jane's narrative in 1802, when she was twenty-six and had just accepted, then rejected, Harris Bigg-Wither's offer of marriage. Her friendship for his sisters Elizabeth, Kitty, and Althea, made the proposal as attractive as his financial security. But by refusing Harris, Jane turned aside from a broad and well-tended path for women of her era into a narrow track that led to unmapped territory. Without the wealth of a spouse and hating her dependency on her brothers, she decided to earn her keep by writing and actively seeking publication of her novels.

If she had accepted Harris's proposal, we might never have known her name.

I followed her over the next fifteen years, and fifteen mystery novels, from Steventon to Bath, Southampton to Canterbury, Derbyshire to London, and a few places in between. I introduced her to Byron, Wellington, Mrs. Fitzherbert, and Carlton House. Rather than a retiring spinster in a limited rural sphere, Jane proved to be a woman of the world: hobnobbing with spies and dangerous politicians, equally engrossed by global politics and trends in high culture. As she moved through my pages, Jane grew older. So did I. She suffered heartache; I had my second child. She settled down in her beloved cottage at Chawton and published *Sense and Sensibility*; I watched my sons grow up and leave for college.

When readers ask why Austen's novels have endured for more than two centuries, I say it is because she teaches us how to live. That's the fundamental reason we humans turn to any story, oral or written, visual or graphic; because we learn from it how to survive. Elizabeth Bennet and Anne Elliott, Elinor Dashwood and Emma Woodhouse, remind us of ourselves in their intelligent and perceptive pursuit of happiness; but as I've grappled with ending this series, I've come to understand that they also teach us how to endure the terrible costs of existence. Austen's work is about surviving the end of things as much as, with each triumphal wedding, she celebrates their beginning.

In her novels there lurks always the long shadow of a missing and beloved character: Anne Elliott's mother;

both of Darcy's parents; Elinor and Marianne's father. Henry Tilney and his sister are, in Catherine Morland's mind, literally haunted by their dead mother. This is no surprise when we examine Jane Austen's life, because death was a constant part of it. Before she herself left the world in 1817, she suffered the loss of her sister's fiancé, four of her brothers' wives, her father, and her close friend, Anne Lefroy. Grief for her father and Madame Lefroy, most Austen scholars would agree, weighed so heavily upon Jane that she stopped writing altogether for several years.

As I sat at my desk one late afternoon writing the last chapters of *Jane and the Final Mystery*, my husband texted me from the airport, where he was meeting our younger son's plane. *Have you heard from him?* he asked. *He's not here, and he's not answering his phone.*

That was the beginning of the worst hours of our lives, when we learned that our son Stephen was dead. His loss came out of the blue, on a stormy October afternoon when he was supposed to be arriving home, and the tragedy of his death at the age of twenty-four destroyed any ability I might have had to confront Jane's end.

I set aside this manuscript and fell into the dark maw of grief. When I was able finally to look at the pages again, I found Jane waiting at the edge of my mind, as I always have. For once, she was silent. But her stoicism and hope in the face of her own decline, her gratitude for the people she loved, and her ability to let go of what she cherished most, offered me a bit of grace. Jane learned wisdom early, and she culled it from the most unforgiving of circumstances as well as the most rewarding. Her stories endure in fact because they *do not* spin fairytales of unalloyed happiness. As I am sure she knew too well, the price of love is sometimes pain.

In the end, we all have our brief passage through the world, in light and shadow, as my version of Jane has had hers in these fifteen novels. It is the words that will outlast all of us.

Stephanie Barron

ACKNOWLEDGMENTS

In 1994, I was pregnant with my first child, a somewhat hallucinatory experience, and I was hearing voices in my head. One of them was Jane Austen's. I had been reading her novels that winter, as I often do when the weather is poor and a good chair beside the fireplace beckons. For reasons I can't explain, Jane's distinctive narrative style lodged in my brain. Rather than questioning my sanity, I decided to use her voice instead—embedded in a classic detective plot—and wrote *Jane and the Unpleasantness at Scargrave Manor.*

Nearly three decades and fifteen novels in the Being a Jane Austen Mystery Series later, I am deeply indebted to the two people who first embraced my bizarre project: literary agent Raphael Sagalyn and the editor he charmed into publishing Jane, Kate Miciak. Your support and combined brilliance have been among the greatest gifts in my life.

Juliet Grames, Associate Publisher of Soho Press, took up the Jane series with enthusiasm and is both a deft and an inspired influence on the most recent books. I'm thankful for her patience in shepherding me through this final installment, despite numerous challenges. Others at Soho—publisher Bronwen Hruska, publicity gurus Paul Oliver and Erica Loberg, Rachel Kowal, Taz Urnov, Janine Agro, Rudy Martinez, Steven Tran, Emma Levy, Lily DeTaeye and Nick Whitney—brought this book to life. A huge shout of thanks to each of you.

And finally, to my son Sam, who I was carrying when Jane Austen first invaded my head, and my husband Mark—my love and thanks. You've helped me understand why her voice remains so compelling and vital to readers two centuries after her death. Austen's stories endure because she teaches us, fundamentally, that the point of life is to love honestly, deeply, loyally, and without calculating the cost. In this final journey with Jane, she helped me understand something equally important—that love survives, and can help ease, even the deepest personal loss.

Stephanie Barron

DISCUSSION QUESTIONS

1) What do you think about Stephanie Barron's depiction of Jane Austen? What qualities, characteristics, or traits does Barron's Jane Austen share with her real-life counterpart? How did Barron blend historical facts and fiction?

2) The novel takes place during England's Georgian era. Did you come away with a greater understanding of what this time and place in history was like? As modern readers, we know that we are reading a story set in the last months of Jane Austen's life. What did you think of Jane's experience with her illness, and the treatments suggested to her?

3) What were your initial impressions of William Heathcote, the boy whose reputation Jane hopes to save? Did you suspect the killer? If so, at what point were your suspicions first aroused, and what evidence led you to your deduction? If not, who did you think was the killer and why?

4) England's public schools—which we would now call elite private schools—provide a very specific setting for this particular murder mystery. How do class tensions and

divisions, such as the separation of so-called Scholars and Commoners, play a role in the rites of passage, cruel hazing, and dangerous pranks at Winchester College? What role do they play in Arthur Prendergast's death?

5) Jane's capabilities are often dismissed because she is a woman. How does Jane work around the hindrances imposed by her gender? Which setbacks she faces would be no problem for her today, and which would be just as challenging?

6) In Chapter 21, Jane takes a moment to pray for her loved ones, including herself. For the last line of her prayer, she states, "Help each of us to meet adversity with calm, loss with peace, and the future with hope." What are your thoughts on Jane's prayer inside the Winchester Cathedral? How does the idea of hope play a role in this story? Is there a difference between hope and faith? In Barron's afterword, she includes historical notes about Jane Austen's life and her death. Does knowing that Jane rests in Winchester Cathedral shed new light on the scene where Jane prays inside the same cathedral?

7) Describe your thoughts and feelings about the Being a Jane Austen Mystery series. Is this book your introduction to the series? Have you read this series from beginning to end? If so, what has that journey been like? Were you satisfied with the ending of *Jane and the Final Mystery*?